# HIGHER GROUND

# GROUND

## A Novel by Perry Oldham

Mercury House, Incorporated
San Francisco

Published in the United States by
Mercury House
San Francisco, California


Distributed to the trade by
Kampmann & Company, Inc.
New York, New York

Mercury House and colophon are registered trademarks of Mer-cury House, Incorporated.

Manufactured in the United States of America

**Library of Congress Cataloging-in-Publication Data**
Oldham, Perry. 1943-
Higher ground

I. Title.
PS3565.L327H5

1987     813'.54     86-21705
ISBN 0-916515-18-4

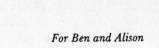

*For Ben and Alison*

# Part
# One

# 1

Whenever they held services for the dead at Dong Xuyen, the rifle reports caught Aaron off guard. He would be sacked out in the hammock, his fatigue pants copper-colored from the dust that infiltrated everything and made the light orange every time a chopper whack whacked down. The mama-sans would be yammering and yodelling like Chinese opera singers, laughing and polishing combat boots out of water-filled lids of Kiwi shoe polish, while a transistor radio blared Vietnamese music. It would be too hot to move, and Aaron would have another attack of dysentery and hotfoot it to the latrine, and while he was curled over his knees a volley of rifle fire would thunder and he'd flash, Oh Christ, not while I'm on the can, and grab the waist of his fatigues in one fist and start out the door with his other shoulder. Then another volley would follow, and by the third round he would realize it was a funeral service, not an attack.

Or he'd be trekking across the camp after a rain. The air would be heavy and full of stinks — mildew and cordite and diesel fuel and DDT sprayed by the gnarled papa-san in a pith helmet and shorts, a cigarette dangling from his tooth-less gums. Aaron would be sweating long, oily drops, and his toes itching inside his boots. As he passed headquar-ters, with its trim patch of grass demarcated by white-painted stones and "Screaming Loons" spelled out on the grass in more white-painted stones, he might see one of the Vietnamese secretaries arrive or depart, oblivious to the heat in a high-collared white or pastel ao-dai, parasol shad-ing a skein of long, black, silky hair that floated behind her like the panel of her ao-dai. He would pass the yawning tin shed where Murphy and his boys were working on a chopper—a Huey or a Loach—on his way to the hut beside the airstrip that served as passenger and receiving terminal. On the way back to the hootch, resenting six fat letters reeking cheap scent addressed to the fucking new guy, he'd hear a barrage like a fist through the thick air and he'd look around for cover. Then a second round of fire, and he would realize before the third that it was a funeral service.

There were more services in the spring, after the onset of the wet season, than there'd been before. Casualties that resulted from losing a couple of choppers a week, not counting grunts medivaced from the swamps and rice paddies; or bizarre incidents like Spec 4 Tiets zapped in his bunk by a clip discharged from an M-16 by troopers posing for snapshots outside with their guns in the air. Cool Breeze, the door gunner, flying with his legs dangling out the open side of a chopper when a giant bird flew in out of nowhere and broke his neck. Red-faced Master Sergeant Miller, who got it downtown in the Tucson when an angel-faced kid lobbed a satchel charge inside the bar, then dodged between two jeeps and was gone. Not counting the goddamn *suicides* . . . .

Aaron eased his foot off the gas pedal. That was a highway patrol car in the rearview mirror. At the funeral this morning, thirteen years after Aaron's return from the war, his brother had looked too . . . composed. The spectacle of Tommy, his smirking younger brother, serene underneath a blanket of sweet-smelling white roses!

Aaron remembered a sprawling pile of ARVN corpses one hot afternoon, missing arms and legs and heads and stinking the gray stink of rotting meat on the back of a deuce-and-a-half truck. He had crooked his arm across the lower half of his face as he regarded the black, burst drum of a stomach glistening with maggots like hungry piglets.

With oversized features and intense gaze, this morning's preacher had struck Aaron as being formidable, but a little incoherent. Except for a few neighbors and old friends, the only mourners had been Aaron, his older brother Rick and sister-in-law Sherri, and their parents.

Later at his mother's house, Aaron hadn't felt like eating. It was weird that after thirteen years, Tommy's death would recall the deaths of a handful of friends in the war. In a way, those deaths still seemed *realer*, for Chrisake, than the death now of his own kid brother.

Damn, Aaron grumbled as he slowed down for a line of traffic stalled ahead. The highway patrol car that had been trailing him the past few miles pulled right onto the shoulder and zoomed by. Aaron's watch showed five thirty-five. He hoped his ex-wife had picked up Kim from the sitter. He hated it when his daughter was left late, the sitter chainsmoking and staring out the window, Kim anxious and tired in front of the television set. He would have his daughter this weekend. She liked his girlfriend, and she liked the room he had done up all in yellow for her.

After the divorce Aaron had not taken much with him to the apartment. Clothing and books, a favorite rocking chair, the carved grandfather's clock he had found at a garage sale, his FM radio-stereo and speakers, his record collection. A few pictures: a pair of color blowups in sleek chrome frames of the adobe mission at Ranchos de Taos, a signed lithograph by Helen Frankenthaler.

He had rented the apartment furnished. Imitation Scandinavian tables and chairs with oversized, detached pillows. The motel atmosphere had suited his mood after the divorce. He'd left the grandfather's clock in the hall closet for two months before placing it in the dining ell and starting the pendulum swinging.

When Nell moved in, she had brought along a cedar chest filled with linens and sachet, piles of clothes and shoeboxes, a collection of Hummel figurines in a lighted glass display case, reproductions of French impressionist paintings in brightly lacquered frames. The mildewed shower curtain she had replaced with a new one in diagonal blue stripes. The cheap drapes in the bedroom had given way to smart, off-white mini-blinds.

She had given the apartment a personality. That was okay with Aaron. Eventually, though, he wanted to move back into a house. He missed the privacy, the quietness of a house almost as much as he missed a back yard to tinker in. There were no plans for that now. Although he enjoyed being with Nell, she was sixteen years younger than he. Young enough to be his daughter.

With jade eyes, flyaway hair pulled back into a tail, and a full, slightly sneering mouth that belied an amiable disposition, she would stand in the kitchen fixing a salad and wiggling her ass to the bass line on a new Rush album. Aaron would remark smugly, "That bass player doesn't hold a candle to Chris Hillman."

Nell would wrinkle her eyebrows and look puzzled.

"You've heard of the Byrds?"

"What'd they do?"

Aaron would place "Eight Miles High" on the turntable and Nell would laugh, "Oh, I remember that from grade school."

When Aaron had turned thirty, Nell had been fourteen years old. This fact never ceased to astonish him. By then he had completed a two-year hitch in the Army, finished his architecture degree, been married three years, and just become a father.

Nell had been in ninth grade. Tommy had been a junior.

Aaron recalled how, after he returned from the service, his younger brother had followed him around hungry for approval. Tommy had mimicked Aaron's loose-kneed, springy walk. The boy had fought with his mother to keep his hair long, like Aaron's, and had appropriated certain phrases favored by his brother — mostly obscenities. Yet the two had never been particularly close. An awkwardness, a standoffishness had characterized their relationship. The fourteen years' difference in their ages partially accounted for that lack of intimacy, but also they were really only half brothers. Aaron's father had died when he was ten.

For a while after the divorce, Aaron shared his apartment with Tommy. When Nell moved in, his brother decamped a couple of miles away to a rented room and they did not see him for over a month. Then one evening, as Nell and Aaron were sitting down to dinner, there was a knock on the door. In slouched Tommy, smirking and looking about as if he was casing the place. They had asked him to eat with them, which he did, gobbling his food with both elbows on the table.

After that he would drop in, always unannounced, two or three times a week. An easy friendship had sprung up from the first between Tommy and Nell, a thick-skinned dialogue of traded insults and obscenities. The alliance had pleased Aaron, but also made him a little jealous. Never had much joking, or any other communication, occurred between him and his little brother.

After dinner Tommy sometimes helped with the dishes. He would tell them about his night job at the Stop-n-Go, or about the latest developments on *As the World Turns,* which he woke up to watch every day at twelve-thirty. On those few occasions when Aaron and Nell had had an argument, she found Tommy an attentive and sympathetic listener. Blood insight enabled him to explain behavior that otherwise would have mystified her.

As he returned to Dallas after his brother's funeral, Aaron wondered for the hundredth time what had been going through Tommy's head when he called the office the afternoon before he was murdered. Would he be alive today if Aaron hadn't been too busy to talk?

He had no answers. With an effort, Aaron turned his thoughts to the Cape-Cod-style house where his daughter and ex-wife still lived. And how he used to pour himself scotch and soda from the the square, cut-glass decanters atop the tiger-stripe oak buffet, sit with feet bare against the cool flagstones of the patio, and listen to the wind blow through the cottonwoods.

# 2

The kids had not been gone ten minutes when Prell and Norma Lou banged on the door. A stately woman with big feet and a prominent chin, Prell swept in with outstretched arms. At her heels, in a faded dress, padded Norma Lou.

"Funeral's over," said Frieda in an irritated voice. "Where were you two?"

"Don't you get huffy with me, Frieda Teague," replied Prell. She peered down her long nose at her sister, who was barefoot. "I hosted a shower at the club this afternoon that's been planned for weeks. Come on, Norma Lou," she gestured behind her to the shorter woman. "Say hello."

Without a word, Norma Lou Hurry waddled around Prell and put her arms around her grieving sister. Eyes wide as a baby bird's hungry mouth and a remarkably long jaw that always seemed on the verge of dropping open gave Norma Lou the look of being perpetually astonished.

"You should have seen the gifts that girl received." Prell began an inspection of Frieda's living room. "Three sets of Fieldcrest bath towels that you can bet cost thirty-five dollars apiece. A pitcher of Waterford crystal I'd give my eyeteeth for. It'd match Mama's crystal bowl I've got sitting on my table. And dishes—my stars, that girl finished her china out. She's got Lennox, a real pretty pattern in blue and orange that costs an arm and a leg. And silver. She chose 'Old Master.' I think she had a lot of nerve choosing a pattern that's so expensive, but there you are. She ended up with a complete service for six. Except for butter knives. I can't believe people spend money like that on presents, but there you are. They've got more money than sense."

Prell looked at her sisters, who had their arms about each other's waists. "O Lord," she exclaimed. "There I go running on again." Prell sat down on the striped armchair.

"Would you like a cup of coffee?" offered Frieda.

"I guzzled coffee all afternoon." With a rasp of nylon, Prell crossed her long legs. "We used the big, silver-plated urn at the club and had those little bitty petits fours with icing on them."

"What about you, Norma Lou?"

"Oh, don't bother," Norma Lou blinked her eyes.

"It's no bother. Sherri made a pot before they left."

Frieda strode barefoot into the kitchen while Prell and Norma Lou exchanged a look behind her back.

"You girls should have been here," Frieda called amid the clink of china.

"How *did* Tommy . . . pass away?" Prell arched one eyebrow as Frieda returned with a cup of black coffee on a saucer. Norma Lou became engrossed in the design around her cup.

"He was stabbed to death," Frieda replied in a steady voice. "In a restaurant."

Prell raised her eyes to the ceiling. "My stars! How did it happen?"

"We don't know. He was in this place and some man pulled out a knife and stabbed him."

"That's terrible!" exclaimed Prell.

"Did they catch whoever did it?" asked Norma Lou.

"No, he got away. But the other customers gave them a description."

"Frieda," said Prell, leaning back her head and talking down her nose, "there was a report in the paper . . ."

Frieda's mouth hardened and Norma Lou once again lost herself in her coffee cup as the intrepid Prell continued, . . . "that said Tommy was knifed in a bar on the south side of Dallas." Prell paused to observe the effects of her remark.

"You can't believe everything you read in the paper, Prell," replied Frieda in a calculated manner. "We were told it happened in a restaurant."

Before her sister could press the point again, Norma Lou blurted, "Did you put him beside Mama and Daddy?"

Frieda pulled an embroidered handkerchief from her waistband and dabbed around her eyes. "Yes, near the top of the hill. So he can look out over the town. Ernest and I will lie beside him. Mama and Daddy just below."

"Have they got Daddy's stone up yet?" asked Prell sharply.

"You know as well as I do, Prell, the money's got to be released from the estate before we can buy Daddy's stone."

Prell snorted and jutted her chin. "It hurts me, that's all, to think of Daddy lying out there in an unmarked grave."

"Do you have the eighteen hundred dollars to buy him a stone?" shot back Frieda. "You're certainly welcome."

For a while the three women sat in silence. Norma Lou finished her coffee, then placed it gingerly on the end table beside her chair.

"You heard from Patsy yet about the estate?" asked Frieda.

"I haven't talked to Patsy for three months." Prell's voice became icy at the mention of their sister. "If that lawyer son of hers would get off his fat butt and get busy, we could get this mess cleared up."

Frieda nodded in agreement. "I don't understand Patsy. The way she's allowing this to drag on. It's not that Ernest and I need the money. Lord knows, we're comfortably off. But my portion of the estate . . . well, it's mine."

At that, Norma Lou stood up, gathered her purse, and padded toward the bathroom.

"I called Patsy a month ago," whispered Prell as soon as Norma Lou had left the room. "I asked her why she didn't push to get the estate settled. And do you know what she did? She changed the subject. Well, I wasn't about to be sidetracked. 'What about poor Norma Lou?' I asked her. 'She doesn't have money for underclothes, and there the estate sits.' "

Frieda leaned forward as Prell continued under her breath. "You wouldn't believe the way Norma Lou has to live. She's using washrags for bath towels. There's not anything but bread and brown beans in her cabinet. Frieda, I honestly don't know how that girl's going to make it through the winter. If her furnace breaks down, I don't know what will happen. She won't accept anything."

"Norma Lou's proud," said Frieda.

"We've got to get those Yahoos moving so we can settle the estate."

"You know, the heart of the matter," Frieda pursed her lips, "is that Patsy and Cody don't want to sell Mama and Daddy's property. They heard there's going to be development out there, and that McDonald's is going to come along and offer us a hundred thousand dollars for that old place."

Prell shook her head in disgust. "To some people, enough is never enough. We've had two excellent offers and I don't see why we don't sell the property."

"I agree completely," Frieda said, "but it takes all four of us to get it done."

Tugging her dress down over broad hips, Norma Lou came back into the room.

"There's food on the kitchen table," offered Frieda. "Help yourself. Prell, do you care for something?"

"I gorged all afternoon. You know, they served caviar on those little rye crisps. Nasty-tasting stuff, if you ask me."

As Norma Lou disappeared into the kitchen, Prell continued. "We're none of us getting any younger. I do not for the life of me know what Patsy and Cody are holding off for. So the kids can fight over it?"

Prell uncrossed her legs and rolled one of her big feet in the air. "We're like you and Ernest, Frieda. Hershell and I

don't require a penny for ourselves. And Lord knows our
Monte doesn't need money. But we'd love to be able to send
Jacqueline to Europe next summer. Her church group is
going, and it would be such an opportunity."

"Well, I'd like to recarpet the den," said Frieda. "Something real nice, maybe a thick wool shag. Something in
memory of Mama." For years, Frieda had kept a notebook
in which she pasted magazine pictures of the things she
wanted in a home: French provincial chairs and tables,
hanging straw baskets of bright artificial flowers, deep-pile
wool carpets, custom-made draperies with scrolled va-
lances, glitter-sprayed ceilings.

"Did you find what you need, honey?" she crooned as
Norma Lou returned with a plate of turkey breast, jello
with fruit, green beans topped with mushrooms, and a slice
of double-crust raisin pie. "I just hope you girls never have
to endure the pain I've had with this."

"I know it must have been awful," said Prell. "But then,
Tommy always has been a heartache."

At first doubtful as how to receive the remark, Frieda
finally acknowledged its justness. "He was my baby. He was
always sensitive."

"Both my children were sensitive," said Prell. "Monte
had asthma, and Jacqueline's an artist. You should see the
pictures that girl has drawn. One she did of our Scottie
that died you'd think would jump out and lick you on the
face. She did it from a Polaroid."

Norma Lou sucked her fingers, one by one.

"Tommy just didn't know where he was going," Frieda
continued. "It was like he was looking for an answer and
couldn't find it."

"Oh, Monte went through that stage," Prell poked her
chin into the air. "Caterwauled around. It's those damn
communists at the university."

"I remember Tommy as the orneriest of your kids,"
spoke up Norma Lou with a smile. "I remember once he

broke a window in the garage when you were at my house. He never said a word about it."

"I never heard about that," retorted Frieda. "How do you know it was Tommy?"

"Martha Early next door saw him do it. She was hoeing in her sweet corn and saw Tommy bouncing a little rubber ball against the side of the garage and it hit the window."

"Why, you never said anything to me about that, Norma Lou."

"I didn't want to embarrass the boy."

Frieda had to laugh."If that doesn't take the cake! When was that?"

"Let me see. . . ." Norma Lou counted back on her fingers. "It must have been about 1967 — not long after Dub died."

"1967. Tommy was only ten years old then. And to think I only just found out about it."

"Monte never was much for baseball. Football was his sport," said Prell. "I remember how proud Hershell and I would be when all the boys and him would run onto the field between a line of cheerleaders and the band members."

"Tommy was living with Aaron, wasn't he?" asked Norma Lou.

"He did for a while. After he came back from New Orleans. That was just after Aaron and Deedee's divorce. We were so in hopes the boys would help one another out."

"I never had much use for that girl," said Prell with narrowed eyes, "after she snubbed Monte's wife when she was carrying Margaret. I wasn't surprised to hear she dumped Aaron."

"She didn't 'dump Aaron'!" Frieda's back was up. "They simply agreed it would be better if they got a divorce."

"I'm just glad Mama didn't live to see it. There's never been a divorce in our family. It would have killed Mama. She was partial to Aaron anyway."

"Well, I don't pretend to understand it," said Frieda. "If I live to be a hundred, I won't understand why two people who have been joined together by God can't work out their differences and live together. But the fact is, they're divorced." She lowered her voice. "It's little Kim I worry about."

"Is she still with her mother?" asked Prell.

"Oh, yes. Aaron gets to see her whenever he wants. But her mother has possession."

"I hope Deedee doesn't poison her against him. That's what happens in a lot of those cases: the one parent poisons the child against the other one."

"Deedee wouldn't do that," said Norma Lou. "I always liked Deedee. Even if she was a little above herself."

"I don't think she would, either," said Frieda. "But then that's their problem. They'll just have to work it out."

"Is Aaron dating again?" There was a grin on Prell's face as she bobbed a shoebox foot.

"I think he's been seeing some secretary." Frieda was noncommittal.

As the other two sisters leaned expectantly forward for more information about Aaron's new friend, Frieda tossed her head and added, "It's nothing serious."

# 3

In the mid-sixties, male college students were liable to lose their draft deferments if their grades fell; and there was a good chance that, after losing their deferments, they would first be drafted into the armed forces of the United States, then shipped off to Vietnam. After an increasingly difficult time at college in Washington, D.C., Aaron Teague had already lost his deferment and taken his pre-induction physical. Essentially, he was marking time until May, when the last of his scholarship money would be gone. His major solace that bleak spring, as well as his major source of torment, was a chestnut-haired girl from Texas.

They had literally run in to each other, coasting down a steep, snow-covered hillside on trays stolen from the campus dining hall.

"You sound like a Texan," Aaron laughed, picking himself out of a snow pile at the bottom of the hill.

"How can you tell?" Deedee smiled up at this good-looking, square-jawed guy who had just careened into her.

"Who else around here makes two syllables out of 'damn'?" Aaron grinned and watched the girl brush snowflakes out of her cropped hair. She moved vivaciously. Her cheeks glowed vermillion and blue eyes glittered between black lashes as she leaned her head over and flicked snow from short chestnut hair.

Over beer at Louella's, an off-campus hangout, the two found that they had grown up within a hundred miles of one another. Aaron was smitten. Sipping a schooner of dark beer, Deedee looked fresh — her hair in damp ringlets and the cuffs of her yellow turtleneck wet with melting

16

snow. Dark blue stones that matched her darting eyes sparkled in her ears.

After leaving Louella's, they decided to go for a drive in Deedee's swanky new Buick. They ended up overlooking the Potomac from the Virginia side. It was a lovely night and they could see clear away to the light on top of the Capitol across the twinkling river. With the windows up and the radio mewing, it seemed luxurious inside the car. Aaron put his arm around Deedee's shoulders and pulled her closer. Without any pretense of coyness, she offered him her warm lips; as he ran his palm up and down over her body then slipped it underneath her sweater, she kissed and sucked his lips.

"Is there anyplace we can go?" she whispered as he fondled a soft breast.

"I don't know anyplace," he gasped; she was groping at his fly. It had been a while since Aaron had been with a woman; now every nerve and muscle stood ready to ring bells. When he sensed that it would hold no longer, he pulled her down on him and came.

With her short hair tousled across his cheek and lips, Aaron exhaled deeply and patted Deedee's shoulder through the sweater as she breathed rapidly against his chest. The softness of her neck, her breasts, her belly. He discerned the smell of face powder beneath rather strong perfume. That he had smelled it before, he was certain, yet he had never been able to identify by name any of the four or five fragrances he knew.

"It's getting cold," she whispered. "Why don't you let the engine run for a while?"

After first rearranging her clothing, Deedee sat up while Aaron turned the engine over. With the windows fogged and the elaborate, green-lit instrument panel, they might have been in the cockpit of an airplane. Aaron flipped the heater-defroster lever and again settled his arm around his companion's shoulder.

There had been girls who desired to chat at such moments, to share delicious confidences. Aaron was gratified that, like himself, Deedee was content not to talk.

When the heater had warmed them, Aaron turned off the motor, and they made love once more on the Buick's ample bench seat.

After that, it had not taken Aaron long to find Deedee indispensable, to become obsessed by her. When she was there with him physically, his pleasure was always flawed by the thought that in a few hours, they would go their separate ways and he would again be alone. When they were apart, he was miserable, breathing only for the time they would be together.

Most evenings during the week they studied together at an office in the engineering building. Deedee came to know the rest of the crowd who studied there, and immediately liked one girl who she said reminded her of her best friend in high school. Hugh, whose desk was piled high with back issues of *Ballet World,* she thought was sweet. He had recently acquired an old phonograph and begun playing a steady stream of classics from the record library. One evening he looked up to find Deedee clasping a spanking new recording of *Giselle* still in its unslitted plastic cover.

"See what this sounds like, Hugh," she had sparkled as his face crumpled in astounded appreciation.

Deedee was intrigued by the brittle, intellectual Karl, whose energies more and more were being expended on behalf of Youth for Trotsky. She admired Karl's capacity for analysis, as well as his ability to act, even to feel, according to what he determined intellectually was the proper course.

An issue she and Aaron thrashed out that Thursday evening, when for once they had the office to themselves, was whether or not Karl was excessively intellectual. In Aaron's eyes, there was something too controlled, too domineering of passion in Karl. However much Aaron might admire that quality, as he might admire a Cubist painting, it finally became boring to him, even repellent. Deedee countered by observing that Aaron was *too* emotional, that he was too often oblivious to intellect. Why, she wondered, did he insist so often on acting like a high school dropout, instead of the intellectual that he was by nature and training? After Aaron mumbled "shit" in reply, she had pressed the point. "That's what I mean, Aaron. Can you imagine Karl saying 'shit' after someone had just made a serious observation about his personality?"

"Well, I'm not Karl," Aaron tossed back breezily.

"And I've never seen anyone so impulsive in my life. I mean, Aaron, if you were walking down the street and decided you were hot, you'd probably drop your clothes right there in the street!"

It was rather pleasant to be analyzed this way. "Go on," Aaron said complacently.

Irritated at his flippancy, Deedee continued, "Granted, it's not good to be out of touch with your feelings, but Aaron, you're drowning in them. You're at the mercy of every whim that passes in front of your nose; you're like a puppy."

"Oh, you don't know what you're talking about," he answered her back.

"I've watched you, Aaron. You'll sit down to study, you'll read two pages, and then you'll go down the hall for a drink and end up gassing for thirty minutes with anyone you happen to run in to. Or you'll come over to where I'm working and bother me."

"I didn't realize I was *bothering* you," grumbled Aaron.

"Well, in a way you have been," Deedee was determined now.

"Aaron, we've studied together every night this week, and I haven't gotten any work done. I'm taking three upper-division courses in economics and statistics this semester, and I have to make A's in them if I intend to get into a good law school. If things continue the way they have this week, I'll be lucky to pass! I mean, Aaron, if you've decided to brush off your own school work, that's your business, but don't assume that I'm in the same boat."

Hurt by her remarks, Aaron sat with his head lowered, then looked over at Deedee. She too, he hastily concluded, must be miserable just now. "I guess I was assuming that we *are* sort of in the same boat," he murmured and reached over to touch her.

"No, Aaron," she exclaimed, "you're mistaken. We're *not* in the same boat. For some reason I'm not aware of, you've decided to waste this year, and you're doing a good job of it. I'm planning to apply to law schools in less than a year, and I mean Harvard and Berkeley and Yale, and I need to make my grades. And goddamnit, Aaron, I intend to do so!"

On a dime, Aaron's mood of reconciliation changed to one of resentment, and he turned back to his desk as Deedee stalked from the office. When she returned, neither of them reopened the matter, and later they walked back to her dorm in silence.

That night he lay awake until after four, rehearsing justifications for his actions and defenses against Deedee's charges, which he had heard before in one form or another from his parents and teachers, yet which until now he had refused to consider seriously.

Deedee's characterization was accurate. He was indeed floundering. Yet what was there for him to grab on to? The draft was breathing down his neck. He would be lucky to make it through the year before he was called up. He had lost interest in architecture, done poorly in his courses, and lost his scholarship. He did not give a rat's ass for business. He would have been interested in a career as a doctor or a psychiatrist, but he had a weak stomach for blood, and besides, he had no inkling of how to pay for medical school.

Yet he had to earn a living. Part-time jobs pumping gas, carrying sacks out at the grocery store, and one summer spent working out under an insufferable Texas sun on a highway construction gang had taught him that he didn't want to earn it with his back. He had thought long and seriously about bumming along the seacoast, picking up money where and when he needed it. Being a beach bum. Underneath the flightiness, though, a wary and irrefutable bedrock of common sense told him no, that would never do for him. That was a pipe dream. The flinty-eyed guardian of safekeeping and banalities decreed, "You may wander to *here*, Aaron Teague, but don't go a step beyond."

Aaron complied. He was not cut out to live that way. While he did not want to live elaborately, he did desire a certain level of bourgeois comfort. Furthermore, he wanted a home someday—he might as well admit that to himself—with a wife and kids, and he wanted them at least to have the things he had had growing up.

Why did he want them? Why was it so important that his kids should have things? Had he been so damn happy because his mother and stepfather had ended up in a tract house with a mortgage and traded cars every three years? Was that the glittering dream he was so eager to pass along untarnished to his own children? He remembered the standoffish way he and his friends and teachers had regarded the grubby, tousled offspring of migrant farm workers, how his parents had discouraged him from playing with them because "they carry lice." No, he did not desire that kind of stigma for his children.

Aaron lay on his bed trying to blank out thought altogether. He had read that one could will one's heart to beat more slowly, or pain to cease, or oneself to fall asleep. He concentrated earnestly on the image of a blank piece of white cardboard, but things kept getting written on it, and he found himself thinking again about Deedee, wishing she were with him.

Then, like a miser stubbornly recounting his change, he found himself going through the events of the preceding evening once again, and his stomach churned like a washing machine. In spite of his bitterness at Deedee's accusations, as he now regarded them, he was bewildered at the notion that she might not want to be with him anymore. Right now she was all he had to hold on to. Everything else seemed to be sliding rapidly away, falling to pieces; Deedee was his only handhold.

On awakening the next morning, his first thought was to go over to her dorm without calling, as if he were merely stopping by between classes—he knew she didn't have a class today until one—and ask if she wanted to go out for coffee. Then they could patch matters up in a natural way. Springing out of bed and throwing on his clothes, Aaron felt better already. On his way across the hilly campus under an ashen sky, he imagined that she was sorry for what she had said. No doubt she would be as eager as he to make up.

In the lobby of her dorm, he asked the girl at the desk to tell Deedee she had a visitor. After a few minutes, the elevator opened and out walked Deedee in cut-offs and a baggy tee shirt. Squinting a smile at Aaron, she asked what he was up to. At his offer of coffee, she looked down and made a gesture as if to present herself, then said, "I really can't now, Aaron. I'm a mess and I've got to finish typing a paper that's due this afternoon."

"Oh well, another time," he shrugged. "How about this evening?"

Scuffing a moccasin-clad foot in a circle, Deedee said, "I think it would be better if we didn't see each other for a few days."

With a deep gulp, Aaron looked the other way as she continued, "I'm not mad at you. I'm really not. But I realized last night that I'm not ready to start giving up as much time as I've been spending with you. I mean, if I could be with you and still get my work done, that would be one thing, but I don't seem to be able to do that. I think we need to be apart for a few days to think things out."

Aaron scratched his head. "Well, if that's the way you feel, of course, that's fine." He was wretched, but managed a weak smile. "I'll call you next week."

"Yes, I'd like that." Deedee bussed Aaron on the cheek then watched as, swinging his arms, he strode rapidly with his low-pitched, athlete's gait out through the double doors of the lobby and down the steps.

It was the worst thing he could have imagined. Aaron's stomach was in knots as he trod back to the house. Pride, a steely determination to hold himself up and not to crawl, fought with desperation in his mind. The leaden morning, his dismal situation in school, all of it suddenly seemed intolerable to Aaron, and he longed for a warm Texas landscape and soft-spoken people. The bleak northern climate, the harsh accents of the people, their abrasive manners were hateful to him now. He wanted nothing more than to be away from there, any place but where his steps were striking the earth. He wanted to be home.

# 4

It was not a pleasant weekend for Aaron. Having resolved not to call Deedee until the following Thursday, he tried to think of other things. He had always been the independent one; he had always called the shots. Why should this time be different?

However, that was not the issue.

No, the issue was that they were splitting up. That's what had happened with everyone he had ever gotten close to. Either the girl had moved, or the relationship had soured like a piece of rotten fruit, or Aaron had lost interest. Would there never be someone he could stick with, who would stay with him?

He was aware of Deedee's determination to enter law school next year. And there was his own draft situation. There was no way they could remain together, even supposing the relationship held, unless they were to get married. And even in his present cockeyed state of mind, Aaron realized that Deedee would not hear of that. Nor, if she did, was he sure that he was prepared to go that far to keep her.

Several times a day, that weekend, Aaron made the fifteen-minute trek across campus to her dorm, where he stared up at her window, then sat watch on a knoll across from the front door to see if she might pass in or out. What he would do if he were to see her, he didn't know. He would rely on instinct.

On Monday Aaron cleaned himself up and went to class. Not since Friday had he washed or shaved, taking a perverse pleasure in his raggedy beard, sticking-out oily hair, verse pleasure in his raggedy beard, sticking-out oily hair, reeking armpits. Today, however, the notion of sitting through a class in Bauhaus design was somehow attractive, and as he took copious notes, he felt almost at peace with himself. On the way out of class, he nodded to the professor, who grimaced back dry as dust.

An envelope from Selective Service lay on the hall table when he walked through the door at home. As he had suspected, it contained the results of his pre-induction physical: Aaron was I-A, fit for service in the armed forces of the United States. Ho-hum. He could give a shit.

By Tuesday night he had almost gotten over his distress and had driven with a friend from his rooming house, Henry Lazarus, to a bar, a box in an alleyway behind a Lebanese restaurant on Massachusetts Avenue.

Stockily built, with a bushy black moustache, Henry Lazarus was a Vietnam veteran. Originally from Ohio, he had been staying at a dorm since the beginning of the spring semester because he could not locate anything affordable off-campus, and he was damn glad to have found the rooming house where Aaron lived. There was something curiously guarded about Henry, Aaron thought. A jaded, dog-tired quality in his face and movements, a tightness around the eye sockets. The two had taken to one another immediately and become good friends.

A husky-voiced Danish barmaid chatted with them over the scrap of bar as a jazz trio played in the corner. "So what do you want to do?" Aaron asked Henry as the barmaid poured them fresh drinks.

"I need to go back and do calculus." Henry shook his head despondently. "What about you?"

"I want to do *something*." On the blade edge was how Aaron felt. He was benzedrine jittery. Everything looked glary. An image of Deedee began to burn in his mind as he swallowed the bourbon. Smooching in some car seat with another guy, leaning back her head in delight as he rode his lips down her throat . . . Christ, it made him crazy to think about it.

At nine-thirty, the two of them slid into Henry's Impala and headed across D.C. The Kinks blasted from the stereo speakers as the car joined the stream of honking vehicles inching along the tumbledown ghetto street of neon signs and barred shop windows. The girls prowled up and down the paper-strewn sidewalks, waving to those inside their automobiles, shouting invitations — one on a streetcorner hiking up her skirt and flashing her buttocks as she stooped forward and looked back laughing over her shoulder — prancing over to strike a bargain whenever a car pulled to the curb and a window slid down.

"Will you look at that!" Henry whistled between his teeth.

There were butterflies in Aaron's stomach. He was game. He motioned toward two lanky girls who stood in front of the iron grill over a pawn shop window, one of them in skintight satiny pants and the other in a short, buttocks-cradling skirt.

"Fine by me," Henry replied, then eased the glistening Impala to the curb. The girls toddled over and, while the one in pants glanced methodically up and down the street, the other girl leaned her short Afro into the cab of the car, opened her coat, and let her jugs dangle in view like pineapples.

"How much you got, honey?" she piped in a high-pitched, little girl's voice.

"Ten," answered Aaron.

"Ten each," she clarified and motioned her companion to join her at the window. Neither of them, Aaron thought, could have been a day over fifteen, both with long lean legs, bulbous asses, and high, round bosoms like softballs.

"Around the corner over there, honey," she pointed left and popped a wad of pink chewing gum.

In the wrong lane to turn left, Henry had to drive up a block then circle back. By the time they got there, the girls were chatting in front of an old, seedy rowhouse.

"Lock the door, for Chrisake," warned Henry as they got out.

Aaron felt ready to explode out of his skin. He stepped across jagged pieces of what had been a bottle of Thunderbird wine and angled across the narrow street behind Henry. Down the block, a cluster of four or five boys leaned idly against a parked car, their hands in their pockets. Experiencing a strong feeling of physical vulnerability, Aaron wished they had brought along knives.

Henry clapped his wide hand on the neck of the girl in pants and started up the worn stone steps to the door, as Aaron followed behind with the one in a skirt. Inside a bare light bulb shone down the shabby hallway with three closed doors on either side. The place smelled like a basement. Aaron's girl squeezed his arm and popped her gum as they continued behind the other two up a scarred and peeling stairway. Looking back to wink at Aaron, Henry goosed his girl, her sateen pants ready to split, before she guffawed and slapped him on the back.

Upstairs, they separated into rooms on opposite sides of the hall. As soon as she shut the door, Aaron's girl stuck out her palm and he forked over a ten-dollar bill. Then without other preliminaries, she stripped and flopped on her back on the iron bedstead with her knees up in a V. Aaron was still tugging at his boots as she hissed, "C'mon honey, I ain't got all night."

As he poked it into her, he was aware of her musky smell, which was strange and familiar to him, and of how tight and slick she was. He remembered the fat woman with conked hair who had banged the members of his high school lettermen's club one night at a beer bust. How after a dozen of them had been at her, he'd stumbled down the sandy road to the rattletrap of a Hudson where she lay dangling her fleshy legs out the open back door, grinning a snaggle-toothed grin up at him, and he had lost heart and gone back to the campfire without telling anyone what had happened. And the woman had not let on. That was forgotten now as Aaron lost himself in the taut, snug embrace of this girl. Soon after it had begun it was over, and already he sat on the side of the bed, pulling back on his boots.

Looking in a wavy mirror tacked to the wall, she smoothed on a fresh coat of dark lipstick, caught his eye, and grinned broadly. Outside in the hall, Henry was waiting by himself. Filing downstairs behind Aaron, he muttered, "Fastest damn lay I ever had."

At the bottom of the stairs, Aaron patted the girl's bum and held open the door.

"You come 'round see me again," she chirped and wiggled down the steps and back toward the corner.

"Whadaya want for ten bucks, Henry?" Aaron insisted after they were back in the car. "For ten bucks you get your horns trimmed, period. The broad doesn't have all night to dally around with you."

"She pissed me off. Telling me to hurry up! hurry up!"

By the time they had put a couple of dollars' worth of gas in the car and were walking up the sidewalk to the rooming house, it was after one. Stars speckled the cloudless sky. Aaron's crazy, frantic feeling, his need to rush away to somewhere, was allayed for the time being. His body ached with weariness and his mind was quiet as he gazed up into the spangled, black bowl of night.

\*    \*    \*

On Wednesday Aaron woke up anxious again, and it was a mighty struggle he had with himself all day not to call Deedee. He lasted it out, though, every hour and minute until four o'clock Thursday afternoon, a time he deemed sufficiently casual.

As he waited for someone to pick up the phone, blood pounded in his ears and he was afraid his voice would shake.

"Hi, Aaron."

God, she sounded cheerful!

At once, the fog vanished and sunlight streamed through. "How have you been?" he asked.

"Fine."

"How has your work been coming?" There was no hint of snideness in his voice.

"Oh, fine. Just fine."

For a few minutes they talked casually of this and that, pretending that nothing had happened. Then, after Aaron asked Deedee if she would like to go out with him tomorrow night, there was a pause and his heart stopped beating.

"Aaron, I've already got something tomorrow with my roommate. It's her birthday, and we're going out to dinner with the girls across the hall."

"Oh." His legs were gone. He couldn't take much more of this.

"Really, Aaron. This has been planned for weeks."

"Well," he began again tentatively, "how about Saturday?"

"I'd like that."

"You would?" Aaron was grinning from ear to ear. "Let's say seven-thirty."

"Okay."

Never had he felt more exhilarated. It had been worth it, after all, the waiting her out. He had known it! Once again, the ball was in his court.

## 5

Friday afternoon Karl, the Youth for Trotsky leader, asked Aaron to drop by for a drink. With his mind now freed of worry about Deedee, Aaron was in a mood to relax.

A tall girl dressed entirely in black asked him into the apartment. Inside, a roomful of student types, only a few of whom Aaron recognized, sat hunched around the floor. Striding in from the kitchen, Karl greeted Aaron in a hearty voice, introduced him to the others, then added that there was wine in the kitchen.

As Aaron was pouring himself a jelly glass of Gallo burgundy, he caught the drift of conversation from the next room. They were talking about the war, and about how Johnson was systematically lying to the American people about what was going on.

"Aaron has already taken his draft physical," Karl announced as Aaron entered the room and squatted beside a poster of Chairman Mao. It was not exactly the blissful atmosphere he had looked forward to this evening.

"How were you classified?" asked a snub-featured, blond boy earnestly smoking a cigarette.

"I just got my notice this week," replied Aaron. "I'm I-A."

"God," exclaimed the girl in the rocking chair. "Are you going?"

"Where?"

"To Vietnam!"

"I haven't been drafted yet."

"Well, if you are drafted and you are sent to Vietnam, will you go?" repeated the girl.

Aaron hesitated, as the others watched him closely. "I haven't thought much about that. I don't know."

The blond smoker peered at Aaron. "But you must be aware of what's going on in Vietnam. How the country is being raped for the benefit of capitalism."

"Don't misunderstand me. I'm not for the war," Aaron began explaining, wishing he were not a part of this tiresome conversation. "It's just that I haven't decided yet what I'll do if I'm ordered to Vietnam."

"I know what I'd do," inserted a lean, red-haired pipe smoker. "I'd split to Canada. There are brothers and sisters up there taking care of resisters. I'd leave in a flash."

Observing that Aaron appeared uncomfortable with the conversation, Karl shifted the subject to the deplorable lack of social consciousness on the part of the student body. As each of the others contributed appalling examples of other students' indifference to anything beyond having a good time and making money, the girl in black sat archly beside the lamp in the corner, smoking and sipping her wine from the only stemmed glass in the room.

It was not that Aaron was unsympathetic to their views. Yet to him they seemed like shrill children, reciting to one another received opinions, rattling them off like litany. He suspected that they got not only their ideas, but their feelings as well, off paper, just as some women get their faces out of paint pots.

As soon as he figured he might decently depart, Aaron excused himself from the gathering and went down to Louella's, where he got drunk standing along the bar with strangers.

By Saturday evening, the exhilaration Aaron had felt since talking to Deedee on the telephone was transcended by a placid self-confidence, a serenity like silken sails.

Not wanting to use Deedee's car and the night being clear and lovely, Aaron suggested that they simply walk around the campus in the moonlight. Then they could stop in somewhere for pizza.

That was fine with Deedee, as she smiled up at him in the lobby after kissing him hello. Strolling along the mossy brick sidewalks, stopping from time to time to sit on a weathered stone bench or on the breast of a hill, they talked about a hundred things, again coming to feel comfortable together. Aaron promised that he would not bother her anymore when they studied together, that he would set his nose to the grindstone. Deedee was astonished at the news of his being classified I-A—far more concerned than he, it seemed.

Later, as they sat drinking beer and eating pizza, Aaron remarked that spring break would begin in a week, but that it didn't matter much to him, since he had no money to go anywhere. When Deedee did not reply, he asked what her plans were. With a bright smile, she said that she was driving down to Florida, Daytona probably, with two of her girlfriends, Sandra and Rosanne.

For a moment, Aaron did not know what to say. His mind was flying. Deedee was going to Florida. He wondered if there was some way he could manage to dredge up the cash to go with them? But he had not been asked. Deedee had not asked him to go. That fact was stark. "When are you leaving?" he inquired with feigned nonchalance.

"We'll probably get up early Saturday morning and drive straight through. It'll be a twenty-four-hour trip with three of us driving."

Aaron no longer had any appetite. Nor anything else to say. That night a mumbled goodnight was all that passed between them when he took her back to the dorm—and the agreement that they would try to get together again to study one night the following week.

# 6

Pride prevented Aaron from making a show of the fierce resentment he felt at Deedee's driving south without him. He knew that she was entitled to go where she wanted and, he supposed, with whom she wanted. He understood that and he accepted it; nevertheless, his blood boiled when he thought of her not even asking him to come along, and when he imagined her with those whores Sandra and Rosanne, lying on the beach, being picked up by guys from God knows where. . . .

It was silly, worse than pointless, destructive, for him to keep thinking about it. He was getting over what he had felt when they first had split. He did not need anyone, least of all some two-timing. . . .

When Aaron returned after class on Friday, the last day before spring break, he was the only person left in the house. Henry and another friend were driving up to New England in Henry's Impala to go skiing. Aaron was stuck, without money and without a car.

Resolving not to sit around feeling sorry for himself, he rifled through his desk for a D.C. Transit Authority map showing the bus routes around the city. The first week he had been in town he had picked it up, then laid it aside. His friends' cars had been more convenient. Now, unless he confined himself to tramping back and forth across the deserted campus for nine days, he would have to decipher the map's code.

By nine o'clock Saturday morning, he was at the bus stop to catch the bus down to the Capitol area. He spent all day poking through the Folger Library, the Botanical Gardens, and the National Gallery. By evening, his feet and calves were so worn out from walking over concrete that he was satisfied to fix himself a couple of peanut butter sandwiches, sip a glass of beer, and watch the television downstairs until he was ready to drop off to sleep.

On Sunday it was ten before Aaron woke up. It felt luxurious to loll about in bed as sunlight poured into the room through sparkly, frost-etched window panes. He wondered what Deedee was doing. By now, they should be in Daytona. They were probably crashing on the beach. They would get sunburned. Damn, he would give his left nut to be there. Aaron felt a fresh surge of resentment.

What would he do today? He didn't want to go into D.C. again, and besides, he didn't think the busses ran on Sunday.

He would take it easy. There were some books he had bought months ago that he'd not had a chance to start: *Naked Lunch* and a crazy war book, *Catch-22,* that everyone but him seemed to have read already.

He could do schoolwork, but that seemed pointless. No one, including himself, expected him to be back next year anyway. Why bother?

After frying some link sausages and two eggs, Aaron took his coffee cup and settled down with William Burroughs in the orange armchair of the sparsely furnished living room and read until one-thirty. Drowsy, he then trudged upstairs to his room and napped for an hour. When he awoke, it was cold in the house; after turning up the thermostat, he shambled downstairs to look at basketball games on TV the rest of the afternoon. He did not like basketball. But he watched with masochistic pleasure, doggedly, until five-thirty, when he went to the kitchen and dragged out a knockwurst and a jar of sauerkraut from the refrigerator and boiled them in the same pot for dinner. God, seven more days of this! He would go crazy.

After dinner he read an insane episode about Dr. Benway that made sense to him, then went down to the basement to work with his weights. As he was lifting, he tried to imagine, as he had done recurrently throughout the day, what Deedee was doing at that moment. Was she laughing it up in a bar? Was she at a party in a motel room? Again the ache in his guts, and he concentrated his attention on maintaining proper breath control.

On Monday he again went downtown, intending to cover the south part of the Mall area: the Smithsonian, which he found over-touted, a jumble of objects; the Corcoran Gallery with its marvelous Whistler exhibits; the three monuments. For the first and last time he climbed the stairs to the top of the great prick honoring the Father of Our Country.

When he checked the mailbox at home, he discovered another letter from Selective Service. With a fluttering stomach, Aaron ripped open the envelope and found what he knew would be there: an order to report for active duty on 15 May. Holy shit! The thing, itself.

Aaron dropped down on a chair in the living room. Since the business with Deedee had been dragging on, he had simply pushed the draft out of his head. What difference did it make, after all, if he were in uniform or not if he didn't have Deedee? Half-realized in the back of his head was the sop that, if they did not stay together and if his school efforts came to nothing, then the Army, as combination taskmaster and wetnurse, would magically erase all his problems. Poof.

Abruptly now, something flip-flopped inside his head. With the crisp piece of paper tickling his palm, Aaron realized that he did not want to be drafted. He *really* didn't want to go. Soldiers were victims—poor, dumb, expendable sonsofbitches tossed like kindling wood into the fire.

Yet what the hell difference did it make, knowing that? The idea that knowledge is a sword, that awareness is the best defense against being made a victim, all the pristine, uncompromising crap handed down from Socrates to the present suddenly sounded flat. At that moment, none of it counted for diddly-squat. He was had. He might as well march in lock-step up the stairs, pull down his collar, and place his head on the block. There wasn't a way in hell, short of leaving the country, to stop the conveyor belt on which he found himself caught. He might as well grab his balls and bend over. A whopping kick in the ass was forthcoming.

It occurred to him to put through a telephone call to his parents, but he nixed the idea. A letter would do. He didn't want to hear his mother shrieking over the phone or his stepfather's wise advice. His stepfather would approve, no doubt: "It will make a man of him." Although he would shake his head because Aaron had not gotten into a *program* to become an officer. Fuck officers. Fuck programs. If he was going to go in, at least he wouldn't be one of the boss's boys.

There was a certain excitement, he admitted to himself that evening as he sat in front of the television eating a baloney sandwich, an ebullience in the notion that he would be somewhere else before long. An entirely new set of rules, a different place, people whose existence he now knew nothing about. Lying in his bed the night before flying to Washington the first time, Aaron had tried to imagine that twenty-four hours from that moment, he would be breathing the air, walking the sidewalks, of a different place. To someone who knew the city, it might have been a toothless whore or a familiar companion; to Aaron, who had never been north of the Red River, Washington was a golden-eyed temptress calling his name through smoky lips.

Now it was a camp follower that summoned him, one who spread her legs for platoons, squadrons, brigades. He harbored few illusions about the virtues of the bitch, expected no lingering bliss. Nothing except a dose of the clap, if he was lucky enough not to contract something deadlier.

\*   \*   \*   \*

Not until Thursday night, when he stopped in late at
Louella's, did Aaron see anyone he knew. At one of the few
occupied tables sat his friend from the engineering office,
Hugh, and a large, carefully coifed girl wearing a black
cape. It was awfully good to see a familiar face, Aaron
thought as he carried a pitcher of beer over to their table.
The girl's name was Alecia; she was a soprano who spoke in
a toney, resonant, singer's voice. She and Hugh had taken
Hugh's mother to a concert by George Szell and the Cleve-
land Orchestra.

"My mother *loved* the Adagio of the Schumann," sighed
Hugh, "but when they played the Mozart, there were tears
in her eyes."

"I agree," said Alecia in bell tones. "When it comes to
Mozart, no one else conducts with Szell's authority."

"I didn't know your mother was out of the hospital,
Hugh," Aaron broke in.

"Yes, I brought her home on Friday." At once Hugh
deflated like a punctured tire. "The doctor told her that
her gall bladder was bad and that she would just have to live
with it." Hugh's pale fingers drummed the tabletop. "He
told me, however, that they found cancer when they oper-
ated. It was so far advanced they sewed her up again and
sent her home. They say it is simply a matter of time."

Alecia shot a bleak look at Aaron. "I'm sorry, Hugh," she
mumbled. Alecia sat draped in her cape, sipping uncomfortably at her beer.

After a few awkward moments, Aaron asked lamely,
"Hugh, are you going anywhere before the break's over?"

"Mother said she would like us to run up to New York,"
replied Hugh. "She wants to take in some shows—she's
been wanting to see *Fiddler On the Roof* for ages, and also
the ballet." He chuckled. "Traveling with Mother, you
know, is such an experience. She insists upon staying at the

old Taft Hotel, off Times Square. Then when she walks
back and forth to the theater, past all the *sights*," Hugh
lifted an eyebrow, "she juts her chin and mutters, 'Nasty!
Nasty!' Her record for one trip is forty-one 'Nasty's.' "

As he laughed at Hugh's account, Aaron was thinking
shamelessly that he could make Alecia if he tried. He
caught her eye and smiled, as if they two were alone at the
table. She tittered and squirmed in her chair. What was she
hiding under that black tent? Was she horribly overweight?
(Her face and neck did not show it, if she were.) Did she
have three breasts?

Why was Aaron pushing this? He found Alecia goosey
and unattractive, and furthermore, he was genuinely fond
of Hugh. He loathed a bird dog as much as anybody did.
Yet just before midnight, while Hugh was in the can, Aaron
arranged to come to her apartment after she was dropped
off.

Later as he waited, shivering, down the street, Aaron felt
very tired and was on the verge of beating it on home when
the couple drove up in an old green Dodge. From behind
his tree, Aaron watched Hugh walk around to open the
girl's door, then follow her (she a good head taller) up the
sidewalk to the mock-colonial doorway of the small apartment house. Then without so much as a handshake, she
passed inside as Hugh returned to his car and drove off.

By the time Alecia showed Aaron into the overheated
apartment, she had shed the cloak. Although she had a
rather full, singer's torso and broad hips, she could hardly
be called deformed, he noted with satisfaction. As she
minced about, flickering her lashes and rolling her eyes,
Alecia chortled that she felt like a coquette.

Aaron followed her into the kitchenette as she whirled
and fluttered. Stepping in behind her as she reached over
her head for two glasses, he cupped his hands over her
breasts. She bleated in surprise. Leaning against the sink,
they pawed each other through their garments until,
grunting in urgency, they tore the rags aside and went at it

slap-bang on the linoleum floor, she protesting the whole time that the draft might harm her register.

Afterwards, their clothes strewn about the kitchen floor, Alecia put on a pot of water for tea, then wiggled on tiptoe out the door and returned in a moment with a jar of Vicks. Squatting with one leg up on the kitchen chair, she rubbed the fumy ointment on her chest while they waited for the water to boil.

"Do you think I have a nice body?" she asked, setting the jar on the table and lifting up her fulsome breasts.

"Yes, very nice. Why do you rub that stuff on them?"

"That helps me retain my register," she replied, dropping her breasts and stroking long fingers along her sinuses.

After tea, Aaron asked if he might stay the night, but was told no, she could not take the chance of the neighbors' seeing him in the morning.

Soporifically assenting to her wishes, Aaron piled on his clothes and his coat and kissed Alecia good-bye at the door — she smelled to high heaven of Vicks — before strolling home alone to the empty house.

# 7

Late Friday night Henry returned from Stowe with tales of powdery snow and beautiful women. And every one of them, according to Henry, was hot to trot.

Saturday morning, Aaron knocked on Henry's door and found him unpacking.

"What'd you do while we were gone?" asked Henry as Aaron moved a dopp kit from the desk chair to the bed and sat down.

"Went down to the Mall a couple of times," Aaron answered with a self-deprecating smirk, "and I watched a lot of television. What about yourself?"

"Fabulous time. We had a fabulous time." As if to confirm delights, Henry was shaking his head.

"You get up on skis?"

"Who had time for that shit? I didn't get out of the lodge."

"How's that?"

"I sat in front of this fireplace the whole time and drank Irish coffee. And the women, you wouldn't believe! Secretaries and nurses, most of them. You gotta go up there."

"Yeah." Aaron pulled on his ear. "Hey, guess what I got in the mail?" Suddenly he felt silly bringing the matter up.

"What?"

"My draft notice."

"No shit!" Henry laughed to himself and shook his head. "You poor fucker. When do you go in?"

"The fifteenth of May."

"Wow, I don't envy you." There was a clear measure of taunting in Henry's response.

"Well, it's just for two years," said Aaron without any resonance in his voice.

" 'Just for two years'! Holy Christ! Do you know how long two years is?" Incredulous at the other's naivete, Henry dropped his jaw and gaped. "One hell of a long time."

Then as if regretting his tactlessness, Henry added, "But you don't need that kind of talk."

"No, that's all right. I thought maybe you could tell me something about it."

"About what?" Henry asked evasively.

"You know. The service. Vietnam."

"What's to tell, man? They grab you by the short hairs and don't let go until you get your discharge papers."

Aaron smiled. "You were in the Navy, weren't you?"

"That's right."

"On a gunboat in Vietnam?"

"Yeah. Up and down canals in the goddamn Delta." Recognizing Aaron's silence as an invitation not to be ignored with decency, Henry observed, "Look man, I'm the wrong guy to come to for war stories. There are guys sitting on barstools all over this town who'll talk your arm off with their fucking war stories if you give them half a chance."

"Forget it," Aaron muttered after a moment; he was offended.

Henry crawled across the bed, propped his back against the wall, and put his knees up. "Like I said, man, I don't tell war stories. I got back with my ass in one piece. I don't have nothing to complain about and nothing to brag about."

Letting fade a mirthless grin, Henry stared blankly for a while at his knees. The matter was closed. Then out of his surly cocksureness, the ex-sailor looked again at Aaron and felt mean. The kid, he acknowledged to himself, surely had reason for wanting to find out anything he could about what might lay ahead, and from the look on his face he resented the rebuff.

"Okay," Henry finally offered in a dry, obliging voice. "What do you want to hear?"

Aaron shrugged his shoulders. "Anything you want to tell me."

After rubbing a palm across his forehead, Henry wrinkled his nose and began, "Well, it's a weird scene. Most of the time you spend sitting around on your ass with nothing to do. Me, I got high most days. I got a fucking A in that course. I used so many damn drugs I wonder sometimes if my mind's not turned to Swiss cheese. Maybe that's why I'm having so much trouble remembering what I read." Under his thick, black moustache, Henry flashed a white grin.

"Fucking grass they rolled on cigarette rolling machines and sold them in the street like Lucky Strikes. Man, I couldn't imagine coming back to the World and having to roll my own joints. And speed. They sold it over the counter in the fucking drugstore. There was this dude I know that did nothing but take speed he bought in the drugstore and smoke grass all the goddamn time. Fucker weighed no more than ninety pounds, at the outside."

With a sneer, Henry shifted himself around to draw out a handkerchief from his pocket and blow his nose.

"Did you get much action?" asked Aaron.

"Say again?"

"You see any action? Get in any firefights?"

Henry laughed. "Hey, man, I saw guys younger than yourself being shoved a rifle in their hands and told, 'Go get Charlie,' and they did." He broke off, recalling for a moment something he chose not to relate. "I've often wondered what happened, what'll happen to those sad fuckers when they get home and can't gun down some dude in the street when they get pissed off at him. You know," he added, dropping his voice, "some of them get used to it, get off on it."

Henry's face wore an icy grin. "When you can do whatever the hell you want to do . . . run people off the road, throw beer cans at Mama-san, blow somebody's head off because he's walking on the wrong side of a line after dark . . . when any goddamn obnoxious thing you want to do, you *can* do because you're wearing the gun, it can get to you, I ain't lying."

Again, Henry sniffled and reached for his handkerchief as Aaron sat wondering, with a twinge of admiration and not a little repulsion, if it would be that way with him.

"Damn. I must have caught a cold." Henry blew his nose as Aaron watched. "Now what else? Well, there's no privacy. None at all. You live with BO and stinky assholes, and you learn not to murder the next guy's miserable ass the minute his back's turned.

"And you learn that most of the shit people worry about here ain't worth worrying about. People get strung out because there's a test, or they've *failed* a goddamn test, or their fucking sweater's got a hole in the sleeve, and you realize that's not worth diddly-shit.

"Plus," Henry stroked the ends of his moustache, "you learn that you never want to wear OD—olive drab—again." With a snigger, he muttered, "Goddamn war stories.

"I remember one afternoon we helped six gook broads repair the bunker at a base camp I was staying over at. You had to take down the old sandbags that were split open and replace them with new sandbags. It was fucking hot like you wouldn't believe. It was always hot. There were six of them. I remember one was this polite old middle-aged broad with round cheeks and a towel wrapped around her head, and there was an old woman with a face like a sack of marbles, and a skinny-ass little chit of a thing with gold caps on all her teeth."

Henry's harsh expression softened as he recalled the slapdash crew. "I can see them as clear as I can see you sitting there. This one broad was strong as a bull, but her eyes were soft, kind of, and she always did the fucking hardest jobs. Her pal was the mouthpiece, she had a wise-ass remark for everything we said. And then there was this good-looking babe who'd just had a kid, she never opened her head. These six broads they moaned and sweated all fucking afternoon lugging fresh sandbags in the wheelbarrow across the yard to that caving-in bunker. The goddamn sun just blazing down on their heads and the wind blowing sand in their faces. They thought it was all funny as shit every goddamn time one of them dropped a sandbag, or got it in the face when a bag broke in her face when she hoisted it up, or when we stopped to rest and gave them rides in the wheelbarrow. They'd giggle and haw-haw and carry on over any little thing."

Henry scratched the back of his neck as his eyes became bitter. "And my best buddy, dude from Boise, Idaho. Came through a year of shit and got struck on the canal by goddamn *lightning,* for Chrisake, two weeks before he was due to go home. Some weird shit.

"But what was weirdest of all was, after living in that shit for twelve months, you come back home and it's just like it was before you left, except *you're* not the same. Most people still don't even know where fucking Vietnam *is,* and me and my buddies. . . ." Shaking his head, Henry gave Aaron a sardonic grin.

"I went to a party the other night," Aaron began after a long silence. "Some cats working against the war. One of them says he'd split the country if he was told to go to Vietnam. Says there are people in Canada who take care of resisters. What do you think? If I'm told to go to Vietnam, should I go?"

For a minute Henry said nothing. "Do you call yourself a resister?"

"I don't think so." Aaron's ideas, and perhaps he had not realized it before, were hardly that grand.

One of Henry's eyebrows flickered before his features assumed the inscrutability of a stone buddha. "Man, I can't tell you what to do. I haven't even got my own head straightened out.

"If I'd known before I went what that year was going to be like, I never would have gone. I would have left the country first. I swear I would have. It was absolutely the *worst* fucking experience of my life." Henry chuckled to himself.

"But you should never believe anybody when they tell you what to do with your life. You shouldn't even ask them. They'll just fuck you up. You know what I'm saying?"

# 8

There was a call from Deedee Sunday afternoon. She was back from Florida, and she had missed him. Aaron was astounded and gratified. Deedee had missed him. And *she* had called. They made a date to go out in her car for hamburgers.

After he hung up the phone, Aaron felt like dancing a jig. He ran the tub full of hot water. A fragrant, steaming bath, then a fresh shave, and flexing his shoulders in the mirror, he was gorgeous once again. Since there were no clean shirts in his drawer, he chose instead a navy blue sweater that brought out the smolder in his dark eyes. Quickly he ran the iron down his jeans to give them a crease and slipped them on still hot. And finally a swipe with the shoe brush across his beat-up Wellingtons. They would have to do. Stepping back from the mirror over the bureau, he smirked approval at what he beheld as he heard the horn of Deedee's car beep out front. Tossing his tweed sportcoat jauntily over one shoulder, he cantered down the stairs.

Behind the wheel of the Buick, brown as a biscuit and grinning for every penny she was worth, sat Deedee. As Aaron opened the driver's door, she threw her arms around him and planted a big kiss on his mouth.

"Oh, Aaron, I missed you so much!"

"Me too." He drew a breath then kissed her again. "You don't know how much."

As they sped across the campus, Deedee told him how they'd had only one really good day at the beach, it being blustery and cold the rest of the week, and how they had run into snow in North Carolina. All the exits had been closed off in Richmond because of snow, and they were afraid they wouldn't make it to Washington without having to stop. Which would have been disastrous because they were down to their last few dollars. Then the snow had stopped and there wasn't a flake on the ground from Fredericksburg north.

As they waited for a table in the sandwich shop, crowded with students back from the break, Aaron told Deedee about his draft notice. She was appalled.

"Oh, Aaron, what are you going to do?"

"What *can* I do?" he shrugged. "I'm going into the Army."

"Have you thought of becoming a conscientious objector?" she asked after they had ordered and were waiting for their food.

"I don't think you *become* a conscientious objector after you receive your draft notice," he replied. "Besides, I'm *not* one."

"Well, if it would get you out of going to Vietnam. . . . What about school?"

"Obviously, I won't be here next year." He was beginning to find her questions tedious. "Look, it's no big deal. I go in for two years then get out, and I have the GI Bill if I want to come back to school."

Deedee wrinkled her forehead and looked away.

"If anything, I may go to Canada," Aaron added in a slightly amused, conspiratorial tone. "I know some people who know some people up there who take care of guys who leave the country."

"Oh, Aaron, that's awfully drastic. You'd never be allowed to come back home to see your parents, or anything."

Aaron was relieved just then to see their waitress arriving with their hamburgers, and he did not bring up again the question of what he was going to do.

It was murky outside on the avenue, swarming with cars whose horns and exhaust fumes billowed through the gusty air.

"Where to?" Aaron asked as he held open Deedee's door.

"Get in. I want to show you something," she said mysteriously.

Sliding in behind the wheel, Aaron found Deedee digging in her purse. Presently she drew forth a shiny brass key and dangled it enticingly before his eyes.

"What's this?" he quizzed.

"Sandra has a sister with an apartment, and guess what—she's out of town. Sandra said we could borrow the apartment, if we wanted."

It was too much for Aaron. "Are you serious?" he exclaimed, then broke into a howl of laughter. "What's the address?"

They drove through the Sunday evening streets, past children in heavy coats and bright caps pulling wagons, young men in pointed shoes on street corners, fat old women on stoops, past brilliantly illuminated liquor stores, up and down hilly streets of grizzled rowhouses the color of dried blood, trees naked to the blue wind, rings of budding girls in flapping skirts, past figures hunched in doorways, past hamburger palaces and ribs joints and pawnshops. Past it all drove Aaron and Deedee, oblivious to everything except each other, reticent in their excitement at what was to come.

They found the refurbished row house on a tree-lined street not far north of the Capitol. After Deedee had gotten out another key to shut off the burglar alarm, they stepped inside and fumbled around for a light switch. The smallish room smelt of bayberry and was tastefully furnished in a mixture of antiques—oak and walnut with marble tops—and sleek Nordic pieces. Making their way back to the kitchen, Deedee reached behind her for Aaron's hand.

"Sandra said there would be beer in the refrigerator. We can help ourselves."

It was too good to be true. If Aaron had sat down seven days ago and tried to imagine The Perfect Situation, it would be precisely the one he was in this very moment.

After scouring the drawers for a bottle opener, they poured their beer into mugs from the cabinet and went back to the living room. On the way Aaron paused to find his favorite FM station on the radio, and when he turned around, Deedee was curled up on the divan. This was near-heaven, he thought as she lay with her head on his shoulder. With the real thing just around the corner.

For a quarter of an hour they alternately necked and sipped their beer until Aaron suggested that they explore upstairs. Already up off the divan, Deedee skipped toward the stairway and called back over her shoulder, "Last one's a rotten egg!"

Upstairs, as Deedee turned back the crocheted spread of the towering, mahogany bed, Aaron went into the bathroom and turned on the hot water. He half-emptied an expensive-looking bottle of perfumed bath oil into the porcelain footed tub. As he sat down on the toilet lid to take off his boots, he filled his lungs with the marvelous, soapy odor.

When he opened his eyes, Deedee was standing in the doorway naked. It took his breath away. Her skin was very white where her bikini had been, her breasts were honey mouthfuls, her bush lush and curly. Relishing his gaze, Deedee sauntered across the white and black tiled floor to the tub and knelt beside it to test the water as Aaron slid out of his clothes.

After soaping and rinsing in the very hot, iridescent water, they lay face to face in the filmy balm and squirmed against one another. Drifting up from the tub in fluid waves and curlicues, steam smeared everything with a dewy film, and both of them were red in the face. Like tiny convex mirrors, beads of sweat clung to Deedee's smooth upper lip. Feeling ennervated and cramped, Aaron gasped, "Let's get out."

With thick, white towels, they dried off quickly before running across the hall to plunge beneath the sheets.

At ten o'clock, against Aaron's groaning protestations, Deedee insisted that they roust themselves out of bed and start back to the campus. Class began for her at eight o'clock the next morning, and she intended to be prepared.

*    *    *    *

Overnight, it seemed, winter began dragging its slow, gray length back into its hole, and spring somersaulted into its place. Buds began to swell on knotted maples and elms as muddy flower beds around the campus sprouted yellow daffodils and crimson tulips.

For three weeks, while mild sunshine fell day after day and clouds trailed lazily from horizon to horizon, Aaron and Deedee dated steadily. In luminous evenings loud with birdsong and motorbikes, they trudged industriously to the engineering building, where they studied until ten, Aaron taking scrupulous care never to interrupt her during the course of the evening's work. On warm afternoons they lay out on the hillside in the sunlight and slept and studied.

And effortlessly, to no one's surprise, Aaron again became so absorbed in Deedee that he wanted to be with her every minute. No idea was worth entertaining unless she shared it, no activity was worth performing unless she were involved. Without Deedee, he was a shadow without a body. The notion that in a month he would be going into the Army he found agonizing. He might just as well be told that in a month he would be executed.

The third Friday night in April, they drove in her Buick out to National Airport to watch planes land and take off. Under a heavily overcast sky, it was almost balmy.

Against the whine of jet engines, Aaron settled back in his metal chair on the deserted observation deck, reached across for Deedee's hand, and followed with his eyes the sleek, glistening birds taxiing back and forth along the floodlit runways. Periodically, the heavy diesel air was shaken by the strident gunning of jet engines preparing for takeoff.

Never one to beat around the bush, Aaron asked Deedee outright what she thought of the idea of marrying him. As if she had been asked if she wanted her fingernails removed, Deedee winced, then thought for a while before saying anything.

"Aaron, I've said from day one that my goal is to get my law degree. I've never vacillated about that, not for a minute. If I were going to think about getting married, it would be to you. You're a sweet guy. We've had great times together. But this is not the time for me to even think about that."

"But if we got married," Aaron submitted, "and I got stationed in the States, you could go to a law school in the area, or . . ."

"Oh, Aaron, don't be ridiculous. You know I want to go to a top school."

". . . or if I got sent overseas, you could go wherever you wanted to, then after I got out I could join you and the GI Bill would help pay for it."

For a minute Deedee watched a slender jet on the far runway soar off the ground and disappear into the black clouds overhead. "There are too many complications," she observed with deliberation. "I don't want to get involved in a situation which, in the first place, is going to draw my attention away from my work. And second, which could become very complicated. What if you got sent to the boondocks where there weren't any good schools? What if I got pregnant?"

"What's kept you from getting pregnant so far?" Aaron asked in a measured voice. "You're giving me all these reasons why we shouldn't get married. What about why we *should?*"

Rather hard, she threw the question back at him. "Okay, why should we?"

After a moment, Aaron cried in exasperation, "God, Deedee, you're a machine! You program yourself to get a diploma so you can go off to Harvard or some other hotshot law school so you can go back to Dallas and work your ass off making money. What then? Is it on your schedule to get married then, or do you plan just to diddle the rest of your life?"

Seeing that Deedee had picked up her bag and pulled out a handkerchief, Aaron continued more gently. "There's something special between us. Or at least I think there is. We need to stay together. There's just not anything else."

Pinching her handkerchief into a tight ball, Deedee dabbed at the corner of one eye, then replied in a low, tolling voice, "Aaron, you are assuming that I share your feelings. That may be a mistake. I'm sorry if in your mind you've made our relationship into more than it is to me.

"I'm ambitious, Aaron. There is nothing right now that is as important to me as law school. Certainly not becoming an Army wife. And yes, there's my life in Dallas. There are a lot of things waiting for me there. I'm not going to throw it all away." Deedee wiped her nose with the handkerchief, then rolled it again into a ball.

"Aaron, you say I'm hung up on running my life according to plan, and you present yourself as such a free spirit. Yet you're the one who's trying to run people's lives. You're asking me to forget what I've worked for, what I've dreamed about since I was a sophomore in high school so I can do what you want. My God, Aaron! Do you think that's fair? You're trying to run my life, isn't that what it comes to? Well, if it's a question of who's going to run my life—me or someone else—it's going to be me."

With that, the conversation ended. For a while longer they sat self-consciously peering down over the airfield at the planes taxiing up and down the brightly illuminated runways. Then without another word, they got up and walked back together through the terminal, past people waiting in transit under fluorescent lights—flipping through magazines, sleeping, watching others walk by. On the way back to the campus, it was still warm enough to leave a window half open. Aaron found a jazz station on the radio: Oscar Peterson, rippling off "All of Me." After they turned off the beltway, Aaron asked, without taking his eyes from the road, "Is this the way we're going to end it?"

Deedee looked across the seat at him as he drove, his profile washed in the headlights of passing cars. Then without a word, she leaned over and kissed him gently on the cheek.

# Part Two

## 9

Late afternoon shadows from the cottonwoods and the purple plum shimmered on a well-tended lawn in Dallas. Bent over a border of marigolds, pink and white phlox, and purple ageratums, Aaron pulled weeds and dropped them into a battered tin bucket at his feet. He was sunburned. His back seemed to drip tea, and his bare legs and feet were splattered with mud.

Frequent rains had produced a chalky, white mildew on the leaves of the rambler roses along the six-foot stockade fence. Before calling it quits for the evening, he would spray the roses with fungicide.

A blue jay soared down from a branch high in a cottonwood and lighted in the plum tree. *Skaak, skaak.* It flapped to the ground and poked its beak into grass so green it was blue.

Aaron smelled honeysuckle that had grown too heavy for the crumbling section of fence across the back of the lot. It needed repacing. And the trim on the house needed repainting.

If he had not gone into architecture, he might have become a landscaper or nurseryman. His earliest memory was of being carried in his grandpa's strong arms up and down rows of flowers in the greenhouse and standing on a rusty metal step stool by the arranging table to compose bouquets from snapdragons and gladioli and maidenhair fern.

Wind soughed high in the cottonwoods and shadows capered on the lawn. A screen door slammed. A naked little girl, yellow hair flying about her head, raced across the grass.

Aaron stood up and stretched out his arms. "How's my girl?" he sang, picking her up and tickling her under the chin.

Bubbling laughter, she flailed him with stubby feet and soft white fists.

"Daddy's dirty," he said, setting her back on her feet. He watched her scamper off bowlegged after two cardinals strutting about the birdbath.

Again the screen door slammed. His wife stood with legs spread on the flagstone patio, brushing out her long hair. "Aaron, when are you getting ready? You'll need to go after the sitter in twenty minutes."

If he didn't spray the roses, they would lose their leaves. And if there were anyplace he did not want to spend the evening, it was at the champagne opening of the new art show at the Dallas Museum of Art. "Why don't we stay home?" he asked, mopping his forehead with a handkerchief.

"We can't very well not show up after we've made reservations."

The Siamese cat crept out from under the green Catskills lawn chair. She arched her back and rubbed against Deedee's calf. "I haven't even fed the cat," she exclaimed and gave a last impatient dash with the brush to her chestnut hair. "Come on, Aaron. While you're showering, I've got to feed Kim and get her ready for bed. And I've still got myself to get ready.

"Kim," she called out across the sun-dappled lawn, "come in now. Mommy wants to feed you and get you to bed.

"Twenty minutes, Aaron!" she snapped before going back into the house.

\*  \*  \*  \*

Wandering in his undershorts into the sunny breakfast

room the next morning, Aaron found Deedee there alone. She was sitting with her feet in her lap at the round, claw-footed oak table. In one hand she held up close to her face a colorful scrap of needlepoint, peering intently at its geometric design, then removing it to arm's length and squinting her eyes, meanwhile humming a made-up tune.

Seeing Aaron, she mumbled a good-morning and put down the canvas. "Coffee's in the kitchen," she said, rifling one hand through rumpled hair. Steadying herself with one arm, she leaned down to pick up the thick Sunday paper off the braided rug. Spreading it in front of her on the table, she began to pick through the sections, pausing periodically to exclaim under her breath in astonishment or surprise at some piece of news.

Aaron stood watching her. Deedee's face was overly square, and more than a little haggard from the demands of her career. Nevertheless, she still seemed lovely to him. She was aging handsomely. In the broad forehead and heavy-lidded, blue eyes, he perceived wit and straightfor-wardness. In the high, rounded cheekbones, pale now without makeup, and pouting lips there was a sensuousness that excited him. Even folded in her chair like this in an unironed muslin gown, cross-legged like a yogi, there was a hint of straight-backed carriage, of easy grace in the way she pointed her shoulders that took his breath away.

She looked like what she was—a woman who had never been denied anything. Accustomed to request and receive, she had never found herself overdressed or underdressed, had never arrived too early for an engagement or too late, been loud or a wallflower.

While he stood leaning in the doorway and looking at her, Aaron pretended to be admiring the view out the bay window. Immersed in the newspaper, Deedee did not acknowledge him again. Remembering how she had slept this morning on her side, cradled into the hollow of his own body, he marveled at her self-containment, her complete otherness.

Aaron filled his coffee cup and sat down across from his wife. Spreading open a section of the paper on the table, he snorted. Then in a mincing, exaggerated fashion, he crowed, "It's the debutantes!"

"Oh, God," muttered Deedee under her breath. She peered across the table to the society page.

" 'The names of twenty young ladies,' " read Aaron aloud while Deedee rolled back her eyes, " 'who will be presented to Dallas Society next November 28 at the gala Belles Heures Ball at the Fairmont Hotel were announced last evening. These young ladies and their guests will participate in an array of events extending through the summer season before departing to their respective institutions of higher learning in the fall. The names of their escorts will be announced in next Sunday's column. The roster of debutantes, who will soon take their place among the Beautiful People of the Southwest, includes the following . . .' "

Aaron broke off and shook his head.

"Who are they?" pursued Deedee with unconcealed interest. She snatched the paper after Aaron disdained to read further.

" 'Kristin Ford Anderson, Angela Renee Curtis, Marijo Lee Denton . . .' " One elbow on the table, her hand combing back her hair, Deedee paused. "Her mother, you know, was Doris Yates. She taught me how to swim one summer after my parents had absolutely given it up. I'd taken lessons for two summers and still wouldn't get my hair wet . . ."

"What's new?" Aaron inquired.

". . . and then Doris Yates, whose little sister Bitsy was in my French class at Hockaday, saw me at the club one afternoon and she asked, 'Can't you swim, little girl?' I remember, that's what she asked, 'Can't you swim, little girl?' I shook my head, no. Well, Doris took me under her wing—she was in Upper School and I thought she was Esther Williams—and every time I saw her at the pool that summer she helped me. By the end of the summer I could swim."

As Aaron smirked, Deedee continued. "Who did she marry? That awful Lyle Denton. Fire-engine-red hair and braces all over his teeth. His father is in oil.

" 'Carrie Sturges Francis, Bunny MacNeice Hirshberger, Valerie Anne Hinton. . .' Hinton Meatpacking. You couldn't miss that nose. We used to call Mel Hinton 'Hatchethead.' Wasn't that *awful*? 'Kirstie Amalie Long . . .' Her grandmother was a Delheimer from New York, and in all the years she lived here, she never once invited a soul into her house. They lived in that mammoth Tudor place at the foot of Hanging Oak Road. Her daughter Meg, Kirstie's mother, had to pay for it, God knows. Meg married a Long, though, and the lights haven't gone off in that house since. Kirstie's turned into a pretty girl. I love her hair. She could stand to lose a few pounds, though."

It had never ceased to awe Aaron slightly that his wife had grown up in Society. Swimming at the country club, driving around in expensive cars with the top down, being presented herself as a debutante. Not long after their meeting in a snowbank ten years earlier, Aaron discovered that Deedee had attended Wellesley for two years. However it was not until after their marriage that he learned of the friendships she had formed there with half a dozen girls who now maintained elaborate residences along the eastern seaboard from Booth Harbor, Newport, and New York to Palm Beach and Key Biscayne. Even now Deedee exchanged letters with a baroness in Madrid whom she helped through the trauma of post-adolescent braces on her teeth.

When as students on Sunday afternoons they had skylarked around Washington in her Buick, seeking out decrepit Victorian rowhouses in shabby neighborhoods and imagining how they might be restored, the discrepancy in their backgrounds had not seemed a problem. Three years later, well after Aaron's return from the Army, and in

the face of lukewarm enthusiasm from both sets of parents — Frieda and Ernest's intimidation at Deedee's wealth,
their stiff-necked former paupers' pride matching in its
disdain the unamused incredulity of the Hartcrofts that
their daughter would be seriously interested in someone
with such a background — the young couple persisted and
were married in a small ceremony in Dallas.

> Deborah Ashfield Hartcroft and Aaron
> Ray Teague exchanged vows in Tinsley
> Chapel on February 21. Serving as
> Matron of Honor was the bride's aunt,
> Mrs. Hardy Frazier of Miami, Florida.
> Best Man was Richard Teague. Daugh-
> ter of Mrs. Benton Fife of Palm
> Springs, California, and Rex Mar-
> tingale Hartcroft, granddaughter of
> the Toastie Hartcrofts, the bride wore
> an ivory wool going-away suit. She car-
> ried a bouquet of white orchids. After
> a trip to Puerto Vallarta, the couple will
> establish a home in the city.

Frieda had laminated the announcement on a piece of
wood cut to resemble a scroll that she bought at Hobby Hut
and hung it in the hall.

"Aaron, why are you sneering?"

"I'm not sneering. I'm just finishing my coffee," he
protested. "I'm savoring your account of the deb-yew-
taunts."

"God, Aaron. You show absolutely no toleration at all in
some areas."

"What do you mean? I haven't said a word."

"You don't need to. If you could see your face. . . ."

"Oh, well. I'm sorry. I obviously can't help the way I
look." Aaron was offended.

"You know perfectly well what I mean. You sit there as though this were the most ridiculous thing in the world."

"Well. . . ."

"I don't make fun of your friends."

"I'm not making fun of anybody."

"Yes, you are. You're making fun of these girls, and you don't even know them."

For a moment, Aaron said nothing and rubbed his thumbnail around the inside of his cup. "No, I'm not making fun of the girls. It's the ludicrous manner in which the whole affair is written up by that silly twat of a reporter."

"Granted, Lana Leigh isn't a great writer. But we're talking about a newspaper column, not a Great Work of Art."

"Horseshit is horseshit."

"Forget it." Deedee folded the paper back and stood up.

"I can't believe you're defending that overwritten garbage," said Aaron.

"I don't see what difference it makes," Deedee was gesturing now with one hand while the other was spraddled on her hip. "We're talking about a silly little society column. That's how they're *all* written."

"I rest my case."

"God, talk about a snit over nothing!" Deedee spun on her heel and strode out into the garden.

The door slammed.

Aaron felt like following her and pursuing the argument. Reason told him, no. Social matters, he knew from experience, constituted a bone of contention between them. Better to let the matter die. Each of them had learned to compromise: he bit his tongue when he sensed that he was becoming acerbic; she did not often insist on their taking part in the doings of local society.

That had been tough for her to accept after their marriage. Brilliant and something of a rebel, Deedee had never wanted to play the Great Lady—to join the Junior

League and the oldest country club, to usher her husband in white tie to society balls four times a year. She had wanted very much, though, to stay a part of her former circle of friends. All of them were rich. Talking money, breathing money, smelling of money.

Among them, Aaron felt out of place — as he had felt when, as an eighth grader, he had found himself one afternoon at a lunch table with a group of rich kids talking about clothes. All of them but Aaron had bought their bleeding madras shirts at the little prairie town's most expensive men's wear shop.

"Where'd you get *your* shirt?" inquired a brawny, crew-cut boy who leered at Aaron's beige shirt.

On the spot and embarrassed, he had named an inexpensive chain department store. He recalled the muffled giggles, the exchanged glances that greeted his news. Aaron felt something of that experience — being a new boy in cheap clothing who ran into a wall built with bricks of wealth and cemented with social position — each time he was dragged by Deedee to some gathering involving her set of friends.

The women were *too* exquisitely made up, heavy golden earrings glistening from hair too well groomed, garments fitting too beautifully. And the men with their well-fed, stupid faces, their talk about Texas football and travel, their aggressive, abrasive egos. Everyone lounging about and being horsey and grinning too much. How Aaron loathed it.

How Deedee missed it.

# 10

Cars. Cars everywhere. With their daughter strapped into the infant carrier, Aaron and Deedee drove down the winding, mimosa-fringed street of little postwar houses. Cars parked along the curbs. Cars underneath carports and lined up in driveways. Cars minus wheels and propped on cement blocks undergrown with dandelions and crabgrass. It was a street of cars.

They had set out across town after lunch to see his older brother and sister-in-law's new baby, Randall, born three years to the day after their own Kim.

Rick and Sherri hadn't wanted the baby. They couldn't afford it. With two other children, there was no more room in their tiny house.

Aaron hoped the baby would not drive them further apart. His brother had been wild after he got out of the Marines, staying out all night, drinking and racing around on a black Harley-Davidson. Then he had married Sherri in a hasty way, and within eighteen months there were two children. His wildness had hardened into sullenness. The irrepressible good humor that had characterized Rick as a youth, the strangeness, the dark good looks that had made others want to look at him, be with him, do for him — all that had vanished. He put on weight, continued the drinking that had begun to trouble him in the Marines, and withdrew into himself.

Sherri became increasingly harassed by his fits of temper and his erratic performance at work, which had caused him to lose four jobs within the nine months she carried Randall. Her eyes grew tight and her smile in company became a fixed grimace.

"Their car's gone," groused Deedee as the tiny frame house came into view down the street. "I knew we should have called first instead of wasting all this time."

However, the front door was hanging open. They swerved into the driveway and halted to avoid a sharp upheaval in the concrete. A doll buggy lay overturned in the middle of the ragged front yard, its dolly among the weeds on its back with hair torn off and one glass eye gone. A wooden playpen filled with moving cartons shared the front porch with an old stove. The screen door had been poked through and the house was in bad need of paint.

Through wide-open windows drifted sounds of a radio and a child crying. Sherri answered the door with a baby in one arm, four-year-old Buddy clinging to one leg, and five-year-old Tamra sucking her thumb and peeping out from behind her mother's other side. She looked tired but happy to see them.

"We brought Kim to see the new baby," announced Aaron. Remarking how big Kim looked beside him, Aaron cooed and admired the wizened, bald-headed little creature while Deedee looked at her watch.

"Come on in," Sherri stepped aside. The hot room was crowded with furniture and smelled of Pine Sol and vegetable soup. "The air conditioner's broken, so we've been in the back yard."

They followed Sherri through the thrift shop of old tables and chairs into the kitchen, where a huge pot simmered on the stove, and out the back door. Around an ailing Chinese elm were gathered a broken kitchen chair and a wooden bench on which rested an infant seat, a tin pan, and a paper sack.

"Aaron, would you bring out another chair?" asked Sherri.

The two women were exchanging the baby as he carried the rusted chrome chair down the concrete stoop to the shade tree.

"He is a pretty baby," admitted Deedee rather grudgingly. Aaron fastened a solicitous eye on Kim, standing at the back of the yard just out of range of the other two children's high-flying swings.

"Yes, he's a fine-looking boy."

Sherri placed the paper sack inside the tin pan and sat down beside it on the wooden bench. A breeze made sitting in the shade pleasant.

"What's that you've got there?" Aaron motioned toward the sack.

"Snap beans. My sister brought them. They'll be good fixed with new potatoes."

"Grandma Hale used to sit on the front porch in the summertime and snap green beans in a tin basin just like that one," Aaron recalled. "Do you remember that, Deedee?"

"Vaguely," replied his wife.

"You kids be careful of Kim," called out Sherri. She looked worn out, thought Aaron. Without any makeup, her skin was dull and crow's feet crinkled the skin around her eyes. Her hair was caught back in a cluster of curls by an orange ribbon that matched her shorts.

"Where's Rick?" he asked.

"Oh, some friends stopped by and they went out to White Rock Lake."

Aaron was silent for a moment. "Well, is everything all right?"

"Oh, just fine." Sherri's expression was a grimace.

"What's he think of the baby?"

She glanced across at the child, nestled into Deedee's shoulder. "He's proud of him. He was hoping for another girl at first. But when he saw Randall, he said he'd keep him."

Kim began to cry. Aaron looked around sharply.

"What's the matter, sweetheart?" he called across the unmown yard. The other two children were continuing to swing.

"She's just upset because she wants to swing," said Deedee. "Ignore her."

"Tamra and Buddy, you get off those swings and play with your cousin," cried Sherri. Turning back to her company, she asked if she could get them anything.

"We can't stay," said Aaron.

"There's Coke or lemonade. Or I could open you a beer."

For a moment, Aaron vacillated, then saw his wife glaring at him. "No, we've got a million things to do. We just wanted to see the baby. Let me hold him," he said to Deedee and stretched out his arms. Carefully he took hold of the child and pretended to weigh him. "What a big boy! How much did he weigh?"

"Nine pounds eight ounces."

"How's Rick liking his new job?"

"He seems to be liking it real well." Again the tightness crept into Sherri's face. "The boss gave him a bonus the other day for handling the most volume of anyone in the store."

"Great," said Aaron, while Deedee motioned for Kim. "You give me a call," he added quietly to Sherri, "if I can be any help. Remember."

Sherri thanked him as he stood up and handed back her baby.

"I think he's about asleep," he said, patting Randall's bottom. As he snuggled onto his mother's breast. "Tell Rick we were here, and keep in touch."

## 11

A year earlier, Aaron had driven south along the beach highway from Galveston, looking for his younger brother, when there he stood — looking like a cover from a surfing magazine, bow-legged and smiling from ear to ear. Long sun-bleached hair, shades lighter than the rest of his lean, amber body, blew about Tommy's head as he extended a narrow hand and flashed a wolfish grin. "I *thought* that looked like you," Tommy grunted. "How're you doing, you mother?"

Pumping the boy's hand, Aaron replied, "Great. How about yourself?"

"Couldn't be finer. What brings you down here?"

"I've had business in Houston and thought I'd drive down here and catch you before I go home. I've got to be back in Dallas tonight." Aaron glanced over at the rusted-out station wagon with two short surfboards on top and asked, "Catching any waves?"

"Ain't bad today, though it ain't been shit for weeks. There are some good rights off that break." Tommy pointed to where a line of foam curled away from an otherwise immaculate, peacock blue sea. "I surfed for an hour then got out because it's so cold."

"Ready to get back in?" Aaron asked, his gray eyes lucent.

"Sure. Why don't you join me?"

"Shit, I'm too damn old."

"Bullshit, you're the one that taught me to surf. I got a wetsuit in the car."

"No," said Aaron, smiling, "you go ahead. Show me what you can do."

Kneeling in the sand beside a fluorescent Webber surf-board, Tommy rubbed it with a bar of clear paraffin. "How's Deedee and Kim?" he squinted up into his brother's square-jawed face.

"Oh, they're fine."

Giving his board a final swipe, Tommy hoisted it up under his arm and trotted into the surf. When the water was mid-thigh, he dropped the gracefully shaped little board with a plop. On his belly, he paddled expertly to beyond where the waves were breaking.

Grinning, Aaron watched his brother catch a fine four-foot wave just after it started to break, slide down the vertical slope and pivot at the bottom, then zoom up the face of the wave and down again, zigzagging across the concave surface until it petered out in the shallows.

"What about that shit!" the boy shouted against the din of waves.

Energetically, Tommy paddled outside on his belly once again. The water looked cold, but the waves were about as good as they ever got in Texas, with its fickle, mushy beach break. Texas waves were for fun, Aaron had always told his brother. It certainly looked like fun today.

As a glassy swell undulated toward shore, Tommy backed his board into position, nose in the air. Then at the crucial moment, he sprang forward, calves kicking the air, and paddled frantically. As he caught the wave, he pulled himself up into a crouch and looked down the slick elevator chute sliding away underneath his board. Down the glossy face he sailed, then shifted his weight onto his right heel at the bottom of the trough and careened back up the trans-lucent wall to the lip where, for a moment, he leaned back onto his left foot, turned, and glided again down the wave's scooped-in side, always moving as Aaron had told him *with* the wave, never against it. As he shot a second time up to the crest, he inclined the board over onto the wave's green back and paddled outside.

The kid was good on the board, damn good. And he looked healthy. In high school Aaron had spent holidays and parts of every summer on the beaches of Galveston and Padre Island. Later, after getting out of the Army, it was he who had introduced his adolescent brother to surfing. Tommy's robust appearance allayed some of Aaron's concerns about his brother's welfare, concerns prompted largely by their parents' fears that, after dropping out of college, the boy would get himself hooked on drugs, or become a thief, or marry a Mexican. It was clear, now, that Mom was being overly protective of her baby. The kid was doing all right.

Aaron watched his brother surf in the frigid water under a brilliant blue sky for the better part of an hour before he paddled back to shore. Rubbing himself dry, teeth clattering behind blue lips, Tommy asserted that it had been great surfing.

South of Galveston, around behind the Perfect Wave Surf Shop, stood a ten-by-ten, flat-roofed, cinder block hut with a door and two windows. Tommy received his rent and some extra money in exchange for helping around the shop. As he told Aaron, it was all he needed.

After lighting the portable gas stove, Tommy told his brother to find a record as he stripped off his trunks and stepped into the bathroom, which was really just a corner of the square room partitioned off by plywood panels that did not reach the ceiling. As steam from the shower wafted over the partition, Aaron put one of the disks from *Exile on Main Street* on the automatic changer. Soon Tommy stepped back into the room, wrapped in a towel, and while they chatted about who had gotten married and who had kids and so on, he put on a pair of cut-offs and a sweatshirt.

Taking a cellophane bag from a drawer, Tommy began rolling two fat joints. Aaron felt a little funny smoking grass with his little brother; it wasn't the big-brotherly role he'd been prepared to play. However, Aaron was no stranger to the weed, and Tommy was, after all, a big boy.

"It's a good life," Tommy proclaimed, walking around. "Here I am twenty years old and I've got a lot of years left before I can't surf anymore. There's people in California and the Islands been surfing all their life and they're in their *forties* and *fifties,* for Chrisake." Tommy took a profound drag on the joint, exhaled through his mouth, then inhaled the smoke again through his nose. "That's gonna be me, man. If I can't live the way I want, I'll just say fuck it and drown."

Part of Aaron sympathized, agreed with his brother. If you can't live on your terms, why bother? He'd once had the same idea. His head was ballooning from the grass; he was seeing very clearly and yet as if cushioned, from a distance. "Whew! What's in this?" Aaron asked, waving his cigarette.

"Columbian grass. Laced with a little hash."

"Some shit!" As they finished their joints and split another, they lost the desire to talk. Aaron lay back in the old mildewed easy chair with his feet up on a table, while Tommy flopped down on his bed, unmade in a corner.

Aaron's mind concocted intricate schemes, including one in which he moved to Greenwich Village and lived with his daughter in the Plaza Hotel. Every morning they would walk down swept steps and go surfing in an ocean that was consistently blue and produced even, four-foot waves.

When he sat up, it was dark and the room had gotten very hot. Turning the stove down, he opened the single cabinet over the sink. Nothing but a can of coffee and an empty cereal box. In the refrigerator, he found a six-pack of Cokes, a jar of pickle relish, and a jug of water. Aaron limped over to where his brother lay sprawled on the bed.

"Tommy, wake up." No response. Shaking him this time, Aaron again called, "Tommy, Tommy, wake up."

Opening one bleary eye, Tommy gazed up and mumbled something.

"Come on, let's get something to eat."

"You go, man. I'm gonna sleep some more."

Giving up, Aaron went outside. The night air was heavy
with moisture and salt. He had to get back to Dallas.
Tommy was doing okay; Aaron would call him tomorrow
from Dallas.

*    *    *    *

All that had taken place a year ago. During that time
Aaron had had no further communication with his
brother.

Now, standing in a high-ceilinged, one-room apartment
on the fringes of the French Quarter, moving a bit to the
right to catch the breeze drifting down from the brown
ceiling fan, the kind you used to find in dry-goods shops,
Aaron peered closely at Tommy and asked, "How did you
find this place?" Over the past twelve months, his brother
had turned into a wraith.

"It was advertised in the paper."

"You ought to hear what Mom says about it."

"Shit," Tommy shrugged it off, "they stayed in a fucking
Ramada Inn."

Aaron could imagine his parents' faces when they first
saw the decrepit building: red-and-white-striped pillars on
the ground floor where a barber shop had gone in; on the
second-floor balcony, hanging baskets of scarlet impatiens
and laundry drying over the railing.

"It's a nice room," Aaron motioned toward the eight-
foot-high set of French doors with wavy glass that washed
the musty room in bluish light. The corner fireplace of
rose marble, its mantle mounded with tape cassettes.

"You should see next door. The guys collect antiques."

Aaron nodded. He could not fault his mother's description; Tommy looked terrible. He had lost fifteen pounds.
His skin was sallow and there were pouches underneath his
eyesockets. His hair was chopped off in a punk style that
emphasized the gauntness of his features. Most alarming,
his spindly forearms were pocked with needle tracks.

"Where are you working?"

"This record shop on Canal Street." Tommy flashed a mouthful of wolfish yellow teeth. "I get a discount on tapes and records."

"What are you listening to these days?"

"Oh . . ." Tommy thought for a moment, "I like Grateful Dead and Boston. Hot Tuna. And I'm kind of into show tunes and," he added with reverence, "Lou Reed."

"Oh, you like Lou Reed? I saw him after I got out of the Army."

"I remember you talking about that."

Aaron recalled Tommy's tagging at his heels in the late sixties. The older brother had been very negative about everything—for a while flamboyantly so—after returning from Vietnam. Tommy's rebelliousness, Frieda insisted, had been due in large part to his brother's example.

Now, however, standing in Tommy's apartment in a neat pullover knit shirt and tropical slacks, an expensive Rolex watch, and neatly trimmed, graying hair, Aaron felt out of touch with the boy. The fourteen-year difference in their ages was worth a generation. Nothing seemed to connect them. That Tommy was guttering, though, was apparent from the needle tracks on his arms. There wasn't much time. Aaron groped for a way to articulate the matter. On impulse, he chose a frontal attack.

"Hey," he began, "I don't want to piss you off, but I'm concerned about you. What the hell's going on?"

Tommy's eyes flared, but he remained silent.

"I mean, I realize it's none of my damn business, but you *are* my brother. I feel somewhat responsible for you."

"Fuck off," Tommy threw back half-humorously, "I'm not your little brother anymore. I'm twenty-one years old."

"Well, let my tell you, my friend, you look like shit. When I saw you a year ago, you looked great. Now. . . ." Aaron grabbed Tommy's wrists and held up the scarred underneath sides of his forearms.

Down in the street, a siren sliced through the late afternoon heat.

"Does that happen often?" Temporarily, Aaron had
abandoned the attack and was tossing about for something
to say.

"You get used to it."

Aaron pursed his mouth and mused. He could figure
the score: from having messed rather heavily with drugs
himself, in Vietnam, Aaron knew that Tommy was unre-
achable unless he allowed himself to be reached. No one
could force help on him. Nevertheless, fatalistically, Aaron
felt compelled to try.

"You know," he began, "Mom and Dad are pretty worried about you."

"I could give a shit."

You little prick, Aaron thought to himself, you're not the
one who gets telephone calls twice a month begging me to
go find Tommy, check on Tommy.

The younger brother took a cigarette from a pack on the
mantle and lit it. "I'll tell you what Pappy dear thinks of
yours truly." Tommy French-inhaled the first drag. "I
swore I'd never set foot in that house again."

Aaron waited for the rest of the story.

"I'd been somewhere. Mom had fixed dinner for Aunt
Prell and Uncle Hershell and she'd wanted me to be there.
Dad was waiting up for me when I got home. 'Your mother
was very disappointed when you didn't show up for dinner,'
he began in this very martyred voice. 'Was there some
reason you didn't come to dinner? Not taking into account
the fact that she cooked all afternoon, and that your Aunt
Prell and Uncle Hershell drove all the way over here from
Fort Worth, don't you think you owe your mother and me
at least the courtesy of calling to say you wouldn't be here?
How do you think it makes us feel when you treat your
parents this way? I know you think I'm just an insurance
salesman, but let me tell you, there are still a few things you
don't know the first thing about. In the first place, it takes

*money* to live, boy, and money doesn't grow on trees. You have to work for it. All you've done, ever in your life, is *take*. That's all you know how to do. Then when your mother asks one thing in return from you, *one thing*, you can't be bothered. You don't do a damn thing except use this house as a place to eat and sleep in. You're too good to come to one dinner your mother fixes when relatives come over, but you're not too good to let her do your dirty laundry.

" 'She doesn't ask much. To be treated with a little consideration, a little decency, that's all. I don't ask that you come back to Bugg and get work, although I'd get down on my knees and thank God every night for the rest of my life if that should happen. No, I just ask that you treat your mother with a little respect, and that you stop making a mockery of everything you've ever been taught. You say you don't believe in God, you say the country stinks, the president is a crook. Come down out of the clouds. How are you ever going to amount to anything with ideas like those? No one's going to hire someone who thinks like that. And don't make the mistake of believing that any decent girl is going to marry someone who thinks that way. Not on your life.' "

Tommy lit another cigarette from the butt of the one he was finishing. "Just as he was launching into the 'You've got a great future, but you can't just sit back and wait for it to happen, you've got to *make* it happen!' routine, I decided I'd had enough and told him to get fucked."

"You did what?" exclaimed Aaron, incredulous.

"I told him to get fucked," repeated Tommy without batting an eye. "I haven't been back home since."

"Shit," muttered Aaron. "You shouldn't take it so personally. We've all heard that speech before. What happened when they came down here?"

"They stayed in the fucking Ramada Inn, like I told you. I had to work most of the time. We met at the motel for dinner once or twice."

Finding himself protective of his parents, Aaron resented Tommy's behavior. Aaron had been furious with his parents before, and Rick had too, but neither of them had ever used language like that.

"What're you in New Orleans for?" Tommy's question brought Aaron back. It was clear he wanted to change the subject.

"Oh, I have three clients who want to put in a group of condominiums," he said cooly. There was nothing more to be gained from talking further about Tommy's argument with his dad. "On Preston Road north of LBJ. They want a New Orleans motif. So I talked them into flying me down."

Tommy nodded at his brother's finesse.

"I thought if you weren't busy tomorrow, maybe you could show me around."

"Sure."

"Deedee's here, too."

"Where is she?"

"At the hotel."

Someone had begun shouting in the apartment next door.

"Don't mind that," said Tommy with a yellow grin. "That goes on every afternoon about this time. I think it has to do with which of them is going to fix dinner. Either one's a good cook. But it's a fight every afternoon to see who's going to be the one to cook dinner."

Not looking toward the sink and the small countertop piled high with encrusted dishes and pans, the first thing he had noticed walking into the apartment, Aaron suggested that they go out to dinner. His treat.

Tommy chose Ruby Red's, a dark, crowded little restaurant with hanging stained-glass lampshades. They lingered for the better part of an hour. Rick and Sherri, Aaron told Tommy, were not getting along well. More precisely, Rick was never home. After work and on weekends he drank beer with his friends. His house was falling apart. Aaron didn't know how much longer Sherri would put up with it.

About his own marital problems, Aaron said nothing.

Since Grandma Hale died, he confided instead, Grandpa had gone downhill. Every day he grew more helpless. Now Mom and her sisters were facing the prospect of placing the stubborn old man in a nursing home. Mom was really upset.

Tommy rolled his lips. There wasn't much to tell about his own life. He worked in the evenings, he slept late, he liked New Orleans.

What did he do in the afternoons? Who were his friends?

He hung around. Yeah. And again the wolfish grin that disclosed nothing.

As they were finishing their hamburgers, a tanned, well-muscled man in a tank top and running shorts that matched his robin's-egg-blue eyes elbowed his way over to their table and planted his right hand on Tommy's shoulder.

"How're y'all?"

"Hey," Tommy glanced up over his shoulder. The newcomer was not as youthful as he had appeared at first.

Very rapidly he began jabbering in a thickly accented voice about a party that was to take place that evening. Occasionally his eyes would stray to Aaron's face and widen.

Aaron soon grew uncomfortable from the fellow's darting looks, his torrent of patois, his hand, which had begun massaging Tommy's shoulder lightly in circles.

Aaron caught his brother's eye. His face wore a cryptic expression. For a moment, as the visitor chattered on, Tommy glowered back. Then his jaw relaxed in a lupine grin. Over the hand on his shoulder Tommy cupped his own hand and rubbed it against his stubbly cheek.

At once, as when a flare quietly pops and produces its umbrella of white light, it struck Aaron—his brother was gay.

"Hey man," Tommy spoke up in the midst of blue eyes' badinage, "I want you to meet my brother."

Aaron sensed that his reactions were being tested.

"China, this is Aaron." Still clasping the tanned hand, Tommy offered it across the table to his brother.

The two shook hands. Stunned, Aaron was reacting on instinct. He asked China to join them. Only then, as China chased off on an involved refusal, did Aaron look again at his brother's face.

Vanished was any hostility. In its place there was a reflective, loose-jawed smirk. Again Tommy abruptly interrupted his friend's repartee. "China's a Cajun."

Stopping in mid-sentence to display a set of oversized, even teeth that were very white, China tossed back his head and gargled a laugh.

"Or pretends to be," added Tommy.

"Kiss my ass," China darted out a pointed tongue.

"Aaron's interested in Southern Things," said Tommy.

"Oh?"

"I'm getting together some ideas for a project," said Aaron, more relaxed now. "I'm an architect."

"I just love old houses," bubbled China. "You really should visit some of the plantation homes. Shadows-on-the-Teche in New Iberia, which is where I'm from, is marvelous."

"What I'm working on is a set of condominiums," explained Aaron, "so I'm more interested in the houses in the Quarter."

China widened his blue eyes at Tommy. "He would love Brian's place, wouldn't he?"

"Mmmm."

"How long are you going to be in town?"

"We're leaving day after tomorrow. Tommy's promised to show my wife and me around."

"Oh."

Tommy made a face at his brother across the table.

Squinting towards the regulator wall clock over the bar, China declared that he had to run. "You coming tonight?" he asked Tommy.

"When I get off work. Wait up, I'll walk you to the door."

After China and Tommy had left the table, Aaron attempted to sort out his thoughts. It was first necessary not to allow the revelation of Tommy's homosexuality to confuse the central issue — his brother's drug abuse.

Tommy's sexual orientation was not a problem, as far as Aaron was concerned. Instead, it provided a chance for Aaron to prove to himself that he wasn't a goddamn hypocrite. He had always held the view that every person has the right to satisfy his own desires, so long as no one else gets hurt in the process. That was his belief, and it applied to Tommy as well. If Aaron's brother was gay, that was his own damn business, nobody else's. Aaron wondered, on the periphery of his thinking, if anybody else in his family knew? He'd had no indication that his parents knew anything.

Next concern: why the hell was his brother sticking junk in his veins? *That* was the issue, let there be no mistaking. (A quiet voice interjected, "Tommy, I don't even know you. We have different fathers. You were four years old when I left home. Now you sit here grinning in that dumb French-cut tee shirt with needle tracks up your arms and think you're cool. I could care less!")

In any case, as Aaron had realized in his brother's apartment, it would be wasted breath to try to dissuade him from using drugs if he wasn't asking for help. If that should occur, and Aaron hoped fervently it would, then he would do whatever he could to help. In the meantime, there simply was not a whole hell of a lot Aaron could do to help his brother besides let Tommy know that he cared about what became of him.

*From Aaron's notebook:*

Wisterias, live oaks, white and red oleanders, camphor trees, palms, palmettos.

Jasmine, camellias, magnolias, crepe myrtles, sweet olives, roses, azaleas, cannas, lilies, poinsettias, wisterias, yellow and magenta begonias, mimosas.

Ivy, palms, oleanders, banana plants (they say the fruit never ripens in New Orleans), plum trees.

Jars on shaded patios. Walls, fountains, trellises.

Rust-eaten wrought iron like great flowering vines trailing from every balcony. Hammered into the ironwork: Cupid's bows and arrows, tulips, morning glories, maize, acorn and oak leaf.

Brick walls covered in cement stucco plaster. Painted in pastels. Deep green shutters. Everywhere the cast-iron balconies and supports which along with the tall windows and French doors relieve the plain flat fronts.

Shaded courtyards approached from the street through passageways paved with flagstone or brick.

We are sitting on the levee, sun behind the clouds, boats hooting along the Mississippi. I am watching my brother out of the corner of my eye. Light-boned, with yellow skin and patchy brown hair. The shadow of a beard ends in a goatee, as if chalked on. His eyes are burned nearly shut.

Deedee refused to lunch at the Jardin Creole, where we'd been told you find the finest crawfish étouffée in New Orleans. The street, she insisted, smelled like a garbage truck.

Otherwise, my dear wife has not spoken two words to me. Why, I wonder, did she come along? She had a brief to prepare. I was hoping that things might take a turn for the better.

Last night's stripper danced behind the bar. Wriggling out of time to the snare drum, swiveling on platform heels to wave her powdered ass in our faces, scrutinizing herself in the smoky mirror, humping the air without blinking a gilded eyelid.

The Quarter shimmers in the heat to rhythms from courtyards and bars, street musicians and tap dancers. Standing still and sitting down, looking for a pick-up. Chatting for a while, touching with hands, walking off singly or together.

# 12

The rungs of the stepladder cut into his shins and the fronts of his thighs. Aaron pressed the brand new ceiling fan with his shoulder up against the hole in the ceiling. He was sweating and his arms were aching. He had returned from New Orleans only a week before.

"You about finished?"

"What?" came the shout from the attic.

Aaron repeated the question.

"Almost."

There was a fumbling with cables and pully on the other side of the ceiling. Suddenly Aaron was relieved of the weight.

"Okay. You can let go."

He lowered his arms. The fan held. Sherri clasped her hands in a victory salute. In a moment they heard Rick climbing down the squeaky folding stairs in the hallway.

"That's one hell of a job. Hey buddy," he slapped Aaron on the shoulder, "I couldn't have done it without you."

Sherri appraised the cheap hanging fan. "It's been so hot," she remarked. "Maybe it will make a difference."

Every house on the block was a five-room efficiency, thrown up after the Second World War to provide cheap housing for veterans. They lacked any shred of insulation between ceiling and roof, between plasterboard tricked out with flowered wallpaper on the inside and white asphalt shingles outside, no down payment for vets who could cover closing costs. In winter the occupants shivered, in summer they boiled. Aaron knew. He had spent the first ten years of his life (and Rick had spent the first twelve) in a series of such houses while their mother's first husband, who died of a heart attack, chased oilfield jobs from town to town.

The floor plan was much the same in all of them: a ten-by-twelve living room with one door opening into a kitchen, the other into a square, tiny hallway that gave onto the bathroom and two eight-by-ten bedrooms.

"Are you going to cover that hole?" Sherri pointed to the three-inch circle cut out of the ceiling, through which the cable connected the fan to a rafter.

"There's a bell around here someplace. . . ." Rick began rifling through the cardboard box in which the fan had come and held up a brown-painted, metal bell.

"Oh, good. I could imagine us losing all our heat through that hole next winter."

"Why don't you hang a fan in each of the bedrooms?" suggested Aaron.

"Well," said Rick, "I would. But the folks only gave us one."

"Will you guys keep an eye on the kids? They're in the back yard," Sherri said. "I need to run to the store."

"Not now, honey. I want to take Aaron out for a beer."

"Oh, don't worry about that." Aaron didn't want to cause trouble.

"No, I insist. A man gives up his Saturday afternoon to hang a fan, he deserves a beer."

"There's a six-pack in the refrigerator," said Sherri. "I really need to get to the store."

"Well, take the kids with you."

"Rick, if you knew how hard it is to buy groceries with three kids grabbing at everything."

"Look, I need to get home," said Aaron. "We can have that beer another time. I know what you mean," he turned to Sherri, "about shopping with kids. I took Kim with me once to the market with a list of groceries and it was murder."

Sherri looked grateful. "I've found that if I can do most of my buying while someone is staying with the children, then I can get by during the rest of the week without going to the store."

There was a sulk on Rick's face. Aaron wished he were somewhere else. He had just been through four days of not talking to Deedee, and he didn't want to be dragged into another fight.

"Look," Rick asserted, disregarding his brother's presence, "if I can bring home a paycheck, the least you can do . . . " His voice had become spiteful. ". . . the very least you can do is to give me some slack when I'm home and not shove the kids off on me so you can do your damn grocery shopping that you should've got done during the week!"

"I'm going to have to run," Aaron backed toward the door.

"You stay here," shouted Rick. "I said I was going to buy you a beer, and that's what I'm going to do."

Sucking her cheeks until she resembled a death's head, Sherri dropped onto a Naugahyde-covered chair just as Rick stepped back onto a toy delivery truck. He kicked it across the floor.

"And while we're on the subject," there were red blotches on Rick's cheeks and forehead, "why don't you pick this place up? Christ, I don't know what you do all week!"

"Would you like an inventory of what I do with my day?" braved Sherri. "I fix you breakfast and wash your dishes, and then," she counted off on her fingers, "I get Tamra up and ready for school. About that time, Randall wakes Buddy up, and I get to change Randall's diapers. Then while I'm fixing their breakfast, I start a load of clothes, which I try to have finished by the time I take Tamra to school, because I can't go off and leave the washer running because it will overflow and flood the kitchen. Which has happened anyway at least once a month for the past year and a half . . ."

Sneering in her face, Rick muttered, "Okay . . ."

"And then," Sherri's eyes blazed, "I get back home and hang out clothes, and make the beds, and watch the kids and try to give each of them a little individual attention. And then if I ever get two minutes to myself, there are the bills to figure out how we're going to pay . . ."

Aaron could not take any more; he bolted for the door. But not before his brother blocked his way.

"I've really *got* to go."

"Come on, buddy. I'm not going to let you go without that beer."

"Oh," cried Sherri, "you two do what you want." Out she strode through the kitchen and slammed the screen door behind her.

* * * *

The two brothers sat hunched over beer glasses. Except for a wrinkled, bleary-eyed old woman in a dirty red tam at the end of the dark bar and the bald-headed bartender with rolled-up sleeves smoking a cigarette as he lumbered around wiping off table tops with a strong-smelling disinfectant, they were the only occupants of the Samoa Lounge. Through beery air floated the sounds of Saturday afternoon traffic.

Propping one elbow on the scarred tabletop and resting his chin on the heel of his hand, Rick exhaled glumly and said, "She makes me so fucking mad. And this job I got pushing tires around . . . by the time I get off work and fight the goddamn traffic home, all I want to do is sack out in front of the TV." The puffy sacs underneath Rick's eyes shone in the dimness of the bar. "And my boss. God, Aaron, he's such a shit! Sometimes, you know, you wish you'd stayed in the goddamn Marines. As much as you hated the lousy food, the shit details, at least you could think about how it'd be when you got out."

Rick scratched his scalp then took a long swallow of beer. "Here I am bellyachin' like a goddamn . . . I never said this shit to anyone else, Aaron, honest to God."

Aaron sat in helpless silence. Everybody had always liked Rick. Everybody had admired him. He was smart. He had made A's in every math and science course he had ever taken. When sides were chosen up on the playground, Rick had always been picked first. He had been Pep Club Beau, Most Likely to Succeed. What had happened to that potential, Aaron wondered, not without a speck of complacency. It seemed simply to have vanished after Rick had married the girl he had gotten pregnant.

Aaron racked his brains for a way his brother might break out of his economic rut. Rick would never accept money from him, he knew that. Yet bills had to be paid, and they had no income other than what Rick provided.

"Have you ever considered Sherri going to work?" suggested Aaron gingerly. "With what she could make, maybe you could go to night school and finish your degree."

"Oh, we've thought of that. Sherri can't do anything except clerk in a store. That won't even pay for day care."

"How many hours do you lack on your degree?"

"Let's see . . . I need about sixty hours for an engineering degree."

"Why don't you aim for a four-year degree? In math, say? That would whittle it down to thirty hours, wouldn't it?"

"I suppose." Rick scratched his nose and straightened up in his seat. His confidential mood had passed. "Enough about me. How are things going with you?"

"Oh . . . okay." Living in a half-million-dollar house and making in excess of seventy-five thousand a year as a junior partner, now, in his architectural firm, Aaron lacked the nerve to voice any of his niggling complaints to his brother. Half guiltily, Aaron sometimes wondered at the degree of his own success, and at Rick's lack of it. Ironically, Deedee had been more than a little responsible — it was part of the

image she demanded. But there was also an inborn com-
petitive, vicious streak in Aaron's character that would not
be quelled, and that would not, now, allow him to admit to
his brother that all was not perfect in paradise.

"How's Deedee?"

"Hunh?"

"How's your wife?"

"Oh, she's fine."

## 13

They seemed to have made a go of it. Deedee and Aaron had settled into the sprawling Cape-Cod structure on a gracious street in Highland Park, not two miles away from the Georgian mansion belonging to Deedee's parents. Deedee rejoined the fashionable set with whom she had grown up, her girlfriends from the Hockaday School and the boys from St. Mark's. It was not difficult for her to pick up the threads, for each season she had flown back several times from Washington to attend social events, and every summer she had spent in Dallas with her family.

However, Deedee was not quite as fashionable as she would like to have been. Increasingly reclusive, Aaron was hardly the ideal social partner. Yet Deedee wanted to claim her place as a leader of Dallas society—which, with plentiful money from the oil boom, was brilliant.

That's why, after a stately old home had burned in Highland Park, she insisted they buy the lot and construct a house. Deedee had encouraged Aaron to indulge his architect's imagination. Initially convinced on the basis of her growing law fees and his profits from the building explosion that they could meet the payments, Aaron had reluctantly pulled out the stops and designed a dream of a house. As he had drawn up the blueprints, then supervised the construction, he had found himself falling in love with the house and the spacious lot shaded by cottonwood trees. Never had Aaron Teague expected to live in such splendor. Heir to four generations of red-dirt farmers, wage earners, and small businessmen, he was nagged by the fear that the house was beyond their means. Deedee did not worry. She was aware of Daddy's money; she was aware that one day it would all belong to her.

While they rarely squabbled, Deedee and Aaron gradually found that they had less and less to say to one another. They rarely touched one another, husband and wife, unless in public or in bed. And the latter became increasingly rare. Night after night, they found excuses to go to bed at different times. When they did retire together, they were usually very tired. This lack of sexual contact constituted a source of embarrassment, of humiliation, to each of them. Something they talked around, pretended did not exist— but a constant presence when they were together.

Nevertheless, Aaron was a faithful husband. All his background had prepared him for monogamy after marriage. Deedee, he recognized, had an eye for good-looking men, and more than once when she was away on business trips, Aaron had found himself wondering if she was sleeping alone. Such suspicions made him furious. He would hate his wife with lethal intensity. By the time she returned home, however, his hatred would have hardened to resentment, and they would continue as if nothing had happened.

Deedee spent what seemed to Aaron enormous sums entertaining the fashionable and powerful members of Dallas society. They attended because of her father's name and wealth, but also because of her own remarkable beauty and high sense of style, and because she was, after all, one of them. In Deedee's house, these oil and gas millionaires in hand-tooled, twelve-hundred-dollar lizard boots, and their wives in designer gowns from Neiman's, drank imported wines and ogled paintings that looked damn near like the ones they had seen in important museums in New York and Paris. They were charmed by Deedee's bare shoulders and diamonds, by her upswept chestnut hair.

Aaron would lurk in the corner somewhere or in another room. And so Deedee's social ambitions were ultimately thwarted. For she was a supremely ambitious woman, this only child of the president of Texas's third largest bank, chairman of the board of eight corporations, civic leader, and connoisseur of art.

Deedee and Aaron had corresponded while he was overseas. Soon after returning from Vietnam, Aaron had flown to see Deedee in law school at Georgetown. He had kept after her. She was flattered; she found herself once again strongly attracted to Aaron, to his springy athlete's walk and lithe build, his straight black hair, his forthright square jaw and piercing gray eyes. In fact, she found him more appealing than she had two years earlier, before he had gone into the service. The boyish charm had been replaced by a more manly taciturnity that she found irresistible.

At times, however, Aaron's lack of expressiveness annoyed her. He could quite easily assume a negative presence, one that glared or moped but that refused to communicate. At other times, inexplicably, he would flare into rages over minor matters. Deedee did not understand Aaron in his moods. He seemed to know neither what he wanted to do nor where he wanted to go, only that he wanted to be with Deedee.

It had occurred to this brilliant and manipulative woman that she could mold Aaron, impress him with the sense of direction he so sorely lacked. Given his obvious abilities, she could mold him into someone worthy of her, of Deedee Hartcroft. Knowing that he was from another social class lent Aaron the appeal of the exotic and made him more of a challenge in her eyes.

She had succeeded, to a degree. After their marriage, Deedee got Aaron to finish his degree in architecture. With this darkly handsome, taciturn unknown in tow, Deedee had returned to Dallas intending to place herself with a good law firm and her husband with an architectural firm. These aims she accomplished. In addition, she managed to smooth some of Aaron's rougher edges. She convinced him to leave his mangy blue jeans, boots, and tee shirts in the closet. In their place he began wearing polo shirts, slacks, and Bass Weejuns for casual and business wear — even Deedee acknowledged that architects favored a more relaxed attire — superbly tailored dark suits and expensive ties for dress.

Aaron was antipathetic at best to the life he was being encouraged to live. Increasingly he was possessed by bleak moods. He took sleeping pills before bed so he would not wake up in the middle of the night and begin thinking. He remembered the endless fantasies he had spun while in Vietnam about Deedee and the life they would share — the cozy house they would live in, the bottles that would fill their liquor cabinet, the children they would raise, the family dinners they would have on holidays — and shuddered at the ghastly parody of those fantasies he was now living out. He remembered how, after first returning from the war, he had often been unable to feel anything, anything at all; how he had remained insensible and mute, or reacted in an offhand, oafish manner to camouflage his frozen emotions; then how he had slowly begun to respond more normally, but had still found it difficult to show outwardly what he was feeling.

Repressing his feelings, he realized, had helped him make it through the war, where too many shocking experiences made responding to them in a normal way a reckless luxury; repressing his feelings again might help him make it through the muddle of his life with Deedee.

Their relationship had reached a point of stasis. While conflicts between them rarely broke into the open, they constantly simmered beneath a discreet surface. Their conversation became limited largely to small talk across the table in front of the child, daily business.

\* \* \* \*

Late one night toward the end of April, Aaron heard a key in the lock. Looking up from the plans for a condo he had been working on, he called out, "Deedee?"

"Hello," answered his wife from the entryway. Kim had gone to bed at seven-thirty. Aaron had been fighting sleep since nine. He had expected Deedee before six.

"Trouble?" He took the taupe overnighter from her and headed for their bedroom.

"My flight was delayed." Deedee rolled her shoulders, exhausted. "It ended up not taking off until eight-thirty." Even in her rumpled, tailored suit, his wife looked wonderful. She was an astonishingly handsome woman.

"I kind of wish you'd called," said Aaron. "Kim was looking forward to telling you goodnight."

"I can't help it if my flight is rescheduled," Deedee snapped.

Aaron lay the suitcase on the bed, then settled in the Windsor chair beside the bay window. "How did your business go?"

"Pretty well." Deedee began undressing, dropping her clothes in a pile beside the closet. "Tompkins is causing problems, though. He not only insists that we press charges against the union leader, he wants us to hire a detective to dig up dirt on his private life."

"Nasty."

"It's just business."

"Aren't we talking about the case where the company discharged a couple dozen employees about ready to retire and cut wages of everybody else by, what, twenty percent?"

"The company is trying to keep from going under."

They're also screwing their employees out of what they have coming to them."

"You're being naive." Deedee wrapped herself in a blue satin dressing gown, slipped her feet into matching slippers, and sat down at the vanity table. "I've known Odie Tompkins all my life—my father gave him his start in business—and he is simply trying to keep from going under."

"And in order to do that, he wants you to dig up dirt on a union leader who's causing him problems."

"You don't have the vaguest notion what you're talking about, and I'm too tired to argue."

Aaron hooded his eyes with his hand for a few moments. Then he looked back up and asked, "How was San Antonio?"

"It was hot!" Deedee was brushing her hair.

"How was your room?"

"Oh, you know. The Menger is tatty, but it's always nice. Everything all right here?"

"Okay. Do you want a drink?"

"Yes, I'd love a brandy."

"Actually," Aaron poured from a crystal decanter on a silver tray, "I'm concerned about Kim. She's been in tears every evening when I've gotten her from the sitter."

"She's playing on your sympathy," replied Deedee. Sparks crackled about her head as she worked the brush. "She tried that on me until she saw it didn't get her anywhere. Mrs. Simpson is very good with her."

"Maybe so," Aaron set Deedee's drink on the vanity table, "but Kim doesn't seem happy. Kids are supposed to be happy."

"Oh, Aaron, you're just talking. The child has everything a child could want."

"She's never with us," replied Aaron dropping again into the Windsor chair.

Deedee caught his eye in the mirror. "Well, she doesn't see any more of her father than she does of her mother!"

"How many times have you picked her up the last month?" Aaron challenged, fighting against an impulse to slosh his drink down his wife's elegant back. "How many times have you dropped her off in the morning? How many weekends have you stayed home to give her attention?"

When Deedee spoke, it was in a composed voice. "You know as well as I do that this has been a horrendously busy month. Mrs. Simpson is an excellent sitter. She certainly charges enough! She takes excellent care of Kim."

Stonewalled. Aaron clattered the ice in his glass. "Let's talk about something else, then. I confirmed our reservations in Corpus Christi for the last two weeks in July."

Deedee laid down her brush and took a sip of the drink. "It doesn't look as though that's going to work out."

"What do you mean?"

"Claude told me on the phone last night that I'll be needed to handle a case in Denver the last two weeks of July."

"Screw Claude! You know we've been planning this trip to Corpus Christi since last fall. It'll be the first time in years we've been able, the three of us, to get away together."

"Well, darling, if my boss says I have to work, I have to work!" Deedee's tone had become arch; the case was closed. "We'll have to go another time."

Aaron's face was flushed. "There's not another time. I'm scheduled to take two weeks vacation in July, and that's when I'm going to take it. My job places certain demands on me, too."

"My God, Aaron, why do you have to try to make me feel guilty about doing my work? I'm a lawyer. I hope to taken in as a full partner. I can't take off work at every whim if I am going to be successful."

"What about our daughter? Doesn't she deserve a little time together with both her parents?"

Deedee rolled up her eyes. "There you go again! Kim, how many times must I tell you, is receiving marvelous care where she is."

"That's not the same as her father and mother."

"You're being obstinate. Stupid." Deedee shot another glance in the mirror at Aaron. "I frankly don't know," she continued in a calculating voice, "why there's this *mania* for trudging off together somewhere on a vacation. I've been wondering for some time now why we don't take separate vacations. That's what several of the men in my office do, and they wouldn't have it any other way."

Aaron's face was expressionless. He stared into his glass. "Don't you think that's kind of like giving up?"

"What do you mean? Every year it's the same predicament, trying to arrange both our schedules so we can go off somewhere at the same time. It's idiotic. There comes a time when one simply has to arrange one's priorities. And certain obligations at work simply cannot be gotten around."

"Yes, one has to arrange one's priorities," Aaron upended his glass. It was clear to him—the whole bloody game was lost.

"I'm too exhausted even for a bath tonight." Deedee began wiping off her makeup. "Are you coming to bed now, or later?"

"Hm? Oh, later. I've got to do some more work before I turn in."

"I probably won't see you in the morning. Claude has called a special breakfast meeting downtown and I'll have to leave the house by six."

"Cheers," said Aaron, taking his glass and shutting the door behind him as he left the room.

# 14

New York
June 17

Dear Aaron,

Bumpy over St. Louis, otherwise a smooth flight. Mitzi and Bunker were at La Guardia. She's put on twenty pounds. Bunker's little bald spot looks like a yarmulke, and he's very tanned. Both send regards.

Last p.m. when Bunker took us to the Rainbow Grill, where Peter Duchin was playing, I felt so dowdy. This afternoon I went to Bergdorf's and found a little black dress for work and a marvelous flame-colored chiffon evening gown.

The plane was in the air before I discovered that I had left my briefcase in the car. Will you be a dear and drive out to the airport and get it for me out of the car (Section K3, my parking stub says). Send it to me by UPS. Thanks.

Love,
Deedee

Dallas, Tx
June 25

Dear Deedee,

Everything goes well here. Two nights ago we had rain so I won't have to water the flower beds for a while.

Had fresh tomatoes and Col. Sanders chicken for dinner this evening. Kim tried one (a tomato) but spit it out then mashed it with her drumstick.

Iris has been sick and sent her sister, whose name is
Tulip, in her place (there's a third sister, she tells me, whose
name is Verbena). She did a fair job cleaning the house,
although I found cigarette ash on the counter in the main
bathroom. Kim has taken a shine to her.

Your briefcase on the way. Give Mitzi and Bunker
regards.

                                        Aaron


                                        Rehoboth Beach, DE
                                        July 3

Dear Aaron,

Got in from NY Tuesday p.m. It's marvelous weather.
You'd love Mitzi and Bunker's cottage. Set upon a dune,
with a great, two-story window (clerestory??) facing the
ocean. The sun rising out of the ocean in the a.m. makes a
lovely picture, all oranges and grays. There's a freshwater
swimming pool set in to the deck so when one gets out of
the ocean one can rinse off.

Oh, Al from my office called me long distance last night
(ten-thirty!). I hate to be a pest, but will you be a dear and
look in the top drawer of my filing cabinet for the folder
marked "Kyle." They are in desperate need of it at the
office. Call Al—742—7698, I think. Look in the phone
book. Better yet, drop it by the office. That's a dear.

You won't know me, I'm so brown. Mitzi and I sunbathe
and play bridge or backgammon in the afternoons. In the
evenings there's a little group of painters and advertising
people and writers that gathers. Oh, I do so want to get a
place up here. It would make the rest of the year bearable.

Tell Kim hello.

                                        Love,

                                        Deedee

Taos, NM
July 16

Rick,

Henry says hi. Fierce black beard and long hair, a little older now than when you saw him last in New York, quite the patriarch. Lives with his wife, Elizabeth, and four kids in a log cabin high on the side of a mountain north of Taos. Primitive: electricity but no water. Makes you wonder why you're wasting your life in the city.

He earns good money making furniture. The wood he mostly salvages from trees that have fallen down. He keeps his drawing board and all his tools in a tin-roofed shed where he designs his pieces—nearly all his work is on commission—and puts them together. There's a kerosene heater in the corner for cold weather. The windows in the shed are thrown wide open when it's warm.

Rick, you'd enjoy the woods. There's a stream not fifty feet from Henry's cabin where they catch fish that they fry for breakfast. The view down the mountainside, a line of blue mountains jutting up across the valley, is not to be missed.

Give Sherri a kiss for me. And will you please check on Deedee when you find time. Looking after the house by herself may be giving her second thoughts about these separate vacations we're taking.

Best,
Aaron

Taos, NM
July 16

Dear Deedee,

Thought I'd mail this now as we won't be back down the mountain for several days.

Henry is much as I remember him nine years ago, except that he's heavier and there are lines across his forehead. I like his wife, whom I'd met only once before. Four children in one house, though, make me glad we have only Kim.

The car broke a fan belt just outside Dumas. Hot like you wouldn't believe. Other than that, no problems.

Don't forget: water the garden and the flower beds. Every other day. Otherwise they'll never make it through the heat. (Here on the mountain, we're sleeping under blankets — ha!)

This part is for Kim: Hi there, darling. The people Daddy is staying with have a four-year-old girl. She says to tell you hello and that her name is Judith. She has a pony named Stardancer, a black cat named Elijah, and two dogs — a dignified German shepherd and a runt. They call them Mutt and Jeff.

Well, Daddy has to go. Work hard on your kick so you can swim all the way across the pool when I get home. Mind Mommy.

> Love to you both,
> Aaron

> Dallas, TX
> July 28

Dear Aaron,

It's been a perfectly horrid week. First, Monday p.m., as I was watering your vegetables, I smelled gas. I called Rick, who said I'd better call a plumber out to look at it. Wouldn't you know — the gas line has to be replaced. There's a trench from the back of the house out to the meter, behind that bush you planted last spring. Three little men with shovels worked one entire afternoon. God knows what it will cost.

Then when I picked Kim up from the sitter on Wednesday, we stopped at the 7–11 and I bought Kim an icey and myself a cup of coffee. I told her to hold the cup as I backed out of the parking place. The clumsy thing ended up spilling hot coffee all over her legs. I ran her straight out to the emergency room, she screaming bloody murder all the way, and they said she had second-degree burns. I think they thought I had scalded the child on purpose.

Then, as if that were not enough, when I got home on Thursday, I found Tulip in the kitchen, watching television and ironing in front of the refrigerator with the door open (!). When I inquired very sternly what she thought she was doing, she said the air conditioner wasn't working and she was "jus' stayin' cool." After I sent her home (Iris, by the way, has been diagnosed as having hepatitis — the contagious kind), I telephoned the air-conditioning people, and they can't come out until next week.

Think of us sweltering here in this hot house and Kim in bandages as you pull up your extra blanket tonight.

Deedee

P.S. Kim says to ask Judith what she feeds Snowflake, or whatever the horse is called.

Dallas, Tx<br>July 29

Dearest Mitzi,

I'm red in the face about not writing. *Chagrins domestique* Aaron is off visiting some college friend in New Mexico, while this house collapses around my ankles.

Oh well. I cannot tell you how much I enjoyed my visit. You and Bunker are my favorite people in the world. I won't forget trying on hats with you at Saks and playing backgammon at the beach. Nothing in the world could make me happier than to find a cottage at the beach or a little flat in NYC. Will you keep an open eye?

After a rather nasty accident involving spilt coffee, Kim is finally learning to swim. *Trying* to learn, I should say. I wonder, are all four-year-olds as clumsy and inquisitive as she? The child chatters incessantly.

I wore my new black outfit to the office when I got back. I must say, I was rather stunning in my tan and my pink pearls. The men in my office would die before they would ever compliment a girl on the way she looks, but I felt stares all day.

Oh, Mitzi, whatever am I going to do? I am simply bored stiff with Life on the Prairie.

As you advised, I returned with an open mind. Aaron met me faithfully at the airport. With Kim clinging to my neck like a growth and Aaron's arm around me I'm sure I looked positively maternal. By the time we got home, though, and I had shut the door behind me, I felt that I had returned to prison. *Sans sursis.*

Aaron is sweet, yes, and intelligent and thoughtful. But he is DULL.

There. I've said it, and it is true. The entire time after I got home and before he left for New Mexico we went out for dinner exactly once (!). That was it! The rest of the time we sat like two bumps on a log in this barn of a house he designed and listened to the clock tick.

My friends invite us to parties. When I mention them to Aaron he looks severely pained and says, "Well, if you want."

Frankly, dear, I have had it. Dragging that man to places where he sits in a corner with a sneer on his face and checks his wristwatch every fifteen minutes. I decided that we would do it his way until he left on this vacation. Then while he was gone, I decided, I would go out by myself.

When Aaron returns, I don't know what will come about. Not that he gives a damn what I do. He could care less that I might go to parties without him.

Oh well, I'm sorry for burdening you again with my little problems. Everything will work out, I imagine. Thanks again for your marvelous hospitality. I adored every moment.

> Love,
> Deedee

Dallas, TX
July 31

Dear Aaron,

I'll bet you didn't expect to hear from me. The reason I am writing is I am worried sick about Rick.

After your letter came, Rick would sit outside on the stoop in the back yard. He'd sit there with your letter in his hands and not say anything. When the kids would ask him to play with them or fix a toy, he'd give them the saddest look. He did this until ten-thirty at night with mosquitoes very bad. He just sat there on the stoop and stared at the Chinese elm. Several times I would go out and sit down beside him and try to get him to talk, but he would set his mouth and not say a word.

This went on for three nights. Then when I woke up the next morning, he was throwing underwear and socks in an AWOL bag.

Where are you going? I ask him, and he says he doesn't know. He just needs to get away from the house for a few days to sort things out.

I was frantic, but I know Rick well enough to know that questions just set him off, so I held in and didn't say anymore about it.

Can I fix you some breakfast? I ask him while he got down his old utility cap from the Marines and put it on his head. We could hear the kids beginning to stir in their room, and Randall would be waking soon, too.

No, he said and put his billfold in his pocket.

Do you have money?

I'm okay.

That's the last thing he said. Just picks up his AWOL bag and kisses me once on the cheek and walks out of the house. The last time I saw him he was rounding the corner on foot toward the interstate.

By the time I got collected, I realized that not only didn't I know where he was going or how he was going to get there, but I didn't know when he would be coming back home. I didn't know anything except he had left.

Aaron, I hate to spoil your vacation, but I don't know where else to turn. You and Rick have always been close, and now it was after he got your letter he jumped off the deep end.

Would you be on the lookout? There's a friend in Galveston that Rick writes to once in a while, and he used to write to a Marine buddy who lives in Montgomery or Birmingham or somewhere in the South. I called the friend in Galveston and would have called you, but Deedee told me there's no phone where you're staying.

Will you let me know the minute you hear something? I don't know that I will do if anything happens to Rick.

> Love,
> Sherri

P.S. I haven't mentioned any of this to your mother.

## 15

"Is this Henry Lazarus' house?" A Marine utility cap drooped across the speaker's sunburnt nose. He was on foot and carried an AWOL bag.

On the other side of the split-rail fence, one of two barefoot little girls searching for fleas in the coat of a German shepherd sitting like the sphinx jumped up and ran into the house. The other put an arm around the neck of the dog, who peaked his ears and scrutinized the intruder.

"Are you Henry's wife?" the man asked a round-cheeked woman in braids who stepped onto the porch. Her hair was brick-colored, and her shoulders were plump and freckled above a muslin peasant top. "I'm Aaron Teague's brother Rick."

Like ice on a griddle, the woman's face relaxed. She smiled and shaded her eyes against the late-afternoon sun. "Come on in," she patted the shepherd's broad neck. "I'm Elizabeth."

Slinging his dusty bag back over his shoulder, Rick opened the wooden gate and hobbled on sore feet across a patch of green bordered by orange poppies. Like a tired old hobo in the limping afternoon, he sank down on the plank step and pulled off his greasy cap. He was beat. The line of his cap shone white against the grime and sunburn of his face and neck.

"Aaron around?" he began peeling off work boots white with dust.

"No, he and Henry are off in the woods. You'd better clean those," she grimaced at enormous water blisters that covered the soles of Rick's feet.

There were now three children on the porch gazing wide-eyed at the visitor—those he had seen grooming the dog and a fat toddler in diapers. Elizabeth sat down in a slatted porch rocker and surveyed Rick with curiosity.

"The three of us spent a couple days together before Aaron went overseas," he explained.

"I've heard about that weekend," Elizabeth said and flicked a red braid onto her back. "What are you doing now?"

"I've been working in a tire center in Dallas." Rick's wedding band flashed in the dry air. "Would you mind if I sacked out here on the porch?"

"Go ahead. The boys will be back anytime." Instructing the children to be quiet, Elizabeth went back into the house.

It was dark when he awoke. For a moment he could not remember where he was. He was cold. He smelled Italian cooking. Slowly Rick sat up, feeling like a pair of leather shoes that had gotten wet and been left to dry in the sun. The blisters on his feet would pop if he stood on them. Gingerly, he pulled himself up by the porch railing and balanced on the outsides of his feet. In this bowlegged fashion, he limped toward the open front door.

Seeing his brother, Aaron winced as the children, including an older boy, burst into squeals of glee.

"Sit down," Aaron said, pulling a chair out from the table. "What the hell?"

"Do you have a needle I could borrow?" Rick asked Elizabeth.

Then Henry was beside his chair, shaking Rick's hand in a firm grasp. The lean, dark, intense-eyed fellow Rick remembered had become stocky and furrowed. A vigorous full black beard and a head full of ringlets made his already oversized head leonine. Dominating his face, as

when the three of them had been on the town with a giddy
kind of angry, hard-edged energy, were eyes like blue coals.

"Oh hell, don't get up," Henry pushed Rick by the shoulder back into his seat.

On the checkered oilcloth Elizabeth placed a bottle of
rubbing alcohol and a sewing needle. Carefully, as the two
little girls stuck out their tongues and wrinkled their noses,
Rick pierced one of the white pads on his feet then pressed
out thin, colorless liquid.

"You must have *walked* from Dallas," remarked Aaron
quizzically. He hadn't a clue what was going on with his
brother—only a kind of dread.

Rick chewed his lower lip while he broke another bubble.

A dark-haired boy had slipped around the table beside
his father.

"You met my youngest three this afternoon," said Henry.

"I didn't get their names, though," said Rick. Grinning
at the younger girl, he laid down the needle.

"This," Henry pointed to the girl nearest Rick, "is Judith.
She's four. And her sister, Raphaela, is six. Joshua, our
baby," he gestured towards a battered high chair where a
child was smearing tomato sauce on his tray, "he's two. And
this," Henry patted the shoulder of the boy beside him, "is
my oldest, David, who's nine."

Without getting up, Rick shook hands in a dignified way
with David.

"Aaron said you have kids?"

"Three. About the same ages as yours."

"Let's not let dinner get cold," said Elizabeth after it was
evident that Rick had finished speaking. She spread her
napkin in her lap and looked at Rick. "I hope you like
lasagna."

He chuckled.

"Start the garlic bread, Raphaela," Elizabeth nodded to
the daughter, whose strawberry blond hair was arranged in
a crown of braids.

Suddenly, acutely, Rick wondered what Tamra, Buddy, and Randall were doing at that moment. Were they missing their old man? "It's pretty country," he offered as conversation. Questions, he realized, must be running through everyone's minds.

"Did you get my letter?" Aaron's eyes asked more than his words.

"Yeah." Rick took a drink of cheap burgundy wine. "Henry, you're not from this part of the country, are you?"

"Cincinnati. We came out here in '68 and never left."

"Where did you stay at first?" asked Aaron.

"We had a little place in Taos. That was nice but . . ."

"Taos is too social," Elizabeth finished Henry's statement for him.

"That's right. Taos is a good place to become known if you want to build custom furniture, like me, or if you're an artist. But it's a cliquey place and there are too many tourists. So we saved our money and looked for a hideout. When we found this place it was just what we were looking for, so we mortgaged ourselves up the ass and bought it."

"Ever been sorry?" Rick laid down his fork.

"Hell, no. We love it here," said Henry, his eyes like blue flames. Elizabeth agreed. "And it's great for the kids. Right?" He ruffled Judith's bonnet of black curls.

After dinner, while Henry and Aaron washed dishes in round tin pans with stream water they had heated on the electric stove, and while Elizabeth took down from the wall a big, galvanized washtub, Rick finished doctoring his feet.

Afterwards the four adults sat out on the porch in the stark light and petted the dogs. The children took turns bathing in the washtub, then stood shivering as their parents dried them off—David darting inside the house to dry himself off—and dressed them in flannel pajamas.

After the children were in bed, the men played hearts around the kitchen table while Elizabeth bathed on the porch. It was dark outside the circle of light, and they sipped red wine from water glasses. After coming back inside wrapped in a long blue terry robe and combing out damp red hair, Elizabeth told Rick she would make him a pallet on the floor. Gathering an armload of clean, faded bed quilts from a cedar chest, she caught Henry's eye. After finishing his hand of cards, he excused himself and followed her up the stairs.

From the stove Aaron transported an iron teakettle-full of boiling water to the porch. "This is for you, slick," he told his brother. "I've been bathing in the stream." Aaron began smoothing a blanket across the cushions of the divan for his own bed, then tucked the corners underneath, while Rick unbuttoned his shirt.

What was he doing here? The unspoken question filled the room. Rick showed no inclination to talk about it, though. Instead he stood up, slipped off his shirt and jeans, and walked alone outside. Far down the mountainside on the broad floor of the valley, dots of light glittered in the darkness the way they did from airplane windows. The night smelled of pine trees. It was chilly. Rick slipped out of his shorts and hunkered in the warm water, the rim of the tub like ice against his spine.

It was only nine-thirty; it seemed much later. He wondered again what Sherri was doing now and if the children were asleep. How they would love this place! Never had his own kids spent any time in the country. When he and Aaron had been growing up, there had been their grandparents' place. His own children knew only fenced back yards, paved streets, an occasional trip to the park where they would run around underneath the trees while their parents kept their eyes open for child molesters. His knees cocked underneath his armpits, Rick sat in the washtub until the water grew cold and his mind stopped racing.

\*  \*  \*  \*

After breakfast next morning, the brothers had their coffee on the porch. An electric saw buzzed from Henry's tin-roofed shed. On the other side of the valley, mountains formed a jagged blue line. Jays quarrelled in the aspens, and a chicken hawk angled lazily down across the sky.

"Here's a list of things I need," Elizabeth said, joining them on the porch. "If you can't find fudge-ripple cake mix, plain chocolate will do. I've got the laundry separated into bundles. You're sure," she smiled at Aaron, "you don't mind?"

With a whoop, Judith cannonballed through the doorway. "Can I ride Stardancer?" Black curls danced about her head as the mutt ran barking in circles.

"Get David to untie her, sweetheart," answered Elizabeth. Inside the house the baby had begun to cry.

Aaron eased the car down the serpentine road in first and second gears, nine bundles of dirty laundry in the back seat. Surely, he thought, Rick would open up now that they were alone. However, the only thing that passed between them was a baffling silence. The air was full of the smell of spruce trees; here and there among the evergreens, straining toward the sun, fluttered green-golden aspens.

In the dusty Chicano village at the foot of the mountain, Rick and Aaron sat in peeling metal lawn chairs in front of the laundromat. Here in the valley, it was heating up fast. Aaron retrieved his battered rain hat from the trunk of the car to shade his eyes.

All Rick's clothes were in the washer; the jeans and tee shirt he had borrowed from his brother fit tightly on his stocky body. A disheveled red chicken was scratching in the sand. Across the street, three men in khakis sat on a green bench in front of a bar drinking from long-necked beer bottles.

When it came time to transfer clothes from the washer to the drier, Rick went inside. A spitshined '55 Mercury with souped-up engine and chromed double-barrel exhaust pipes backfired down the dusty street. Three brown-skinned youths in dark sunglasses and oiled hair shared the front seat. Then a second car, a later-model red Pontiac lowered to within six inches of the ground and likewise containing three teenaged boys, pulled alongside the first car and stopped in the middle of the street. Aaron watched the drivers of the cars call to one another in Spanish and absentmindedly gun their engines. Casually, arrogantly, six heads turned to regard the stranger.

Abruptly, the Mercury hung a U-turn and, with a furious burst of throttle, pealed out. The Pontiac began again its slow passage up the street. The three drinkers in front of the bar continued drinking.

Aaron watched the scene in front of him, but he was thinking about Sherri and how much he liked her, and about his brother. Rick was in transit; he radiated a sense of displacement. Aaron brooded on the terrible rootlessness all of them were afflicted with right now. He was intimately acquainted with that feeling. It reminded him of the time he, Henry, and Rick had honked and splashed up Riverside Drive in the rain to Forty-ninth Street in Henry's Impala, then turned east toward the Hampstead Hotel off Times Square. It had been the Wednesday before Thanksgiving. On the following Saturday, Aaron had to report to Travis Air Force Base in California, on his way to Vietnam.

Rick had seemed reckless and full of good spirits as they joined the group on the sidewalk in front of the Metropole, gawking inside at go-go dancers behind the bar. Aaron felt strange in civies, and without any hair his head was cold. Further down Times Square, they ducked into a dark, narrow bar with murky, green light like an aquarium. There was nothing but standing room along the knife-initialed bar. Glasses clinked and rough laughter rang out as two whores eased in among them and cadged drinks from the two brothers, while Henry, who had driven up from college to see Aaron off, gazed insouciantly around the room.

As Rick's girl Frenched his ear, Aaron's insinuated her crotch against his hip. Teased, bleached-out hair, sooty eye makeup, and white lipstick made her look hard as the street, but it was a young girl's voice that asked him if he was in the Army. "I could tell from your hair," she explained after his affirmative reply. "Where you stationed?"

"Nowhere at the moment. I'm going overseas on Saturday."

"Vietnam?"

"Yeah." Aaron felt awkward talking about it, as if it were cancer.

"Jeez!" She hugged him around the waist. "Hey, ya wanna take me home?"

"Not tonight."

"Twenty'll buy you a good time." Slowly she raked herself up and down his hipbone. "Fifteen for you. I got a place a block away."

Aaron punched Rick. "What's going on?"

Rick's eyes were swimming. "This girl's in love with me." Like his brother, Rick's hair was cut to the scalp. On leave from Camp Lejeune, he himself expected orders for Vietnam at any time.

"Come on, man. Let's shove off," said Aaron. Rick leered at the redhead beside him, then said to his brother, "You go ahead. I'll meet you guys later."

"Come on. You don't want to go off by yourself."

"This is my kid brother giving me the advice," Rick was talking to the redhead. He turned back to Aaron. "So you come with me. You and Blondie, there."

Aaron put an arm around his brother's shoulders and spoke into his ear. "I don't have much cash."

"My treat," Rick leaned back from the bar. "The hell if a man can't buy his little brother a shot of leg before he goes off to fight the war."

"That's all right, you go. I'm not really in the mood," Aaron replied mirthlessly. "But be careful, for Chrisake."

As Rick made a face and told the redhead it was no go, Aaron sank his elbows into the bar and drooped his head.

All his energy had vanished; he was dead. There was nothing in the world he wanted so much as a clean bed in which to sleep out the night.

Waking up before Henry or Rick next morning, Aaron slipped on his clothes, left a note that he'd be back by noon, and crept out the door.

This was to be his morning. In two days he would be on his way to California. Then would begin his Great Adventure. Shit. He wondered what Vietnam would be like. What would his quarters be like? Who would he be living with? Would he be getting shot at? How would he react?

A raw wind pinched Aaron's scalp as he joined the crowd lining Broadway for the Macy's Thanksgiving Day Parade. A high school band was prancing by, plumed helmets, zits on the red cheeks of the clarinet players, and short-skirted twirlers with goose bumps on chubby legs. Then the sailing balloon figures of Dumbo and Pluto and Mickey Mouse, enough to scare the wits out of some little kid, followed by a float with Steve Lawrence in an overcoat buttoned to the chin, blowing kisses. "Rots a ruck," he seemed to be saying, to Aaron.

Turning back the way he had come, he walked over to Fifth Avenue and strolled north, past St. Patrick's Cathedral and Radio City, where he turned in to watch the ice skaters, then on to the Plaza Hotel. The fountain was dry; four puffy-eyed kids were sitting on the rim swinging their legs, one of them picking a guitar. A badly scratched hansom cab with a whiskery brown horse and no driver waited beside the curb. A gust of wind blew grit into Aaron's face as he gazed up at the hotel.

Then he padded up the steps and through the lustrous, brass doors of the Plaza Hotel. A red-faced old man in a tightly buttoned dinner jacket was sacked out in one of the chairs, head back and mouth gaping open in inaudible snores. A woman in an expensive tweed suit and a snood was conversing discreetly with the desk clerk while her porter stood whistling alongside charcoal-gray luggage.

The porter sneezed, and then blew his nose. Aaron watched everything. He was a giant eyeball registering indelible impressions on its retina, storing away memories for the coming year. He felt as if the doorman, the desk clerk, everyone in the lobby, were peeking surreptitiously at him, waiting only for some flimsy pretext to give him the bum's rush back onto the street.

On his way back toward midtown, Aaron met waves of people washing up from Times Square after the parade: families with children, dads leaning back against the weight of hanging bellies, harried mothers yelling at their kids, frowzy panhandlers, larger-than-life moustachioed policemen on horseback, stony-eyed prostitutes, clusters of giggly, rowdy teenagers, wobbling drunks with red eyes, a pair of shrieking homosexuals, attractive young women with clean skin and well-brushed dark hair, sexless mournful old people shuffling along in isolation. Through them pushed the insolent taxicabs and belching busses.

After gobbling a steak and onion sandwich while standing up at a lunch counter, Aaron ambled down Eighth Avenue, scanning the lewd marquee bills, ignoring the guys with hungry eyes leaning up against plate glass store fronts and in doorways, to Forty-second Street, where he elbowed his way grinning through the whores and dudes with greased-back hair and turned-up collars, whores black, yellow, and white, in tight skirts, nylons and high heels, in sprayed-on jeans and leatherette jackets, one in short shorts and a Hawaiian shirt, oblivious to the harsh, gritty wind, "Hey Joe, whadaya know?" The twenty-four-hour movie houses, one after another in a row, reeking the familiar, bus-station disinfectant smell that was the smell of home in this place.

It was nearing noon as Aaron walked up to Forty-fifth Street, looked in last night's corridor bar—Blondie was not there—then sauntered over to deserted Fifth Avenue and circled back toward the hotel on Forty-ninth. Aaron remembered that it was noon on a holiday. That his family would be gathered at someone's house and now, after stuffing themselves on turkey, mashed potatoes and giblet gravy, and an entire table of desserts, the men would lie out in aluminum yard chairs underneath the elm trees, the women would be swapping news and dirty jokes in the kitchen, and the kids would be getting sleepy after running and cramming cake in their mouths all day. And he felt vagrant on the dirty pavement, years away from Texas, where he remembered everyone in shirt-sleeves and drinking orange juice every morning with their coffee.

Ahead of him a flock of blue and gray pigeons were scavenging the gutter for scraps; they scattered in circles in the air as he approached. Yes, you got by, hustled your bread one way or another. You had to eat. Aaron wondered if he would still be alive next Thanksgiving. Would he still have all his limbs intact? And where did he stand with Deedee? When they had talked on the phone just yesterday, she had assured him she would write, but he had failed to detect any real warmth in her voice. Hungry, Aaron trudged down Forty-ninth Street to the Hampstead wondering what, just what, would become of him.

At Birdland that night they met Hilary and Tish sitting next to three empty chairs in the sort of listeners' gallery behind the corded-off area of tables. Mose Allison was drawling one of his cool tales and the boys had seen the three empty seats, Aaron grinning with his eyes, Rick giving Henry a leer and pointing to the girls.

They were down from Bennington, the boys learned between sets. The taller of the two, Hilary, was auburn-haired and very slender, her face rather hard and too like a fashion model's as she sat intently listening to the music, but softening into a wide, almost buck-toothed smile and with huge eyes that sparkled when she engaged in conversation. Tish, like a full-blown blond rose, was all billowy curves and fragrance. Both girls' hair was parted in the middle and glistened richly down their backs, and both wore close-fitting jeans and sweaters.

After Mose's set, they had all gotten drinks, the girls insisting on paying for their own and seeming unphased by Aaron's and Rick's unfashionably short hair. By the time John Coltrane was blowing long riffs, improvisation of the freest imaginable sort, flowing from vertical squiggles and spirals of rushed notes to honks and skreeks of unalloyed bitterness, they had decided to drive together in Henry's car down to the Village.

It was jumping as they wandered along Eighth Street, Hilary like a long-legged thoroughbred, lustrous hair rippling down her back, Tish beside Henry, like All-American high school sweethearts but handsomer and more experienced.

Motorcycles baroomed up and down the street in and out between honking cars with glaring yellow lights. High school girls already wearing the look of predators, in tight pants and boots, clustered along the sidewalks, pausing from time to time for moments of jabbed discourse with long-haired guys goofing by, the rhythm of it fast and ragged. In Washington Square underneath the Arch, people were singing "The Times They Are a-Changing." Hilary held hands between Aaron and Rick, hummed the melody and tossed her head from side to side in time. Then down McDougal Street, where they listened in front of the Cafe à Go Go and clapped in time to a black youth's tough New York step and turn.

Across the street, Tish saw Fred Neil's name on a poster and exclaimed that she had seen him last winter in Cambridge and that he was really good. Wanting to see him, they crossed the street to the grimy little club and sat at a table against the wall. A sloe-eyed waitress in a black turtleneck brought them drinks, while under a tight spotlight, Fred Neil drooped over his guitar and sang in a raspy, mellow voice about broken love affairs, waking hung over, and being blue.

Well, I'm just a country boy,
I got sand all in my shoes.
You know, I got stuck in the big city,
Gotta sing the big city blues, city blues

They had two rounds of drinks and it was past midnight. Aaron was dozing against the brick wall when Hilary poked him in the ribs and stuttered with laughter, "Aaron, stop him!"

Fearless as a linebacker, Rick was standing on the bench and trying, unsteadily, to step onto the doubtful, oblong table. Hilary cried again in mock distress, "Oh, stop it, Rick!"

"You said I wouldn't do it," he called down, elevating his arms and gingerly placing a foot onto the table like a tightrope walker testing a rope.

A little embarrassed, Henry demanded under his breath that Rick get down. Tish sat open-mouthed and Aaron waited in amusement to see what his wild older brother would do.

Now atop the table and with the other customers turning to stare and the bartender putting down a shaker and starting around the bar, Rick teetered and turned to face the wall. Hands at his belt, he boomed out, *"Full Moon,"* bent forward and dropped his trousers.

Hilary shrieked and collapsed in helpless laughter while everyone else's mouth dropped open.

Holding the pose only an instant, Rick again stood up, thundered, *"Double Hog-Back Growler,"* then bent over and spread the cheeks of his ass. By the time he had announced *"Red Eye Snake,"* salaamed, and poked his dick back through his legs, the bartender and a bouncer had clapped their hands on him and jerked him roughly down off the table, sending the drinks crashing to the floor.

Neither Tish nor Henry drew a breath. Hilary's eyes were enormous, her hands over her mouth.

Springing up, Aaron touched the bartender's shoulder. "He's had too much to drink, that's all. Let me take care of him."

Nasty but very cool, the heavyset, long-haired bartender spat back, "This your pal?"

"He's my brother."

"You don't want him in jail, you get the bastard outa here, see?"

Having sense enough not to open his mouth, Rick buckled his belt and waited for Aaron to take care of things.

"We're leaving," Aaron assured them, as the bouncer shoved Rick into the table, then turned on his heel and swaggered away with the bartender.

Hilary, Tish, and Henry were already on their feet as Aaron pushed Rick ahead of them out the door. When he was safely on the sidewalk, Rick winked at Hilary and growled, "See, I told you I'd do it!"

On the way back up Fifth Avenue to their hotels, Rick was content for the most part to listen to the easy conversation flying between Hilary and Aaron, yet not feeling left out, serving as an authority when called upon, feeling that although Hilary was talking to Aaron, she deferred to him, the older brother, and that she really liked him.

Winter lay ahead with exams and money problems for Henry; within seventy-two hours Aaron would be landing at Tan Son Nhut Airport, and Rick would follow within six months. The war that had already changed Henry would leave its lasting impression on the Teague brothers, as well. But that Thanksgiving night none of them was thinking of much besides the marvelous girls they had just told good-night.

# 16

There were sandwiches waiting for Aaron and Rick at the cabin when they returned. After lunch, while Henry worked in his shop and Elizabeth folded and put away clothes, Aaron and Rick followed David down a wooded trail to the meadow he and his father had begun to clear. Walled about on all sides by pine trees, the rolling stand of ground was dotted with aspens and junipers. While Aaron and the boy, dextrous and strong for his age, dug out a stubborn juniper bush, Rick ripped a fallen tree trunk into firewood with a gasoline-powered chain saw. After a while his shoulders ached with the weight of the machine. Nevertheless, Rick enjoyed doing this work in the crisp air with the smell of wood in his nostrils.

Late in the afternoon, Judith meandered through the forest on the back of a small pony whose inky coat matched her own mop. Aaron and the boy grinned at her as Rick flicked off the chain saw.

"Mama wants to know when you're coming in," she announced.

"Old David here says we have to finish clearing this meadow before we quit."

"The whole thing?" Judith gasped.

Rick had strolled over beside the pony and was patting its flank. "We'll finish it tomorrow. Will you help me?"

"I can't saw," she said seriously. Then perceiving the merriment in Rick's dark eyes, she giggled.

"Come on, guys," he turned to the others. "Dinner's ready."

Next morning, while Elizabeth sliced thin slabs of bacon
with a knife that resembled a machete, the men wrapped
towels around their waists and went off through the pines
to the stream.

The fresh snowmelt caused Rick's feet to cramp as he
stepped from rock to rock. In the middle of the stream,
just where sunlight pierced the tall trees and the water
tumbled over a great, moss-covered stone, he squatted and
inch by inch immersed his buttocks. Once dulled to the
shock of icy water sluicing over his genitals and thighs, he
lathered himself with a bar of soap. For the first time in
months, Rick felt completely awake. He felt a flash of love
for this place.

After bacon and paper-thin flapjacks doused in sor-
ghum, Aaron left for Taos, where he planned to spend a
day studying adobe engineering before leaving for Dallas
next morning. Henry went out to his shop. Rick did the
dishes before plodding fifty steps uphill to the outhouse.

Where his obligations lay — where he belonged — that
Rick knew. But he could not imagine himself back there.
Each day he missed his children more intensely. And the
way Elizabeth laid her hand on Henry's shoulder, the sound
of her voice, the way the gold hoops in her ears peeked
through the fall of her hair evoked within him fierce flashes
of lonesomeness for Sherri. The blue uniform, though,
the leaving for work six days a week in traffic at seven-thirty
with the sun in his face, working his ass off hoisting tires
around from one place to another, saying yessir and yes
ma'am to rude bastards he would rather have slapped
upside the head, waiting the clock out until five when he
would fight the traffic home against the sun — all that, he'd
had his bellyful of it.

After lunch Rick ventured into the tin-roofed shed
where Henry was rubbing oil into the wood of a fine oak
coffee table. His curly black beard and unruly hair bristled
in sunlight filling the room from open windows on every
wall. Clad in a sawdust-covered pair of cut-offs, Henry

looked thoroughly at home amid the crazy collection of hand saws and power saws, drills, bench press, screwdrivers and awls, cans and bottles, tool chests, and a hanging calendar from Nutt Lumber Yard.

There was a justness of proportion about the table, a gracefulness that moved Rick. Henry showed him how the thing was constructed entirely with dowels and precision fitting, how fine the grain of the oak was. He had done nothing with the finish except to rub on a very light coat of sealer, then coat after coat of oil to enrich the color and throw the grain into relief.

When he had begun showing his work in Taos, Henry explained, he had resolved never to use nails in his furniture and never to cover it with heavy, slick varnish. He had lost a few commissions (*"No nails?"* screeched one old woman weighed down with turquoise bangles. "How's it gonna stay together?"), but he had persevered. Now, Henry reported modestly, his work was commissioned a year ahead. You make quality products, he declared, and your clientele will seek you out.

Squatting in the corner in the sunlight, Rick watched Henry pour a yellow, citrus-smelling oil on his cloth and rub it vigorously into the wood. With disgust he recalled the cheap, formica-topped tables in his own front room. How honest, how fine, in contrast, seemed this piece of furniture. How it suggested satisfaction. Independence.

"Man, you've got it made," Rick observed in a quiet voice from the sunny corner.

Henry smiled and rubbed on the table. "You haven't been here when it's ten below and there are five feet of snow on the ground, you're running out of supplies, and there's a sick baby in the house." He shot a penetrating glance at Rick. "Also, ticks can be a nuisance. And we're unhappy about the kids' schooling."

"How's that?"

"There are only five Anglo kids in the whole school. It's a Spanish-speaking village, and the other kids speak very

little English. We try to work with them here at home,
but . . . "

Henry screwed the cap back on the bottle of oil and
stepped back to admire his work. "Ain't bad," he admitted
and began cleaning his tools.

"I was wondering," Rick began, "if I could make myself
useful around here for a while."

Henry stuck out his lower lip. "You know you're welcome
here as our guest for as long as you want."

"I don't mean that. I want to earn my keep. For starters,
I was thinking I could finish clearing the meadow."

A troubled expression overspread Henry's face. He had
not questioned Rick about why he had wandered onto their
place, or why now he wanted to stay. There had been two
other friends — one from the Navy, one he and Elizabeth
had gone through school with in Cincinnati — who had
stopped over with them and then decided they had to stay.

Henry had not encouraged them. If they wanted it bad
enough, they would establish a foothold on their own, and
he would welcome them as independent neighbors. But
there were no free tits. If Henry became convinced of
something, he grabbed on and could not be shaken. He
was no idealist. In Rick, as in the others, Henry perceived
an idealistic, star-gazing quality he didn't trust. As the
brother of a good friend and as a fellow vet, Rick had
Henry's goodwill; besides that, he was a likeable guy. Now,
though, he reminded Henry of a baseball that had just
been walloped by a long hitter: no one knew yet which side
of the fence it would land on.

It was dusk when Aaron drove in, gravel clattering
against the floorboards. As soon as he stepped out of the
car, he asked his brother to walk out with him into the
meadow. Dismissing any attempt at small talk, he pulled
Sherri's letter from his breast pocket.

Examining the letter, Rick remained expressionless.
Refolding it along its original creases and handing it back,

he peaked his eyebrows. "What are you going to do?" he asked.

"I called Sherri from Taos." Aaron's tone was flat, noncommittal.

Rick shrugged his shoulders and stuck his hands in his pockets.

"I thought you ought to see the letter," Aaron said finally.

It was a long while before Rick spoke. "It was my fault every bit as much as hers that we had to get married," he admitted. "I accept that. It's just that, more and more, I find myself blaming Sherri for everything. I can't help it. After your letter came, I thought about Henry living here and being his own boss, and I thought about it more and more. I realized I'm getting older. Man, don't you know, my possibilities are disappearing. If I'm ever going to make a break, I have to do it . . . soon, or it'll never happen.

"I talked to Henry today about staying on here. It'll only be for a while. I'm not walking out on my family, you understand. Not permanently. I just have to get away for a while. See what it's like." Rick slapped at a mosquito. "We'd better get back," he said. From deep in the woods flared the scream of a bobcat.

"Look, I can understand what you're saying," said Aaron when they were in sight of the house, "but . . " he groped for a way to phrase the unmentionable, "but I don't know how they're going to manage financially." It was chancy, Aaron felt, but it needed to be said.

Rick had nothing more to say.

But the next morning when Aaron slipped the car into gear amid a flurry of hand-waving and shouted good-byes and began the descent down the zigzag dirt road toward Dallas, his brother sat beside him in the front seat.

## 17

"You're looking well, my dear."

"Thank you, Claude. I love your sweater."

"This?"

"I love the color. Where did you get it?"

"In Scotland last fall."

"Cashmere?"

"Oh yes."

"I love cashmere."

"You sound like Marilyn. She refuses to look at a sweater unless it's cashmere."

"Marilyn's a nut."

"Ha ha ha."

"I love their pool."

"It's unusual."

"I wonder how much it cost."

"More than *they* can afford, no doubt." Claude Manners leered with reptilian eyes while Pal o'Mine Belcher snorted into her cocktail glass.

"You're awful."

"Don't forget, I sign Deedee's paycheck."

"Oh?"

"Ha ha ha." Manners loved to tantalize Pal o'Mine. "It's fortunate for her that Daddy's got a bank."

Reeking of expensive cologne, the sleek attorney smirked as they were joined by Pal o'Mine's husband, Tom, and another, more athletic-looking man.

"How you doing, Claude?" Belcher spoke in a gravel voice.

"Well. And you?"

"Couldn't be better. You remember Bart Shelton?"

The tall, prematurely gray man with deep chest and narrow hips offered a tanned hand to the debonair lawyer and smiled a self-confident smile.

"Bart's with Dunn and Bradstreet. And this," Belcher enfolded the fading, still handsome blond whose carmine lipstick overran the natural line of her lips, "is my little woman, Pal o'Mine."

Within ten minutes, Belcher's wife had disappeared with Shelton to sample the French onion dip.

It was seven months now since Aaron had returned from Taos and in a surge of optimism had drawn up plans to enclose the patio, surrounded on three sides by wings of the U-shaped house. In the center he had installed a swimming pool.

Tonight was its unveiling. A small circle of friends — which meant mostly Deedee's friends — had been invited: the senior partner in her law firm, Claude Manners and his wife Marilyn; banker Jack Hamilton and Bijoux; civic leader and local business tycoon Tom Belcher and Pal o'Mine; banker Matthew Meyer — his wife, Anne Benson Meyer, was one of Deedee's oldest friends, they had been debutantes together; sporting goods magnate Taylor Bendix and Lela; Harriet Legget, who after her husband's death had become chairman of the board of Max Industries; Glenn and Miriam Gilstrap — Glenn was an architect in Aaron's firm; fashionable gynecologist George Lish and Shirley Szigetti — she had retained her maiden name after their marriage; stockbroker Bart Shelton; advertising executive Blake Quigley and his wife Jonnie; former president of the Junior League, now executive director of Civic Volunteers, Gypsy Levin. And ludicrously, thought Deedee, Aaron had asked Rick to drop by.

By ten-thirty, everyone except Rick had shown. Just as well, she thought, circling the pool with fresh bottles of scotch and vodka. Ever since Rick and Sherri had separated, barely a month after his return from Taos with his tail between his legs, he had engaged in increasingly bizarre behavior.

"Will this do?" she asked the bartender.

"Yes, ma'am." His black skin glistened against a starched white jacket.

The party was going precisely as Deedee had planned. Like a gray Mercedes or a street-length mink, neither too bright nor too dull, it was elegantly relaxed. She was terribly disappointed that the enormous, blooming hibiscus had not been delivered. However, hanging baskets of Boston ferns drooped appealingly, and flats of red and yellow tulips gossiped on either side of the sliding glass door to the living area.

Everyone seemed pleasantly occupied. Except for Shirley Szigetti, trapped in a corner by that awful Glenn Gilstrap, who was probably boring her with motorcycle stories. Back around the pool strolled Deedee to Shirley's aid, pausing along the way to admire how nicely Jonnie Quigley's purple silk blouse set off her complexion, tease with Tom Belcher, and put the poodle back out into the yard.

Where was Aaron? She had not seen him since he had stood beside the hors d'oeuvre table with Anne Meyer, running her fingers back through that frightful hairdo now, and talking with Jack Hamilton.

"Hi!" Deedee was the gracious hostess.

"Oh, hi." Skinny Glenn Gilstrap turned around in his short-sleeve nylon shirt, whereupon Shirley Szigetti smiled a grateful smile.

"I like what you did with the patio," said Glenn.

"I think we're going to like it," acknowledged Deedee. "When are you and Miriam leaving for Canada?"

"I don't know if we're going this year," Glenn shrugged bony shoulders. "Miriam has been having female trouble, and she wants to stay close to home."

Deedee touched Shirley's wrist. "Dear, I want to show you the shoes I found at Neiman's to go with my lamé jacket." The two women turned away from Glenn Gilstrap.

"That man!" exclaimed Shirley. With elongated, fragile bones, tiny head capped by a chignon, and exotic, peach-colored gown, she looked like a flamingo.

Deedee was about to reply when her mouth dropped open. Between the flats of tulips stood Rick, handsome and rather too informally dressed in Levis, boots, and cowboy shirt. Beside him, like a flagpole, was some painted creature with long, teased, silver-dyed hair and double-knit stretch pants so tight the line of her panties was apparent. Already they had become the object of sidelong glances as Aaron led them halfway around the pool to the bar.

"Who is that?" asked Shirley in a nasal voice.

"Oh, that's Aaron's brother," Deedee whispered. "The woman I've never seen in my life. Come along, dear." Grasping her friend by the elbow, Deedee said, "I want to show you those shoes."

From across the room, Aaron watched them sweep from the scene. Tit for tat, he told himself. He had made little effort to be convivial. In fact, for the last hour he had hidden out in the kitchen while Tulip constructed canapés.

The bartender poured beer into a glass for Rick and mixed a stinger for his companion. With great black eyebrows scrawled upon a white powdered face, Donita looked like an Egyptian mummy case, an impression enhanced by her towering height and the garments in which she was tightly swathed.

"Are you from Dallas?" Aaron asked her.

"No, I'm from Cuero."

"Donita works at the Kountry Kitchen," Rick explained.

For the first time, Donita's mask was replaced by a timid, sweet smile. Aaron noticed her long, pale fingers fiddling with the stem of her glass.

"Why don't we find a place to sit down?" He led the way through a phalanx of expensively clad backs.

"I like your pool," said Rick.

"Thanks."

"Are they going to try it out tonight?"

"I hope not." Aaron had not seen Rick for several weeks. He was living alone in a one-room apartment and sending Sherri each month a sizeable chunk of the money he made in his new job as a printer. She had remained with the children in the house and, to everyone's amazement, was managing somehow to take a course at a junior college to become a keypunch operator.

Rick perched awkwardly on an uncomfortable bench, at first sprawling, then crossing one ankle over the other knee. "How's Kim?"

"Oh, she's fine. How are your kids?"

"Great. They're doing great."

Unable with Donita between them to ask about Sherri, unable to think of anything else to say, Aaron said nothing. They finished their drinks and watched the others in the room.

"Well, we can't stay," said Rick.

"Don't run off."

"We're on our way to the Blue Moon," Rick winked at Donita, who responded with a blank stare.

"I wish I could go with you."

Rick looked at his brother and perceived the seriousness of the remark. "Well, why don't you?"

Aaron gazed around the room. "Shit, man, I can't leave."

* * * *

The Westminster chimes of the hall clock could be heard striking twelve-thirty. More than half the guests had left shortly after eleven. The late partiers—Tom and Pal o'Mine, Bart Shelton, Taylor and Lela Bendix, Jack and Bijoux Hamilton—might hang on until dawn.

Then like a reprieve, after they had played several hands of Royal Rummy for twenty dollars a chip, Taylor Bendix proposed that everyone drive over to his place to watch *Star Wars* on his giant-screen TV. Through a friend, he had managed to obtain a video cassette of the film, probably years before it would be available to the general public.

After everyone had departed laughing into the night except Bart Shelton, who had remained behind to finish a conversation with Deedee and help clean up, Aaron excused himself. The hired bartender and Tulip were gathering wadded-up napkins, cigarette butts, and empty glasses.

Aaron turned on the overhead light in the bedroom and shut the door. He was fatigued, but not sleepy. Muzzy from bourbon, he stripped off his clothes and stepped into the shower.

It had not worked out. He was ready to admit that now. Last fall after returning from New Mexico, there had seemed a chance that the marriage might work. They had sat up late in the evenings, heads together over blueprints, Aaron hoping the project might placate his wife's desire for a vacation house on the East Coast. It had required a second mortgage to add the pool and enclose the patio. Business had been poor the past several months. How did she suppose they could afford a second house half a continent away?

Aaron was frankly tired. Tired of the bickering, tired of the pretensions, tired of Deedee. What for several years had seemed merely a brittle surface, a patina which he found foreign, but through which he had always been able to see, underneath, the girl he had met once in the snow — that surface seemed now to have hardened. He could no longer see beneath it. It had become the fact. Deedee had become what once she had only resembled: a sleek and complacent society woman.

She, on the other hand, did little to disguise her impatience with her homebody of a husband. To make up for their lack of rapprochement, she had come to rely more and more on relations with friends.

Tonight's party, Aaron decided as he dried himself off with a thick Turkish towel and slipped on a plush cinnamon-colored robe, had demonstrated once again—no, had demonstrated finally—how little they had in common, he and his wife.

For the first time, as Aaron sat down at the desk built in to the bay window of their bedroom and faced his reflection in the panes, he accepted the notion of divorce as the best answer to their problems.

It had occurred to him fleetingly before. He had toyed with the notion and dismissed it. For one thing, there had never been a divorce in his family. It simply was not something that his people had done.

More important, there was Kim. Five years old, she and her father adored one another. Deedee would retain formal custody. That was customary, although he was certain that Kim meant more to him than she did to Deedee. Both parents would remain in Dallas, though, and Kim could see him whenever she wanted. Perhaps they could share custody. Deedee would not be one to make problems.

In fact, he was surprised that she had not suggested a divorce before now. It was common among those of her set, after all. She was no happier than he in the marriage.

For over an hour Aaron tried to concentrate on a set of plans for a clinic he was designing and waited for his wife to return to their room. He thought of Deedee alone somewhere else in the house with that stockbroker said to resemble Omar Sharif, and he grew furious that he could not demand a divorce from her right then. At that instant, he felt driven to do that tonight and get it over with. He was ennervated from the way their relationship had been dragging on, sucking away his life's blood. For the past—how many?—years, he had expended far too much of his energy counteracting the effects of his disastrous marriage. The strain was murdering him; it was the poisonous kiss that put him to sleep at night and woke him each morning.

At two-thirty Aaron flicked off the desk lamp and felt his way over to the bed. Nauseated at himself for not venturing out of the room to discover the pair, offended deep in his man's pride, for though he had decided to wash his hands of his wife, that is what she remained at that moment—his wife—he pulled back the covers in the dark room, crawled into his side of the bed, and tried to go to sleep. The smell of Deedee's perfume was on the sheets.

Aaron began thinking, then replaying, a drive he had taken with Henry Lazarus north just out of Washington along the river to the rapids at Potomac Park. It had occurred the afternoon after he and Deedee had called it quits—he had thought it would be for good—at National Airport, and she had left him with one forlorn, ambiguous kiss.

Aaron and his friend had sped along a winding, sun-dappled road through a forest, sunlight streaming down at an angle through spanking new greenery high in the reaching trees, warm air gusting in through the open windows, ruffling their hair, whipping their shirt-sleeves. In its loveliness, the afternoon had seemed to mock Aaron's misery.

Near the falls, Henry had parked the car and, carrying a bottle of wine, followed Aaron along a cinder path toward the rushing sound of the river. As they stepped out of the trees, there it was at once, roaring and vigorous, a leaping torrent of chutes and whorling water, surges tumbling over boulders and swirling into eddies, then flinging off in undercurrents and crosscurrents and breaking again further down river upon other rocks, working through the torrential process again and again.

Leaving the path, Henry and Aaron picked their way through the brush along the riverbank until they came upon a sun-washed overlook and sat down. As they passed the bottle back and forth, they spoke few words. It was enough to sit on the warm earth with spray and sunlight on their faces and the din of the rapids in their ears.

Aaron watched a glistening black log tumble down the cascade, become caught in the run, then dash against a rock up into the air end over end, like a twirler's baton, and fall back down into the flow, which sucked it into a whirlpool round and round where it went under the surface to bob up again several yards downstream. From there it rushed through a sluice between two enormous boulders to become absorbed in yet another purple vortex, which held it but an instant before shooting it again downstream.

When they met the bottom of the wine bottle, the two friends got up and dusted off their pants, then made their way back along the river to the cinder path. Although Aaron found himself slightly buzzed by the wine, he felt remarkably clearheaded.

Remembering the river soothed Aaron's nerves as he lay alone in bed in one of the rear wings of the house in Highland Park, just as sitting on the sands of Galveston Island had used to calm his adolescent griefs. However, this time there was no river to project his misery on to, and no friend to share it with; only the river flowing in his memory. Having worked its way through swirls and cataracts, it was flowing smoothly now. Flowing peacefully, purling and soothing, beyond all the tears he had refused to shed, the hard looks, gilded ambitions, grief over the death of friends and grief over the deaths of elders, fears of getting old, bitter betrayals. For the time being, glisters on the surface of the water had replaced the overwhelming and finally lulling weight of all that had passed and was to come.

# 18

"We have ignored it. We have pretended there was not a problem. It's time now to have it out!" Sitting very straight at the claw-footed oak table in the breakfast room, Aaron glared at his wife.

"What are you talking about?" Deedee had just come in carrying a steaming, oversized mug of coffee. "Give me a chance to sit down before you pounce."

Aaron watched Deedee take her seat across from his at the table, shake out her loose-hanging hair, and pinch her silk robe closed at the throat.

"Now, what's all this snoot about?" she said pettishly.

Aaron took a deep breath; his gray eyes glittered. "Where did you sleep last night?"

"Oh, God. Aaron, sometimes you are so . . . middle class." Looking over at her husband, trying to gauge the effect of her words, she continued. "It was nearly three when we finished up, and I didn't want to wake you, so I slept on the couch in the den."

"And what were you doing until three o'clock?"

"I was talking with Bart Shelton, if you must know. I'm not used to having to account for my movements." Deedee was preparing to seize the offensive.

"And I'm not used to being made a fool of in my own house. That goddamned oily stockbroker. . . . I'm sure he's just your type." Aaron could feel himself rapidly becoming overwhelmed by his wrath. He made a vain effort to regain self-control.

"I don't believe we're having this conversation," Deedee replied more loudly.

"Keep your voice down," Aaron said. "I don't want Kim to hear."

Deedee pushed her chair away from the table, "Well, I don't wish to continue this . . ."

"Sit down!" Aaron shouted. "We should have had this out a long time ago. I am not going to put up with any more of your crap. That's my message."

Shocked by the unexpected vulgarity of his tone and words, Deedee curled her lip and put her fingers to her throat. "When you get in one of these moods," she said in a haughty voice, "I find it very hard to remain patient with you. Now what, precisely, are you suggesting?" Deedee was maneuvering now, instinctively, from the well-bred assurance that certain matters are never referred to, certain charges are never made — never, under any circumstances. These matters might be tacitly assumed, they might be talked around and insinuated, but never are they *named*. To do so would constitute an act of unthinkable vulgarity.

"I'm suggesting that you fucked that oily sonofabitch under our roof last night," Aaron spat back. He experienced a perverse thrill at his wife's appalled reaction to his most ungentlemanly revelation. "When I woke up at three-fifteen and you still weren't in bed, I went around looking for you. You might at least have locked the door."

Deedee's face was the color of putty. "You're mistaken. I can't believe that we're talking about this."

Leaping out of his chair and grabbing a rich handful of Deedee's hair, Aaron brandished his other fist in her face. "Do I have to rub your nose in shit to get you to admit that it exists?" he snarled.

Deedee snatched the cup of hot coffee off the table and splashed it up into Aaron's face.

Yelping like a dog in surprise and pain, he caught his face in both hands.

"Don't you *ever* lay your hands on me again!" Deedee screamed and started for the door.

"Come back here," Aaron shouted, wiping his palm across his eyes. His skin was red where the hot coffee had splattered over it. "We're going to get through this matter. I'm not going to have it drag on any longer."

There stood Kim in a quilted robe in the doorway to the kitchen, her yellow hair hanging down, her five-year-old's eyes frightened.

"What are you doing up?" Deedee asked the girl in a controlled voice.

"I heard noises." The little girl burst into tears.

Kneeling, Aaron hugged his daughter as, over her shoulder, he glared at her mother. "Don't worry, sweetheart," he said helplessly, "Mommy and Daddy were just discussing something. Why don't you go back up to your room and get dressed, and Daddy will take you out for breakfast."

"Can we go to Hardy's?"

"Anywhere you want." Aaron pointed his daughter back toward the door. "Do you need help getting ready?"

"No, I can do it by myself." After looking again uncertainly from one parent to the other, the girl started back to her room.

Exhaling heavily, as if he had just finished a foot race, Aaron sat back down at the table and tested his cheek with an index finger. His face stung. His fury had vanished. He felt exhausted, and he wished fervently that the business with Deedee were over. Stronger than that desire, however, was the overwhelming need he felt to conclude the matter.

"We obviously can't work out the terms now," he said after a few moments, "but let it be established that we are getting a divorce."

"I couldn't agree with you more." Deedee stood very tall and patted her hair. "I wish you'd have your things out of here as soon as possible."

Feeling his anger flare again and not desiring another outburst, Aaron bit his tongue and watched his wife walk out the door.

# Part
# Three

# 19

The cabinets were empty. Before he went any further, Aaron drove to the store, walked up and down the aisles, and without a shopping list tossed everything into his basket he could imagine needing, from Saran Wrap to sugar, iodized salt, and coarsely ground pepper.

Arranging it all in his tiny kitchen made him feel efficient. Everything fit. After frying bacon and eggs, then browning two slices of whole-wheat bread in the skillet — he had no toaster — Aaron sat down with a cup of instant coffee and surveyed the kitchen. It was his. Alone. The few dirty dishes from the set of cheap pottery purchased at Woolco he loaded into the dishwasher.

There was laundry to manage. After sending everything tied in a dog-eared bedsheet to the cleaners and receiving it minus a sock and with holes in his handkerchiefs, Aaron decided to wash his own dirty clothes in the laundry room of the apartment complex. Only dress shirts would he send out.

There was the apartment to clean. For years, they had depended on housemaids to scrub down the kitchen and bathrooms, vacuum the carpets, dust the blinds and table tops. Now with child support to pay and exorbitant rent for the modest apartment, a maid was out of the question. One evening a week he spent with dust cloth and can of spray wax.

Always, there were groceries to buy.

There was the car to maintain.

There were long evenings to fill.

Yet it was mainly relief he felt now after the divorce, emerging from a sandstorm of pretense that everything had been okay. A man of wide acquaintance and few close friends, Aaron had previously discussed his marriage problems with no one except Henry Lazurus, one night as they sat on the front porch and drank beer after everyone else had gone to bed. He had chosen to keep this matter secret even from Rick. Only after the final scene in the breakfast room did Aaron confide to his brother the bones of the affair. His wounded pride, wretchedness, and humiliation spoke for themselves.

The worst moments had come while he moved out his things. Rick had helped him dislodge the standing clock from the hallway and bear it prone like a coffin outside. Aaron remembered when he was seven and they had been transferred to another town. The moving was all excitement and packing things away in huge orange cartons until the rooms were empty and unfamiliar and he had run down the street to tell his best friend Rex good-bye. Then through the smudged back window of the car, watching the white-shingled box house grow smaller, he had thought he couldn't stand it.

Months later Aaron had received a letter from Rex. They too were moving. They would stop through for a visit. For the rest of that summer Aaron sat in a chair in the front yard, waiting for a brown '49 Hudson to drive down the street. One afternoon as he was playing with his wagon, a brown '49 Hudson did drive by and he ran into the house crying, "Mom! Mom! Rex drove by! But they didn't stop." Frieda said that surely it wasn't Rex; Aaron knew that it was.

Aaron remembered all that as they eased the standing clock around the corner of the hall, through the front door, and lengthwise into the van. Before they drove away, Aaron studied the house. He had designed it. He had selected every stone and board. Everything about it—from the bay windows in the master bedroom and the breakfast room that surveyed the back yard, to the natural oak woodwork

and plank flooring, the glistening New England win-
dowpanes — reflected his tastes. He knew the garden would
go to weeds. Deedee never stuck her head outside except
to walk to the car. She could care less. She would hire
someone to mow the lawn; the flower beds she would
ignore. It made him sick to think about.

Several evenings after moving into the apartment, Aaron
busied himself with putting things away in drawers and
cabinets. For an hour or two each night before going to
bed, he was keenly aware of being alone. There was no
movement in the apartment.

He would put records on the phonograph — reflective
songs by Paul Simon, Tim Hardin, Billie Holiday — and
holding a book in his lap, he would analyze how his wife
and he had grown apart. Or he would dig out old rock
albums — Jimi Hendrix, Led Zeppelin, the Stones — that
brought back Vietnam and he would remember with bitter
pleasure how his old buddy Len would come back to the
hootch from downtown in his shades, a wide grin on his
face, and lie stoned on his bunk while his huge Sansui
speakers pounded out "Sgt. Pepper's Lonely Hearts Club
Band."

He remembered the tinny speakers in the Paradise Bar,
open to the street with its grille rolled back, squeezed in
among the other bars and massage parlors, where he had
sipped 33, the local beer, splashed over ice, for afternoons
on end. He remembered the faces of the bargirls, slight-
boned, city-born  Eurasians in skin-tight pants and mini-
skirts whose loveliness transcended the heavy paint on
their faces. Flat-nosed girls from the rice paddies with
pock marks across their foreheads, bad teeth, and brown,
splayed feet. Middle-aged Nguyen, who had migrated
south from Hanoi in 1955 and who smoked opium-dipped
cigarettes that made her pupils loom enormous in the dim
back corner of the room. Sharp-eyed Mama-san, hearty
square bones in her face and a dry voice like a cicada.
Grunts in from the bush, their faces sunburned, their hair

oily and rumpled, their eyes tight and jittery, red-rimmed.
GIs from the base camp, free-spending and loud, moustachioed, all-American boys gone to seed. Angular, black-
thatched Vietnamese children who played about the blister-
ing sidewalk, edging over the line into the shade of the bar,
their eyes missing nothing. Beggars, ancient papa-sans
mutely holding their bowls toward you, and younger men
without limbs, destroyed by the war, hating you for your
wholeness and for fucking their women, panhandling
from table to table until being chased out by Mama-san
onto the sidewalk like stray chickens.

He remembered the first day he had gone there, newly
in-country, with another soldier who was going home in a
couple of weeks. How a grunt with eyes that looked like
bulls-eyes had collapsed in a horse laugh at the spectacle of
Aaron's stateside haircut. His shock when after downing
beer after beer all afternoon, that hollow-eyed GI had
stumbled out onto the sidewalk, unbuttoned, and urinated
in the street. How no one had seemed to give his action a
second thought.

His favorite times at the Paradise had been rainy afternoons during the monsoon season when he would have all
afternoon to sit at a table with his knees up and drink 33.
Falling in heavy straight sheets, the rain was like a curtain
through which soldiers would plunge inside laughing and
cursing. A cheap-scented warmth would radiate from one
end of the bar, where the bargirls were gossiping and
grooming themselves. They would saunter over to new
arrivals and lace their arms around the men's shoulders
and sit in their laps and ask them to buy Saigon Tea. In
cracked, sing-song voices, they would chatter and pull out
scraps of paper on which they would want to play tic tac toe.

Periodically, a couple would disappear through flowered
curtains at the back of the bar. Upstairs, as Aaron had
discovered with Ba, a sparrow-boned hostess whose long,
black hair hung loose down her back, the afternoon could
be made to run quickly. Already *boo-coo si,* pretty drunk, he

would find the wiry bargirl a steady support as she guided him up the tile stairs, giggling and clasping his arm across her shoulders with one hand, supporting his back with the other. Inside one of a line of tiny cubicles, the girl would turn on the blue Japanese oscillating fan and aim it at Aaron, who would already be sitting on the side of the single bed unlacing his boots. The air from the fan would feel cool on his sweating skin; it would ruffle the curtain that separated the room from the hallway, where girls were laughing in harsh tones and there was the odor of cooking.

In a flash Ba would be out of her clothes, her skin golden in light muted by the bamboo shade hanging down over the window. With a tin basin of water, she would soap his cock and inspect it, then push him back onto the cot while she climbed on top. For a while she would wriggle in his grasp as he licked and sucked her small breasts, then they would reverse positions and he would bang bang away until finding release in spasms of pleasure from this place into the pure moment of the present.

\* \* \* \*

One evening not long after moving into the apartment, Aaron visited a fashionable bar where he had heard there was plenty of action. Wearing jeans and a tweed sports coat over a blue oxford-cloth shirt, he recognized that it was a younger crowd. He smiled to himself. What had he expected?

Carefully barbered heads of young men with moustaches and gold chains around their necks and women with magenta lipstick and Farrah hair shimmered in plate-glass mirrors. Greenery spewed down everywhere, and little neon signs in Art Deco glowed the names of drinks—GIN, VERMOUTH, AMARETTI—behind the mahogany bar. The voice of Bette Midler spiraled from a rainbow Wurlitzer juke box.

Aaron found a place at the bar and ordered a bourbon and water. The place was too stylish, too bright, too Deco. He acknowledged a kind of snobbery towards these beautiful, bright-faced children. He felt contemptuous of the men with their smooth-skinned, pretty faces and gold chains, their immaculate short hair and conservative garments.

Two comely girls in jersey dresses falling well below their knees occupied stools beside Aaron. The one nearest him had lustrous raven locks, layered as most of the girls had their hair, in a tumbling mane that just kissed her shoulders. A clingy, mulberry-colored dress cupped large firm breasts and a hambone hip that swirled into a shapely thigh and calf.

"Nice evening," he remarked in the girl's direction and folded his hands upon the counter.

Supercilious, she looked around. "Are you talking to me?"

"I said it's a nice evening."

Without changing her expression, the girl turned back to her friend.

Did he look too old? Technically, he *could* be her father. Nevertheless, he had maintained his athlete's build, of which he was more than a little proud. Surely, he must look more interesting than the boys flitting around this place.

"Excuse me," he decided to give it another try.

Again the girl looked around with a haughty expression. "Um. I was wondering if you work around here?"

"Fuck off, gramps," she sneered and turned back to her friend.

In a momentary fit of rage, Aaron wished he had a knife: he'd rip the bitch's throat out on the spot. He inhaled deeply. He'd better get a hold on himself. He was thankful for the tinted lights; he knew his face was red. As he finished his bourbon, a muscular young man with the short dark hair, the gold chain, the Burt Reynolds moustache inserted himself between Aaron and the girls and leaned an elbow on the bar.

"Hi," he said to the girls in a deep voice and cocked two fingers to his forehead.

Neither girl said anything. They smirked at one another.

"I was watching you ladies from across the room and thought I'd introduce myself. I'm Jeremy." A dazzling smile erupted beneath the rugged black moustache. The girls tittered and one of them responded, "I'm Donna. This is Penny."

Aaron's mouth dropped open.

"That's my friend Chris over there at the table in the corner." The three looked over their shoulders, where a blond counterpart of Jeremy waved back at them. "Why don't you all join us?" The fellow straightened back up and followed the girls back towards his friend.

"Well, fuck me!" said Aaron to himself.

He didn't go out again for two weeks. After work he would fix himself a drink, which he consumed with a lot of ice-cube shaking while looking through the newspaper. Then he would put something in the microwave for dinner, something he had prepared and frozen on the weekend. While that was heating, he would change out of his dress clothes into an old pair of jeans or corduroys and a sweater.

The portable television was connected on the counter in the kitchen so he could watch it while he ate. That was his most vulnerable time, the hour when if he wasn't careful, he would tumble over into the blues. By the time the dishes had been rinsed and placed in the dishwasher it was seven-thirty or eight. For an hour or two, he would read a novel or if there were work he had brought home, he would toil underneath the black, wrought-iron chandelier that hovered like a great spider over the dining room table.

At nine or nine-thirty—if he had been successful, and his mind had not strayed into bramble fields of memory—he would change into a jock and gym shorts and work with his weights for an hour. Or he would walk two blocks to the high school track and run four miles at a 7:30 pace. At ten he caught the news and downed a beer before showering and falling wearily into bed.

By following this schedule, Aaron hoped to avoid feeling sorry for himself. Experience had taught him the value, in bad times, of keeping busy. Doing this and doing that. Optimistically, he knew that this was bound to be a low period, but that he would live through it. He knew—and it was necessary to repeat this to himself when things looked bleak—that he would live through it, that there would be good times again. That's what he told himself.

Then one Friday night when Kim was in France with Deedee's mother for three months, he fought against it until nine-thirty. He was suffocating. He didn't feel like reading and there was nothing on television. It was Friday night. He did not want to clean the apartment or work out. Flying high these days with more than one woman, Rick was not home when Aaron called. He had to do something or he would go crazy.

In the Anchor, two couples were drinking in a booth along the wall, the men on one side of the table, the women on the other. Three longhairs in shades hunched over beer glasses at the end of the bar, eyeing a middle-aged rinsed blond whose mascara had run like inkstains down her cheeks. As Aaron took the stool beside her, she upended her beer glass and shoved it forward. When the bartender, who reminded Aaron of a fellow he had hated in college, short and squatty with a flattened nose, slid glasses of beer in front of them, Aaron paid for both.

Without smiling she squinted at him. "Thanks," her voice was boozy. "Can I borrow a smoke?"

"I don't smoke." Aaron was apologetic.

Morosely, the woman turned back to her beer and circled the bottom of the glass with the fingers of both hands. Her teased hair was rumpled and matted and you could see black roots. She was wearing a plain white blouse with stains down the front, designer jeans, and lizard-skin cowboy boots. On her left hand glittered a Tiffany-cut diamond solitaire.

"I can buy some cigarettes, if you want," he offered. The woman reached down by her feet and almost lost her balance. She sat back up with a brown leather purse in hand and began picking through it.

"That's really not necessary," Aaron started toward the cigarette machine that stood beside the door.

"Here," she pulled out a five-dollar bill and slapped it down beside Aaron's beer.

"So what the hell do you want?" she blurted after taking a deep puff on a cigarette from the pack he had bought. The five dollars remained untouched on the bar.

"What do you mean?"

"Just what I said—what do you want? What are you after?"

"I'm just passing time." Why did these matters have to be so complicated. "No sweat." For a long time they sat without saying anything else. One of the longhairs put money in the jukebox and a country song began to play. He had decided to order another beer. "I'm Aaron Teague," he said looking at the woman, who was nodding her head with eyes closed in time to the mournful tune. "What's your name?"

She drew a deep breath and forced it out through her nostrils. Opening her eyes, she peered at Aaron as if she were sizing up something she wanted to buy.

"Fran." A hint of a smile was trying to break out around the corners of her mouth. She reached for another cigarette. This time she held onto Aaron's hand for a while after the cigarette caught fire. Her palms felt soft. She smiled and spiderwebs around her eyes caught the tint of the match. She blew it out and squeezed his fingers.

They drank beer until midnight. Aaron learned that Fran was married to a meat-packing executive and that theirs was a marriage, as she put it, in name only. He nodded his head and kept her beer glass full.

After the divorce he had begun buying *Playboy*, then *Penthouse* and *Hustler*. Like some horny adolescent boy, Aaron became increasingly preoccupied with the women he passed on the street or sat across from in waiting rooms. Not since his first year as a penniless, white-walled GI in the sixties had he gone for so long without a woman.

"Why don't we stop by my place?" he suggested. In spite of hours of steady drinking, Fran seemed no more or less drunk than when he had first sat down.

She took a deep breath and coughed. In the white blouse she extended her arms on either side and stretched lazily like a cat. Then she turned her face with its splotches of mascara toward him and, pursing her lips, blew him a kiss.

She followed Aaron in a Corvette. Riding through the dark streets, he watched in the rear-view mirror as her car weaved back and forth across the road. He hoped she would not get stopped by a patrolman. He was irritated at himself for getting involved in the shabby affair. He hoped he didn't catch a dose of clap. Already he had an erection.

When he clicked on the overhead light, he swore to himself that she was forty-five. Her frowsy hair was a nest, and there were discolored pouches under each eye. In her short rabbitskin jacket, the sort high school girls were then wearing, in her boots and tight jeans, a strap purse dangling over one shoulder, she looked like some ludicrous, overage runaway.

"Come in," he mumbled. He turned on a lamp beside the divan and turned off the harsh overhead track lights. "Sit down. Can I get you a drink?"

Clutching her coat around her as if she were naked underneath, Fran scanned the room before lighting on the divan. "Nothing for me," she said and pulled her jacket tighter.

"I'm going to have a bourbon," called Aaron from the kitchen. "Sure you don't want any?"

"I'll share yours," she smiled when he sat down beside her.

"Are you cold?"

"No."

"Why don't you take off your coat then?"

As she leaned forward, Aaron helped Fran out of her coat, then dropped it on the rug. His arm around her, he put down his drink and kissed the woman. Like an over-ripe peach, her mouth fell open and she poked her tongue into his mouth. Her body was soft, and her arms pressed his back.

Like a tree dropping leaves, she shed her clothes in the middle of the bedroom while Aaron tested the water in the shower. Her skin was pulpy. Out of her jeans, Fran's hips were mottled and her belly pouched, making her swaybacked. On his wife there had not been a superfluous ounce.

They embraced underneath steaming spray. She felt slick and warm. Where water splashed off the crown of her head, the blond hair showed black in the part. Lightly, Aaron massaged her back, her breasts. She closed her eyes as he washed her face. Her skin shone brightly now like enamelled fruit. He lathered her brown pelt, gently, thoroughly, working his fingers through the hair and up her vagina. Gasping, she leaned into the tile and flexed her legs.

In bed, Aaron pulled the blanket up and prepared to mount her.

"Hey, baby," she whispered. "Can we lie here for a minute first? I just want to lie here." She reached around his shoulders and gently guided him over beside her. "I just want to lie here for a few minutes," she repeated, patting him on the back like a baby she was cuddling. "This is what I miss." The woman had begun to cry softly. She cradled Aaron in her arms. "This is what I miss."

## 20

"So some dude knocked on the door last Friday and asked if this is where Richard Teague lives. I said, 'You're looking at him,' and he asked if that's my Mercury parked in the lot and I said, 'Yeah, why?' He said he was there to repossess it." Straddling a straight chair, Rick bit off the end of a pretzel then took a swig of beer as Aaron finished his bench presses, sat up, and gingerly laid the barbells on the floor.

"What'd he do then?"

"Hot-wired the car and drove it off."

"Shit." Glistening with sweat, Aaron walked over and fiddled with the dial of the portable radio. From its single speaker wound the scraping of a country bow and fiddle.

"So does that clean you out?" asked Aaron.

"Huh?"

"That wipe out your cash?"

"Yeah. I had to borrow from the credit union to pay Sherri's house payment."

"Do you remember that MG you helped me pick out?" Aaron said with a grin.

"Helped you pick it out, shit. I told you not to buy it." Rick hooted and lifted his beer bottle. "That was a fucking fiasco."

They had driven into Dallas one Saturday morning when Aaron was a sophomore in high school, and Rick a senior. In that morning's classifieds, Aaron had passed over the Buicks, Chevies, Dodges (old lady cars), Fords, Mercuries, Oldsmobiles, and Plymouths (no class), to the sports cars. He could never afford a 'Vette, but an Austin Healey would be a bitch. "We're Looking for People Who Need a CHEAP and Dependable Car." That was him, definitely. Louie's Limos, on Fort Worth Avenue. There was a '53 Healey ("good body, good mech, cheap"), a '55 Alpha Romeo with no price, a '54 MG ("runs good, as is, $750"), and a couple of Triumphs out of his price range.

Red and green plastic flags flapped on lines between telephone poles along the avenue in the wake of truck and car exhaust, and wooden signs along the other three sides of the car lot proclaimed No Down Payment, Low Interest, We Got the Cars You Get the Savings, Real Bargains, You'll Never See Them This Cheap Again, Sell Out, We Finance, Save Bucks. Over the ramshackle office, a red, neon disk flashed out "Louie's Limos."

"Aaron, you gotta be kidding," Rick had sneered.

"Just drive, James."

After parking Rick's Plymouth, the two had strolled around the lot in their white tee shirts and cuffed Levi's. Old Fords and Chevies, Jaguars, MGs, Volkswagons, Buicks, a parking lot full of dilapidated vehicles. Aaron folded the newspaper over to this morning's ad as a paunchy, sweating salesman with rolled-up sleeves and a fuming cigar in his mouth made his way through the cars to the boys. "Hiya, I'm Frank. What can we do for youse guys?"

"I want to see the '53 Healey and the '54 MG you advertised in the paper."

"The Healey's sold. MG's back this way." Motioning with his head, Frank led Aaron and Rick to the rear of the lot, where a salmon-colored MG was squeezed in between a Ford pick-up and a 1952 Cadillac.

"So what's wrong with it?" Aaron asked.

"They ain't a thing wrong with it. Why you think they's somethin' wrong with it?"

"Seven hundred and fifty dollar's not a lot for an MG."

Withdrawing his cigar with his thumb and beringed first finger, Frank tapped the ash onto the oil-stained pavement. "I tell you, my friend, Louis La Coste is in this business to make money, make no mistake. But he's found over the years that the best way to make a buck is to play fair with his customers, and that's no shit." Frank lodged the cigar back between his teeth, inhaled slowly and deeply, and puffed a perfect smoke ring. "What Louis does is this, he bases his price on what the car costs him. If he pays a lot, he charges a lot. If he gets it cheap . . ." Frank shrugged his shoulders, smiled toothily, and rolled up his palms.

Aaron scratched his head. "Where's this car come from?"

"This is a repossessed model. I shit you not, it was owned by a guy worked in the public library downtown, some bald-headed guy. He drove it six months and got behind in his payments."

"So what then?"

"Say again?"

"What happened then?"

Frank inhaled again and blew another smoke ring. "It sat in the warehouse, that's all I know. They finally got tired of it being in the way and Louie took it off their hands for a song. I swear to God, that's the truth."

Rick had walked around to the side of the car. "Where are the side panels?"

"Ain't got none."

"Ain't got side panels?" Rick shot back. "What the hell are you supposed to do when it rains?"

"You can pick them up for a song at a salvage yard. Don't sweat the small stuff."

Aaron stepped around to the driver's door and tried the handle. The door did not open.

"Needs a little oil on those handles," Frank apologized, yanking on the door handle with his right hand as he reached through the window and pushed out from inside with his left.

Aaron slid into the tan, kid-glove-leather-soft, bucket seat. A bitch. How he would dig cruising around in this. It was fucking beautiful. "Can we start it up?"

"Sure thing. Let me go get the key."

As Frank strode back to the office, Rick bent over and gaped at his brother. "Your head's further up your ass than I think if you buy this pile of shit."

"Watch your mouth, this is my car."

"Get serious. You haven't even looked under the hood. What the hell do you know about a car?"

"So what's there to know? I can drive one."

"Have you ever investigated how to take care of one?"

"They got books on how to maintain a car. So I'll learn."

"I tell you, man, you're crazy, you're just throwing your fucking money away."

When Frank returned, there was a key swinging from his right index finger. "You know how to start one a these dudes?"

Aaron grinned. "How?"

"First you work the choke like *this*. . . ." Frank reached across Aaron and pulled out a knob to the right of the steering column. "Then you tromp the clutch a few times and turn on the switch and give it the gas."

Aaron worked the clutch pedal twice, then turned on the key and stepped on the gas. The motor turned over once, coughed, and quit.

"Try it again."

The second try was like the first.

"Why don't you slide out and let me try? This car ain't been started for a few days and it's a little cold."

After Aaron crawled out of the tiny car, Frank squirmed his way in. Catching his brother's eye, Rick shook his head and motioned thumbs down. After considerable priming and tickling the choke, popping the clutch, flicking on and off the starter, and giving it the gas, Frank finally brought the engine alive with a shrill stuttering skirrrrrrrr, like a gasoline lawn mower engine in need of a tune up, punctuated by flatulent backfiring.

"Sounds good, eh?" he peered out the window at Aaron and grinned broadly.

"Let's see the engine," Aaron replied, while Rick covered his ears.

Frank pulled the hood release, and eased himself delicately out of the car. Then after he propped up the hood, they all bent over the vibrating motor. "It's a beaut'. I shit you not, friend, you're not gonna find more for your dollar than you got in this honey. It's a stud automobile."

Aaron straightened back up and walked slowly around the car, kicking each of the tires. "What kinda terms you got?"

"What do you need? You got some cash?"

"Three hundred. Can you do something with that?"

Rick laid his hand on Aaron's shoulder. "Man, let's do some more looking."

Shrugging off the arm, Aaron continued. "I think six-fifty ought to buy it."

The stub of Frank's cigar dropped to the pavement and he squashed it with a greasy black shoe. "That seven-fifty's firm, my friend. Louie priced it according to what he paid for it. We're just trying to meet expenses on this one."

"What kind of terms do you have?"

"We finance out of a loan company up in Grapevine. You got a job?"

"Yeah, I work part time at the Conoco in Bugg."

"You get paid regular for that?"

"Yeah man, what do you think, I do it for free?"

"Well, we'll have to do a background check. But if you measure up, the car is yours."

Aaron gazed at the jazzy pink sports car, patted a shiny fender, and grinned. "Let's go see about it."

Remembering all these years later how the MG's engine had blown after two weeks, Aaron resolutely grasped the barbell, then pressed it quickly over his head several times in succession before letting it down. "I'm too fucking old for this shit," he mopped his forehead with a towel. "I tell you what else. I went to the doctor this morning and found out I have the clap."

"No shit!" Rick winced and laughed. "Where'd you get that?"

Aaron shrugged his shoulders. It had to have been Fran, although they had not met again.

"This your first dose?"

"Yeah. Ever had it?"

"Fucking A. When I was stationed at Camp Lejeune. Not counting 'Nam."

"Any trouble getting rid of it?"

"Hell no. The doc shot me up with penicillin every time, and that was that."

"Shit." Facing the bar, Aaron went through another set of standing presses.

"You got pus?" Rick asked when the set was finished.

"Yeah. Hurts like hell when I piss."

"Jeez!" Rick chomped down on another pretzel. "So who'd you get the clap from?"

"It's not important."

"Shit. Who'd you get it from?"

Aaron snorted.

"Come on, what happened?"

"Some cunt I ran into in a bar."

"Damn," Rick sneered, "you should be more careful."

After finishing his last set of standing presses, Aaron took a swallow from a bottle of ginger ale beside the radio, then breathing deeply, paced back and forth with his hands on his hips as he asked, "Seen Sherri?"

"Yeah, I saw her at Parents' Night the other night at Tamra's school."

"How's she doing?"

"Oh, fine." Grinning, Rick raised his beer bottle. "In fact, she looked real good. She done something with her hair or something."

"You gonna start seeing her again?"

"I might, I just don't know."

Aaron grinned. "You could do worse."

Rick smiled reflectively.

"Who else you been seeing? What about that dental hygienist you stopped by here with the other night?"

"Yeah, she's all right."

Sitting down on an old shag rug, Aaron hooked his toes underneath the barbell and did fifty sit-ups before resting on his back. "She got a friend?" he asked.

"Whadaya mean, she got a friend? If she did I sure as hell wouldn't introduce her to a degenerate like you," Rick mocked. "You'd fucking give her the clap."

"Kiss my ass!"

"Bare it!"

"Shee-it," Aaron laughed and warned, "you better watch it or you'll end up married again."

Rick cocked an eyebrow and grinned. "You don't think it'll happen to you?"

"No way. Man, you get married again, you might as well hang it up." Aaron added ten pounds to each end of the bar, then hoisted it onto his shoulders and began his squats.

"Damn squats'll ruin your knees. I knew a guy in the Corps that ruined his knees doing squats," Rick cautioned.

Saying nothing until he finished the set, Aaron wiped the sweat out of his eyes and said, "I don't go all the way down." He stepped over to the radio again and turned it off. "This dental hygienist, does she live by herself?"

"Naw, she's got a kid lives with her."

"She's got a kid?"

"Yeah, a little boy, two years old."

"What's she do with the kid when you come over?"

"Whadaya mean, what's she do with the kid? He *lives* there, for Chrisake. I go over and she fixes supper and then after supper the kid goes to bed."

"She's a good cook?"

"Great. She makes chicken noodle soup that's good as Grandma Hale used to make."

"I tell you, man, you're gonna end up married again before you know it."

Rick chuckled softly and finished his beer.

# 21

When Aaron's secretary, Gloria, flew to Cancun for ten days, Nell appeared as her replacement. She was in her early twenties, this girl with wispy, caramel-colored hair brushed back casually from a part down the middle. The ends floated about her head like goose down as she ducked to make out something on a report then sat back up straight and squinted at the sheet in the typewriter. Her nose was long and perked at the end. A square jaw, the sort prized by fashion photographers, dominated a broad, full mouth that sloped downwards, giving her something of a sarcastic expression. Heavy, unshaped eyebrows, overhanging eyelids, and lucent green eyes made her gaze probing but drowsy, as if she were oriental or had just been woken up. She was wearing a paisley dress with padded shoulders, and the flowing emerald scarf encircling her neck and hanging below her braless bosom complimented her eyes and made her complexion look ivory.

Aaron introduced himself. Leaving the typewriter running, she returned a cursory greeting. Later in the morning he found occasion to request a file from the girl, whose name he learned was Nell Graves. Her wiseacre's smile disarmed Aaron almost as much as her height—in high-heeled, maroon suede boots, she stood half a head taller than his own five feet nine. An assortment of rings glittered on long fingers as she searched through the files.

Two evenings later, they had dinner together at Marco's. Nell was from Normal, she explained smirking at the name, a little town in Illinois a hundred and twenty miles southwest of Chicago, where her father taught economics at the college. She had graduated in English from the University of Chicago only four months ago. The diploma had produced no job. Then one afternoon after three fruitless weeks of jobhunting, she received a letter from a girlfriend who had gone to work in Dallas. Because of an oil boom, jobs were plentiful. Nell had sat with legs propped on the bed, a cold Stroh in one hand, her friend's letter in the other. And she thought. About the Sun Belt and margaritas. The next morning she checked out of the shabby off-campus room where she had lived for the past two years. After stopping overnight in Normal, she loaded her Toyota with possessions and left for Dallas. She moved in with her girlfriend temporarily, and bought a *Dallas Morning News*.

There were jobs for engineers, geologists, computer specialists, cocktail waitresses, secretaries, and nude models. For English majors it was not so bright. Temporarily, until she found what she was looking for — preferably something in broadcasting or journalism, something that ultimately could take her back to Chicago — she was doing secretarial work.

She was very young, Aaron thought as he listened to her and sipped red wine. Yet not callow or glossy. Nor did she convey the utter, mad egotism of so many Bright Young Things. The way she had of projecting her jaw to smile, the worldly shadows underneath her eyes, made her seem almost his contemporary.

For her part, whether out of loneliness or attraction, Nell appeared to be enjoying herself. Her shamrock eyes laughed in the candlelight, and her rings glittered as she turned the stem of her wineglass. A wry smile never left her face.

That weekend they went to the stock car races. Nell loved motors; rather, she loved the *sound* of motors. In jeans, a hip-length llama-skin jacket, and a long purple scarf that matched her suede boots, she grinned and clapped her ringed hands at the roars and blatttttttts that sawed their way out beyond the stadium into the clear autumn evening.

After the races they stopped at an old ice-cream parlor in a run-down part of west Dallas, where ceiling fans recirculated the warm air that had risen from the radiator as they ate hot fudge sundaes and talked about themselves. Aaron explained that his brother Tommy had recently moved in with him. When he had first arrived on the bus from New Orleans, he looked awful. His forehead and cheeks were blotched with angry-looking boils. He was emaciated. There were sores up and down both arms. While admitting to shooting speed and smoking grass, Tommy claimed to have avoided harder stuff. He was not addicted, he insisted. What he required from his brother was a place in out of the cold where he could drink plenty of milk and orange juice and get himself back together before spring. From random comments, Aaron had pieced together that Tommy had lost his job at the record store not long after their visit three years ago. Since then he had worked as a bartender, trash collector, window washer, gardener.

"Haven't you been in touch at all these past three years?" Nell asked.

Aaron had sent Tommy several letters, but none of them had been answered. The last one had been returned, "No one of this name at this address" scrawled in Tommy's handwriting across the front of the envelope. Once a year, at Christmas, Frieda and Ernest had received a picture postcard informing them that Tommy was alive. That had been all. From time to time, Aaron and his other brother, Rick, had talked about Tommy. They agreed that one of them should go back to New Orleans to track him down. Nothing had gone beyond the talking stage.

So for three years Tommy had lived God knows how or where. It had been one more nagging source of unease and guilt, while Aaron had witnessed the dissolution of his own and his brother's marriages. With a tight smile he conceded that it had not been the best of times.

"How has he been doing since he's been living with you?"

"He has good days and bad days. I don't think he's using anything—I told him there would be none of that stuff in my place; that's the only condition I laid down—and he's put on twenty pounds. He just hangs around the apartment, though. He sits in there with the door closed and plays records."

"Christ," whispered Nell. "Does he have any friends?"

"No one that I know of. Oh . . . once or twice he's stayed out all night." Aaron paused. "But I don't think he has any friends."

Both of them had finished their sundaes, and when the waiter returned they ordered coffee.

"Does your brother help with the bills?"

"No. My parents send money for his keep." Aaron's jaw tightened. "In a way, I think that's what's wrong with Tommy. The kid's nearly twenty-four years old. He's never finished a damn thing in his life that he's started. Now Mama and Daddy are paying his board. I frankly don't understand him. By the time I was twenty-four, I had a couple years' schooling under my belt and was in the Army and on my way to Vietnam." Aaron broke off, hoping the last statement hadn't sounded too much like boasting.

"Do you really think that's fair?" said Nell. "From what you say, the guy has been knocked down, and he needs some help to get back on his feet."

"Oh, I'm sure you're right," Aaron agreed, then thought for a long moment before continuing. "It's always been that way, though. Tommy's always had everything given to him. I've wondered many times if it wasn't to prove to himself that he could make it on his own that he quit school and went off by himself. The problem is, he found out he *couldn't* make it on his own. Now I don't know what's going to become of him."

The waiter was bringing coffee in thick white crockery mugs. "Do you two talk much?" asked Nell. The coffee was too hot to drink.

"Not much. We never have. With the exception of a few details, the things I've told you, everything I know about Tommy's last three years I've pieced together through observation and deduction. It's as though there's a distant relative living in the apartment with me, one I barely know but for some reason find myself responsible for."

"Does he know you're willing to help?"

"He showed up on my doorstep, didn't he?" Aaron laughed. Then he said, "Yeah. I've told him I want to help however I can, and I'll listen whenever he wants to talk. I don't know what else to do."

Nell knitted her heavy eyebrows and took a sip of the dark coffee.

With a start, Aaron realized how he had allowed himself to run on. Embarrassed and curiously happy, he reached across the round table top for Nell's hand.

After Gloria returned to the office sporting a Mexican sunburn and Nell departed, the two continued seeing one another. Aaron passed along her name to an acquaintance who was looking for someone skilled in communications, and she began soon thereafter doing public relations work at three hundred fifty dollars a week.

He shamed Tommy into spending Christmas at their parents' house, while Aaron and Nell flew to Fort Lauderdale for the holidays. They stayed in a whitewashed stucco apartment a block from the beach, and bought a table-sized plastic tree that they decorated with seashells and the labels off champagne bottles.

During the afternoons they lay on the sand underneath pale blue skies watching one another's bodies turn from white to brown. They either ate dinner out, their favorite place being a hofbrauhaus run by two immigrants from Hamburg where they gorged themselves on sauerbraten and dark beer, or they cooked for themselves in the tiny kitchenette of their apartment. Spaghetti and meatballs, broiled sirloin steaks and baked potatoes, scrambled eggs and fried bacon. Aaron had become a good basic cook

since moving into his own place. Nell's speciality was
sauces: hollandaise for eggs, a marvelous brown herb
sauce for steak. They would pat and nuzzle one another as
they edged around the kitchen. After dinner they walked
along the beach letting the cool waves wash in and out over
their bare feet.

While they never seemed to run out of things to say to
one another, time and again Aaron was struck by the chasm
of experience between them. One evening as they sat in the
sand talking politics and watching hermit crabs scamper
about, he had mentioned Eugene McCarthy's name.

"Who?"

Recalling the political traumas that had constituted 1968
in the life of his own generation, Aaron was staggered. Nell
was not stupid, he reminded himself, nor noticeably unin-
formed. But all that had occurred before she had reached
an age of political awareness. It was nothing more than
history to her. It had not been a part of her life.

In bed they were perfect companions. The musty apartment smelled of mildew; the sheets smelled of Nell's
cologne. She would stand with one foot on the commode in
the brightly lit bathroom and pat cologne lightly over her
body—in the hollows of her arms and along the sides of her
full breasts, on the insides and outsides of her thighs, then
run her fingers up through her long hair. As Aaron lay
watching her from the bed, he thought he had never before
been so happy.

Their last glimpse of the beach, as the rented Pontiac
turned toward the causeway joining the strip of beach to the
mainland, was of two little girls in brightly colored swim-
suits chasing one another out of the surf and up the narrow
stretch of white sand. As they leaped and frisked about like
hummingbirds, their laughter floated and burst in the
golden morning.

It was cold but dry when they landed at Dallas/Fort
Worth Airport, a gray, overcast, winter afternoon. On the
loop around town, Nell rolled down her window. An old

Chevie ahead of them with a caved-in fender and no muffler was being passed on the right by a green TR6, a razor-cut dark-haired man behind the wheel, while behind them a teenager in a red Dodge was honking his horn at a Cadillac nosing through the traffic like a barracuda through a mass of lesser fish.

"Get your damn head in!" cried Aaron. Like a puppy in hot weather, Nell was hanging out the window, her scarf billowing after her. "For Christ's sake," he griped after she pulled herself back into the car. "Didn't you ever see that movie where Vanessa Redgrave played Isadora Duncan and she strangled to death when her scarf got caught in the wheel of a roadster she was riding in?"

"I was just listening to everything," said Nell a little huffily.

"Well, listen to it with your head in the car."

When Aaron opened the door to his apartment after dropping Nell off, it was six-thirty. Tommy was sprawled in an armchair watching television. The room stunk of cigarettes; empty soda and beer cans and pizza boxes were strewn about.

"Hey," mumbled Tommy without taking his eyes from the game show.

Aaron set his suitcase down on the carpet and closed the door behind him. "How was your Christmas?" he asked.

"Yeah." Tommy's gnarled body seemed boneless.

"Did Mom and Dad enjoy it?"

"I didn't go." Tommy's eyes remained fixed on the television screen, which now displayed a commercial for drain cleaner.

Aaron sat down on the divan and wrinkled his forehead. "You didn't? I thought you were going home for Christmas."

"It would've been a hassle," Tommy glanced at his brother. A yellow-fanged grin washed across his jaws and was gone. "You know?"

"Hell, man, I just hate to think of you spending Christmas by yourself. Plus," Aaron said rather sharply, "I think the folks had been looking forward to it."

Tommy shrugged his shoulders. "That's the way it goes, man." Once again the game show was on. "Oh," he said a little more loudly as Aaron stood up, "you'll be happy to hear: the kid got a job—*de dah!*"

"Yeah?" Aaron raised an eyebrow. "Where?"

"The Stop-n-Go down the street." Tommy watched the antics on the television screen as he spoke. "They pay good. But it's dangerous work. There's a loaded *pees-tole* on the shelf under the cash register."

"That's good, man. What are your hours?" This was the first really positive move Aaron had seen Tommy make.

"Eight to four . . . *a.m.* I leave in about an hour." Aaron had picked up his suitcase and was starting with it towards his room. "Well, you be careful. It's dangerous out there at night."

"Tell me about it." Tommy grinned to himself, a wolfish grin that bubbled over into an eerie, sucking laugh.

After Tommy went to work, Aaron cleaned up the apartment. The place was filthy. Dirty pots and dishes filled the sink and covered the cabinets; pizza was ground into the carpet; a beer can lay on its side in a foul-smelling bog where the contents had drained. Aaron pitched the dirty clothes into Tommy's room and shut the door. He would let the kid stay there, but he'd be damned if he'd do his laundry. The bathroom he attacked with a can of Ajax, a scrub brush, and a roll of paper towels. He swore the whole time he was cleaning the room.

A few evenings later, Nell looked lovely in a pair of scarlet heels she had brought back with her from Florida and a revealing jersey dress. She was wearing cologne and her eyes glimmered a jade hello. They had decided to dine inexpensively at a little Vietnamese restaurant, then make the 8:45 showing of a new Fassbinder film.

"Guess what?" Nell frowned as she closed her menu. "They're raising the rent."

"How much?"

"A cool hundred a month. Just like that. Can they do that?"

Aaron shrugged. "Isn't there a rent council or something? Why don't you call?"

"Oh, shit. It's not worth it. We're so cramped as it is. I've never unpacked half of my things. They're in boxes out in the storage shed. And I think Sheridan is ready for me to find my own place."

Garlanded with smiles, a Vietnamese girl arrived to take their orders.

"Where are you thinking of moving?" Aaron tried to sound casual, but the plan that was hatching in his mind made his gray eyes dance.

"I'd like to find a garage apartment in that pretty, old neighborhood behind where I work. I love the big old live oaks and the brick sidewalks. Somewhere, ideally, I could walk to work."

Aaron smiled and poured both of them tea from the clay pot their waitress had brought. Steam coiled up from the little cups without handles. It smelled faintly of flower petals. "Why don't you move in with me?" he proposed. There it was, without trumpets. Aaron's eyes searched Nell's face.

She looked surprised.

"I'm serious," he added.

"I honestly wasn't fishing for that, Aaron."

"Why not think about it?" He was amused by her befuddlement, and he felt very happy.

"It hadn't occurred to me."

Aaron grinned and touched her under the table with his ankle. "Think about it."

He didn't wish to crowd her. He was astonished at his own impetuosity, although the notion of their living together had occurred to him before. It was a case of the

opportunity presenting itself, and of his seizing that
opportunity.

It had seemed like an awfully long time since Aaron had
shared quarters with anyone other than his brother. And
with his daughter on weekends. At first after the divorce,
he had enjoyed the freedoms of a single existence: the
bottom line being not having to care for the needs of
anyone but himself. However, that had gotten old quickly,
and now he wanted to share his life again. Living alone had
allowed him to make clarifications, to find out again what
life could be like without the constant anxieties attending
an unhappy marriage. But it had also been a time of
desperate loneliness: going to movies by himself, night
after night eating only a sandwich and soup, since there was
no one with whom to enjoy a meal. He had learned that
without someone else, he was conscious of nothing so much
as of merely growing older, of time filtering away like grains
of rice sliding one by one out a hole in the toe of a
gunnysack. He needed someone as a reflector, as a comple-
ment to divert his attention away from that fact, and to give
him the sense that something besides time slipping away
was real.

A week passed before Aaron again brought up the matter to Nell. It was a windy eighteen degrees outside as they
drove the Central Expressway downtown. Inside the Su-
baru all was snug.

"You understand," Nell said, "don't you, that I'm not
ready to make any sort of commitment?"

"Nobody's mentioned a commitment." Periodically their
faces were illuminated by headlights from oncoming cars.

"I think so much of you, Aaron, I really do. But I'm not
ready to make a commitment to anyone."

Aaron was silent. He would let her work through this.

"And there's your brother."

"What about him?"

"Wouldn't it be awkward for him if I were there?"

Aaron chuckled. "He won't know you're around. He's working nights and sleeping during the day. The only time I ever see him is at dinner. The rest of the time he stays in his room."

"I don't know. I'd feel a little funny."

"Believe me, Tommy's not a problem. Next objection?"

Nell laid her wrist on the back of Aaron's neck and fluttered her fingers. "I don't really have any, I guess. When can you help me move in?"

Aaron reached up beside his cheek and rubbed Nell's hand with his own. "Lady, you just tell me when you want to move."

Tommy was shaken by the news. "I'll find another place," he said immediately.

"There's no need for that," responded Aaron. "We'll have my room and you can stay in your room. There's no reason we can't all live here."

"Sounds kinky to me," Tommy snickered. "No, man. I know when it's time to move on," his eyes narrowed over the yellow grin. "I'm not gonna get in anyone's way."

Aaron was thinking. It would be a relief to have his brother out of the apartment. And not only for the sake of the new arrangement. Tommy's slovenliness, as well as his habit of playing either his record player or the television every waking moment, had been wearing on Aaron's nerves. The kid had a steady job, he wasn't using any chemicals, except for the couple of beers he upended before dinner each afternoon. It was high time he flew the nest. He would make it on his own this time.

"Where would you move?" Aaron asked matter-of-factly.

"Oh, I'll find a room someplace. Don't worry about it." Tommy gave a sidelong glance at his brother. "Hey, man, not to worry. I'm happy for you. I really am."

Chuckling in his strange, sucking way, Tommy slid his hands into his back pockets, ducked his head, and shuffled barefoot out of the room.

# 22

When Frieda and Ernest woke up on Christmas eve morning, it was eight degrees Fahrenheit outside and fifty-two degrees on the thermostat in the hall. "What are we going to do?" Frieda wrung her hands. "A houseful of company on the way and no heat!"

Ernest shook his head and called Mr. Huddleston. The furnace man was making no house calls until after Christmas. Clucking around like a chicken, Ernest told his wife, would not help matters. He filled the fireplace with split logs and started a fire.

After breakfast Frieda brought a scalding cup of spice tea into the den, where Ernest was sitting on the hearth polishing a pair of brogans. She pulled her cardigan tightly around her shoulders and shivered. "I hope this house warms up by the time the kids get here. It seems like everything that could've gone wrong has gone wrong."

"All your worrying's not going to help a thing."

"First Aaron flies off to Florida with that . . . chippy," Frieda said bitterly, "and Rick and Sherri not together."

"They're together for today," Ernest reminded his wife gently. "Be thankful for that."

"You're right," Frieda agreed and sipped her tea. "I just wish they'd *stay* together."

Ernest pursed his lips, but before he spoke, Frieda continued, "I'd jump for joy if Aaron and Deedee would even get back together for Christmas. When I think of what's gone on between those two, it makes me sick. I don't know when we'll be able to give little Kim her present. Aaron should have brought her out here for Christmas. Poor thing's not going to remember who we are."

"Aaron's been real good about bringing that little girl out to see us," said Ernest. "And he's been awful busy. Kim's not going to forget who we are."

"We'll see. I bet you a nickle Aaron was ashamed to bring that *girl* he's living with out here to meet us. I bet he feels like a damn fool, which is exactly what he's acting like. Any girl that would live with a man old enough to be her father . . ."

"We haven't even met her," cautioned Ernest. "Don't throw stones."

Frieda gave her husband a withering look. "If it wasn't for Deedee, Aaron wouldn't be where he is today. You know as well as I do, when he came back from Vietnam, he wasn't fit for shooting. Sitting around the house all day the way he was, raising hell all night. Deedee put him back on the track. Whatever you can say against that girl—and there's plenty can be said against the stuck-up thing—you have to give her that: she put Aaron back on the track."

"I'd give some of the credit to that guidance counselor Aaron had in high school, the one that set up the scholarship."

"Hmph. Lot of good it did him—flunked out of college and had to go in the Army."

"Well, hell, that wasn't the counselor's fault! The kid was immature. Besides, the Army wasn't all bad for Aaron—it made him grow up."

"I've got my doubts about that," said Frieda. "It taught him how to drink and God knows what else. I don't even want to think about it. I'll say it again, he was on his way to the gutter when Deedee got hold of him and put him back on the track."

"There wasn't such things as scholarships in my day," said Ernest. "Or at least we didn't know anything about them. I was the first one in my family to finish high school."

"We did the best we could with what we had," said Frieda. "We have no reason to feel ashamed." A thoughtful look spread over her face. "Baby, do you remember when I first married you after the boys' father died, how Aaron wouldn't have anything to do with you for over a year? Rick took to you right away, but Aaron held back."

"Yes, I do remember that."

"He always was the brain of the family; I guess it's fitting he's the only one to finish college. In some ways he was my favorite," Frieda mused. "Although I've never understood him. It's because of Aaron that Tommy went off half-cocked, though. Tommy worshipped the ground his brother walked on."

Ernest nodded in agreement.

"Do you remember how the first thing Tommy would do when he got in from school while Aaron was overseas was ask if a letter had come? Then when Aaron came home, my Lord, that kid was in hog heaven! The way he lapped up every word he said. Then when Aaron grew his hair long and Tommy had to be a copycat, that's when we started to lose him. I believe to my soul that Aaron has to bear some of the blame for what's happened to Tommy."

"That's not fair to Aaron," said Ernest. "A man has to be responsible for his own self. I may not be educated, but I know that much. The fact is, Aaron could play with fire and not get burnt. Tommy couldn't. I maintain it was the Army that made Aaron able to take it." Ernest buffed the brogan's toe to a high sheen. "Aaron's a survivor; he always has been. Tommy's always been a whiner from day one. He's my own flesh and blood, and it hurts me to say it, but I'm afraid the kid just doesn't have what it takes to survive. He never has. I wish he could have had the opportunity to go in the Army, like his brothers. That might have been the answer for him."

"Maybe," said Frieda, unconvinced. "I still say that Aaron had the power of influence over his little brother, and he could have used it for good or for evil purposes."

"You're just talking now. Besides, I believe that Aaron is trying to make up for some of that by looking after Tommy now."

"Thank the Lord for that!" Frieda finished her cup of tea and set it down on the brick hearth. "I hope Tommy looks as good as Aaron says he does."

"Just be kind of low key when the boy gets here," said Ernest. "We don't want to scare him off again."

By four-thirty, when Rick and Sherri arrived with the children, the den was cozy as a fresh panful of biscuits. There were gas fires burning in both bathrooms, and the oven had run all day.

For the holidays Rick and Sherri had called a truce. Christmas, they agreed, was for the children and the grandparents. Rick was impressed by his estranged wife, who was working as a keypunch operator while she continued to take night courses two evenings a week. Her hair was shorter and back behind her ears, which were tipped with gold crescent moons. Her complexion was bright and she held herself with an assurance he had never seen in her before.

Looking like Grandma Hale in the doorway, Frieda hugged Sherri and went on about how pretty she looked. Then she kissed each of the children, and gave Rick a look that was at once encouraging and disparaging. "There's no heat!" she exclaimed. "You may want to keep your things on." But the children already had wriggled out of their coats and were rousting through the pile of brightly wrapped presents around the Christmas tree, which twinkled with colored lights.

While Ernest helped Rick carry in several armloads of packages from the car to add to those already under the tree, the women disappeared chattering into the kitchen. Frieda and Ernest had stood firmly behind Sherri throughout the ordeal. Their son, Frieda confided to whomever she was talking to, was in the wrong in this matter. He was turning his back on a good home, a good wife. It was not like him at all. Sooner or later, he would come to his senses.

The children hung on their father. Tamra, a chubby girl with a loud, hoarse voice, wanted to look through the photograph album with him. As if she had never seen the pictures before, she laughed at the funny-looking people and insisted in her husky voice that Rick tell her the stories behind each one. Buddy was embarrassed because of a new haircut, which he said made him look dumb, while Randall was content to sit beside his father and be patted and stroked.

"Have you heard from Aaron?" Frieda called out from the kitchen. The house smelled of the Christmas tree, fresh bread and turkey dressing, pumpkin pie.

"Not since before he left for Florida," answered Rick. Aaron's trip south had not set well with his mother.

"Well, I wish that Tommy would get here." Frieda came to the doorway, drying a plate. "How long has it been since all of us were together for Christmas?"

"Let's look at the tree," Rick laid the photograph album on the coffee table and took Tamra by the hand. "This drum," he pointed to a tiny red ornament hanging near the top of the tree, "is one I made in Cub Scouts."

"I just got my Wolf badge," Buddy tested his cropped hair with the palm of one hand.

"Well, congratulations." Rick patted his son's thin shoulder blades.

"There's gonna be a winter camp-out in a few weeks. It's for the guys and their dads. Are you gonna come?"

"You bet."

"See!" Buddy made a mouth at Tamra behind their father's back. "You said he wouldn't come."

Her face red as a holly berry, Tamra slapped at Buddy. "I did not. *Mother* said he might not be able to get off work."

"And this star," Rick fingered an ornament on the tree, "is something your Aunt Prell brought back from Mexico."

"I love it," said Tamra and bent down the branch for Randall to examine.

"The angel," Rick pointed to a blond-haired doll in a white gown at the top of the tree, "used to hang on top of your Great Grandma Hale's Christmas tree."

Buddy was on his knees shaking a heavy box from his father. For each of his children, Rick had bought one special gift: an electronic game for Buddy, a dresser set with amber handles for his daughter, a box of oak building blocks for Randall. For Sherri, he had found seed pearl earrings.

In many ways it had been a discouraging winter for him. Twice he had been down with flu, and his car had suffered one breakdown after another. His work had been going all right—he liked his boss at the print shop. But he missed his family.

When he lived at home, he had found the children a nuisance, always hanging on him, wanting him to build with them, read them stories, buy them shoes or stuffed animals or toy trucks. Then when he was away from them, he was miserable. Watching children with their parents on the street or in restaurants or supermarkets, he would think guiltily of his own daughter and sons, of how they were without their father.

And he missed Sherri. The women he met in bars or at work, so different from one another, blonds and redheads and brunettes, all of them reminded him in some way or other of his wife. The way one of them stood stirring soup on the stove with her weight on her back leg, the way another would tug on an earring, the way a third laced her hands around his neck or gasped when he first entered her. They were like Sherri, all of them. Yet they lacked her strength, her silent vulnerability. Seventeen months ago, his wife seemed to be smothering him. Now he was wondering if there were any real possibilities for him without her.

Then he would recoil. If it weren't for Sherri, if it weren't for the children, he might be making fifty thousand a year as an engineer. Or a hundred thousand. They had wrecked his possibilities. For the rest of his days he would be nothing but a peon, earning money to pay their bills.

What an ass he was, he would then conclude. It was no one's fault but his own that he was where he was. Whatever Rick Teague was, he told himself with grim satisfaction, he was no shirker. He would shoulder his responsibilities, as he had done in the past. And like wet clay in the sun, his emotions would harden. The circle of his thoughts would begin to roll again.

By six-thirty Tommy had still not arrived. Frieda called the apartment. Her face darkened as she spoke quietly for a while then hung up. "Let's go ahead and eat," her voice was toneless. "Tommy's not coming."

"Why not?" Ernest was worried.

"I couldn't make out why. He said he's going to stay at the apartment."

Sherri and Rick looked at one another, while Frieda returned to the kitchen and Ernest took down the poker to stir the fire.

It was nearly midnight when Rick dropped off Sherri and the children at their house. Thin ice pellets sprinkled the road like grains of rice. He had enjoyed the day. Tremendously. He could not get over how terrific Sherri looked. Working obviously suited her. And the kids were wonderful kids.

He recalled a conversation with Aaron late one night at his place. The expression on his brother's face had soured as Rick had waxed nostalgic about the Marine Corps and Vietnam, then had recounted once more his dream of living the good life in the mountains of New Mexico.

"Hey, my man," Aaron had interrupted, his tongue thick with Scotch, "don't get pissed. I wanta tell you something. It's not New Mexico you're missing. Or the mountains, or the fucking Marines, or whatever the goddamn hell it is you think you're missing. It's your youth. That's what you're missing."

At the time, Aaron's remark had not meant much. But Rick had not forgotten it. Tonight as he drove back alone to his apartment on Christmas Eve and somewhere else his family was getting ready for bed, he weighed his brother's words.

Early the next morning, he called Sherri to ask if he might drive over. She was wearing the green velour robe Frieda and Ernest had gotten her for Christmas, and Rick's pearls shone in her ears. Glad that their father was eating breakfast with them, the children sat grinning at one another. Sherri's expression was guarded. She had baked a Swedish tea ring—Aunt Norma Lou's recipe. In spite of Christmas clutter, the house was immaculate. The children were washed and brushed; Sherri was freshly bathed and sweet-smelling. She was proud of her domain.

After breakfast, she and Rick bundled up in heavy coats and walked alone up the winding street of tract houses. Mimosa trees shivered in the wind, and rime etched the windows of cars and pickups parked in driveways and along the curbs.

"What I came over for," said Rick finally, his breath white plumes, "was to ask if I could come back."

Sherri's eyes widened slightly, but she said nothing.

"I've missed you. I know I haven't done right by you. Although my intention was never to hurt you. You have to understand that."

Sherri was working hard to control her face. "If you knew the hell you've put all of us through!" she muttered. "If you had said this two weeks after you walked out, or six months after, I would have probably said yes. Immediately. I've had to pull things together for myself. The children. Money. Baby, you'll never know what you left me with."

Rick dug his fists in his pockets.

"I was so mad then," Sherri continued. "There were days when I could have slit your throat if you'd walked through the door. Slit it knowing I would have gone to prison. You not only hurt me and the kids, but you destroyed any chance I would ever have. I hated you.

"Then I'd feel guilty. The kids didn't have an easy time of it, you know. It's my responsibility to protect them from hurts they can't handle. I couldn't do that. So I must have been doing something wrong. And I must have been doing something wrong for you to want to leave. I'd look at myself in the mirror. Had I gotten ugly? Was that it? Hadn't I been good enough in bed? What had I done to drive you away?

"I kept remembering when I told you I was pregnant with Tamra. You never flinched. 'I guess we'd better get married,' you said. And then you kissed me." Sherri drew a handkerchief from her pocket and wiped her eyes. Her knuckles were blue.

"Then after eight months of utter hell, I woke up one morning; the tears were gone. I knew I'd cried long enough. I knew I'd better get busy. My children needed me. Even if you didn't. And we needed money. That afternoon, I went over to the community college and enrolled in a night course. I didn't know how I was going to manage it. I just knew that I *had* to. And I came back and fixed dinner, and I felt better. No," there was gristle in Sherri's voice, "I felt *good!* For the first time since you left, I felt really good.

"I finished that night course, and I found a job, and now I'm taking another course. Things are going good for us, Rick. Too good to throw over on a Christmas whim."

As they turned around and began walking back towards the house, Rick placed his arm around Sherri's waist. "All I can tell you," he said in a quiet voice, "is that this is not a whim. I give you my word. I'm proud of you for the way you've taken care of yourself and the kids. I wish I could say the same for myself." He broke off.

"You give me one year," said Sherri back in front of the house. "If after a year, you still want to get back together, then we can." She disregarded the frown that began to spread like a cloud across Rick's face. "In the meantime, you're welcome to come over whenever you like."

Her eyes glowed. She was awfully afraid to hope. Her wounds had taken a long time to cover over; the scabs were hard. She did not want them ripped off. Maybe, though. Just maybe.

\* \* \* \*

During the first week in March, Rick took the day off and drove to Jessup, a town where they had stopped over once on their way back from somewhere else. Both of them had been charmed by the brick, tree-lined streets of lovely stone and frame houses; the campus of the small, parochial college dotted with weeping willows and Georgian buildings; the quaint, friendly downtown built on a square around a limestone courthouse. Someday, they had promised themselves, they would return.

He had no connections in Jessup. In fact he did not know a soul. After parking his car outside a bakery on the square, Rick bought a newspaper off the rack and over a cinnamon roll and coffee perused the help-wanted column. He marked three ads with a ballpoint pen: one for a salesperson at a hardware shop, another for a checker at a supermarket, a third for a printer at the newspaper. The printing course he had taken in high school already had stood Rick in good stead in his current job. Thinking of Sherri, he also marked two ads for keypunch operators, one of them at the college.

The supervisor at the newspaper was working double shifts. Pushing up a green eyeshade, he told Rick he could begin immediately. Whistling to himself, Rick checked the paper again for places to live. Rent was very high—higher even than in the city. And there weren't many houses for sale. One of them, though, took his eye when he drove up. A roomy, three-bedroom, white-frame bungalow from the twenties. A broad, covered front porch with a porch swing. A small, enclosed back porch that was plumbed for automatic washer. A detached single-car garage. There was an old-fashioned floor furnace that would be warm to stand over on cold mornings, and a footed, porcelain tub that, like the rest of the fixtures, was original with the house. Mature maple trees badly in need of pruning shaded the front yard, and two enormous cedars of Lebanon grew in the back. The place was dowdy and needed paint inside and out. There was not a shred of insulation in the walls or in the attic. But he loved it, from the L-shaped living room with bookshelves on either side of the artificial fireplace to the yellow, built-in breakfast nook. With two salaries—he had no desire for Sherri to give up her job—and with the down payment they would realize from selling their house in Dallas, they could swing it.

Rick's head was racing with new plans, new possibilities as he drove the ninety miles back to the city that evening. He would call Sherri as soon as he got back. No, better yet, he would drive right over. Surely, she would not insist on another ten months apart when she heard what he had found. It had been there, under their noses, all the time! Why hadn't he thought of it before? Never had he been dissatisfied with Sherri, or with the children, per se. It was the situation, the sense that he was locked in a box with no exits that had driven him crazy.

To live in Jessup! There were excellent schools. He remembered from his own high school days the high reputation of Jessup schools. If she wanted, Sherri could continue going to school while she worked. He could go to school. He doubted if the modest liberal arts college had an engineering program. But no doubt there would be something Rick could finish a bachelor's degree in. And there were the roomy old house and the trees.

Rick turned off the car radio to sing his own song.

# 23

Aaron sat slumped on the side of his lower bunk, feet on the floor, orders to return to Vietnam on his lap. All about him in the open-bay barracks, GIs with white sidewalls were transferring their belongings from footlockers into green canvas duffel bags. Aaron was wearing baggy, government-issue drawers, which he detested, and tropical combat boots with green fabric shanks and steel plates in the soles. It was a helluva situation: he was too old; he'd already served a tour in Vietnam; he couldn't leave his daughter; he was involved with a woman.

Click, click, click. Like the slow ticking of a clock, Aaron's drill sergeant, a lifer named Iglinsky, was pacing the length of the bay. The creases in his fatigues could have sliced cheese. His boots, remarkably tiny — no larger than a size seven — for a man of his bulk, Aaron suspected had been shellacked. Scraped whiskers gave a bluish cast to heavy jowls. As he paced he leered from side to side, his eyes like balls of hard, green candy.

"Get the lead out," Iglinsky demanded, approaching Aaron's bunk.

Aaron mumbled under his breath.

"Say again, troop?"

"I didn't say anything."

"You best get yer ass movin'," Iglinsky popped his eyes at Aaron, "or you be in a *world* o' hurt."

No, he wouldn't go again. Already Aaron could feel the great weariness of marking days off a short-time calendar: three hundred and sixty-five days to get through without stepping on a land mine or a Bouncing Betty that pops up waist-high like a bouncer on a trampoline before blasting your balls off. Three hundred and sixty-five days to get through without being wasted by a bomb in a market place, by a satchel charge, by a car bomb that explodes after you drive back onto the compound or when you turn the key. Three hundred and sixty-five days to get through without being picked off by a sniper as you walk dully along the perimeter or sit on top the bunker passing the pipe. Three hundred and sixty-five days to get hooked on fine fine superfine dope, Cambodian Red, speed that you buy over the counter in the drugstore, opium, the big O like a vanilla snowcone, like ice in a tin cup of ditch water. Three hundred and sixty-five days to get your shit blown away, to get mortared, done a job on, to get dusted, snuffed, wasted, three hundred and sixty-five days to get it, to get greased, become a grease spot, get zippered into a body bag.

Never happen, my man, Aaron whispered after Sarge's starched back. *Sin loi*, tough shit, tough titty. This time I am not your man. Next time you look I be gone, I be *dee-dee mau*.

Quietly, without drawing attention to himself, Aaron stood up and shuffled towards the latrine. Poor white-walled sonsofbitches humping away so Sarge won't come back and bust their asses. Outside the door, Aaron sidled through the darkness and soon, his stomach a tub of elation and anxiety, he was loping along a shabby backstreet in Dong Xuyen. In his OD drawers and combat boots, he was ignored by the old mama-sans chewing betel nut and sweeping sweeping sweeping with fan-shaped brooms.

Then he was in a crowd of Vietnamese teenagers—cowboys and coke girls. The boys had long hair and weasel butts, the girls were wearing cone hats. They paraded Aaron through the street. He was wearing a leather dog collar, and the leader of the group, taller than the others, more muscular, and wearing a red kerchief around his brown neck, was leading him by a leash. Aaron ate with a spoon from a can of dog food, and when a wizened old mama-san with a face like a walnut tried to snatch it from him, he bared his fangs and clasped the can to his chest. The children were singing snatches of songs and laughing, and Aaron was aware of playing the role of clown. It was a disguise he felt comfortable with.

When they reached the base camp, the sentries waved them through to a corrugated-tin hootch just inside the gate. There, a tired and cynical-looking woman with her hair in a net told them to line up. She could talk to them only one at a time. While they were not paying anything today for workers, she said, it would be necessary to work today in order to be considered for employment at the camp tomorrow.

"Never happen,"

"Fuck you,"

"Number ten," were responses from the cluster of boys; their girlfriends had shoved their way into the hootch behind them and were jangling their golden bracelets.

"It may be number ten," returned the woman in a patronizing voice, "but that's the way it is. If you don't like it, leave. There are plenty who will work if you won't."

Amidst the yammering and shuffling around, the tall youth with the red bandanna elbowed through the crowd to stand before the woman's desk. Smiling in an ingratiating manner, he dug in his shirt pocket and pulled out a laminated identification card. Complacent, the woman watched the other youths line up behind him to add their names to her list of workers.

Through the back door of the hootch appeared the head of Sgt. Iglinsky. "How's it goin', hon?" he leered.

The woman spread her arms and smiled about her. Sarge winked at the woman, light sliding down his blue jowls, then disappeared back out the door.

"Wha' the fuck you think yer doin', trooper?" bluffed Iglinsky when Aaron confronted him outside with a German Luger.

Without hesitation, Aaron raised the pistol and aimed it at Iglinsky's heart. Bang, went the gun, as Sarge's eyes popped out on stems like daisies and his blue jaw came unhinged.

Bang, Aaron shot another round into the man's chest, as he stretched out beefy arms and foundered forward. Bang. Bang. Bang. Like a tank or a wounded rhino that keeps loping for you after you've pumped your last round into his shoulder, Sgt. Iglinsky groped toward Aaron, who realized he was dreaming and made himself shake his head back and forth, back and forth, back and forth.

Aaron's heart was pounding and goosebumps covered his skin. There was light across his face, an aching in the small of his back. He was cold and remembered he was not in Vietnam and blissfully pulled the clean cotton sheet up around his shoulders.

Aaron flexed his toes against the footboard. The room was bathed in amber light. Nell was lying on her side, her back to him, hips shoulder and head forming three graduated hillocks. She was breathing so shallowly that Aaron placed his hand lightly on her rib cage. Deedee he remembered inhaling profound, regular diaphrams-full of air in her sleep, as if getting her money's worth, breathing in and out, in and out deeply and ponderously through flaring nostrils.

On his back underneath the sheet, eyes shut again, Aaron rifled light-fingered down through the hair on his chest and belly, through his coarse pubic hair, testing easily his morning hard. Rolling over on his side, he put out his hand again and touched Nell's hip, gliding the palm of his hand over her silhouette as she lay sleeping, over her sharp hipbone down into the valley of her waist, the skin soft as the underside of an earlobe. His palm floated up her ribcage, lightsome fingertips testing the silken skin underneath her breasts. Up and down her spine now Aaron ran his hand with a delicate buoyant touch, swirled his palm over a sprawling buttock then stroked the slack inside of a thigh. Shifting positions, he cradled her body with his own.

Her eyelids fluttered open and she mumbled something. Worrying his hand underneath her arm, where it was warm as an incubator, Aaron caressed her breast and nuzzled her blowzy hair. Smiling and twitching her shoulder under his kisses, Nell rolled onto her back, stretched both arms over her head, and enlaced her fingers like a bow on a package.

\* \* \* \*

Twelve hours later Aaron stood in front of the sink, washing lettuce for a salad, while Nell scurried about the apartment with a wiping cloth and a can of spray wax. At three-thirty that afternoon Frieda had phoned to say that she and Ernest were in town shopping; they would stop by later for dinner. He was not to go to any trouble.

Nell's response had been to cover her face with her hands and say that she would eat out.

The doorbell rang. Hurriedly Nell scoured one last table top and hid the can of spray wax and the wiping cloth in a drawer. Aaron boldly flung open the front door.

"Hi!" bawled Frieda and threw an arm around Aaron's neck. She clutched a stuffed brown paper sack to her breast like a suckling. Behind her stood Ernest with sacks in both arms, grinning through his teeth.

"I thought we'd never find this place!" She stepped back to appraise her son. "You've lost weight," she scolded. "Aren't you getting enough to eat?"

"Here, let me take that," Aaron held out his arms. "You didn't have to bring groceries, for Chrisake."

"You just be quiet. I know that you work . . ." Frieda shot a glance in Nell's direction, ". . .and we're not about to barge in on you expecting dinner. Show Dad where to put those sacks."

Aaron pointed toward the kitchen and smiled. "I'm sorry. Mom and Dad, this is my friend Nell."

With a toothy grin, Ernest bobbed his head as Frieda started towards the kitchen.

"Have a seat, Mom. Dinner's almost ready."

"I said we're not going to barge in on you," proclaimed Frieda over her shoulder. "Is there an apron in here?"

"Go sit down," Aaron stepped into the kitchen and attempted to turn around his mother by the shoulders and direct her toward where Ernest had begun to leaf through a magazine. "Nell and I have dinner already prepared."

"We'll just add some of these things we brought along: brown beans and hamhock, iced tea," Frieda said, pulling out of the sack a one-gallon jar, "fresh tomatoes and green beans from our own garden, summer squash, sliced breast of turkey for sandwiches." She withdrew an aluminum-foil wrapped bundle and a loaf of sandwich bread. "And there's a pan of fudge brownies in one of these other sacks, somewhere. I would have baked an angel food cake — I know it's your favorite — but I didn't know how it would travel in this heat." Frieda cackled at her son's speechlessness.

"What's in the other two sacks?" asked an incredulous Aaron.

"Oh, those are just some things from the garden we thought you could use: tomatoes and green beans and some plum jelly I put up."

"No, that's okay," Aaron said. "Don't take it out now. I wish you hadn't brought all this."

"Now you just be quiet," chided Frieda, as Nell came up beside Aaron. "I'd like to know what mothers are for?"

"Have you checked the stroganoff?" Nell asked.

"No," he peaked underneath the lid of a small pot on the front burner. "When should we put on the noodles?" he asked, while Frieda began emptying the other sacks onto all available counterspace.

"Any time." Nell clearly did not know what to make of the intruder.

"Uh, Mom," he seized Frieda by the arm and began tugging her out of the room, "I insist now. You go sit down in there with Dad. Nell and I will get dinner."

Scowling at the younger woman, Frieda allowed herself to be shunted into the other room.

"Now," Aaron sighed in relief, "can I get you drinks? Dad, what about you?"

"Oh . . ." chuckled the red-faced man, pulling down the waistband to his sansabelt slacks so it did not ride across his stomach, ". . . you have any bourbon?"

"How do you want it?"

"Why don't you mix it up with some Coke?"

"What about you, Mom?"

"Just fix me some of that iced tea," she sulked. "In the gallon jar."

In the kitchen, Nell was wringing her hands. "Are we having all this?" she whispered.

Aaron considered for a moment. "We'll slice one of the tomatoes," he concluded, taking out a heavy chopping knife from the knife block and choosing a tomato from the half dozen Frieda had spread out beside the sink.

"Be sure to wash that," Nell pulled out a pan from underneath the stove and began filling it with water. Since she had read an article hypothesizing that an accumulation of pesticides in the body causes cancer, they had eaten only organically grown vegetables.

"Can you take care of this?" Aaron remembered the drinks. "Just work around these things," he motioned to the food scattered over the countertops.

Taking the bourbon and the iced tea back to his parents, Aaron swallowed hard. "Mom," he said, "I want you to be extra nice to Nell. She's nervous, you know."

Wide-eyed, Frieda protested, "Why, haven't I been anything but nice to the poor girl?"

"Damn, this stroganoff is burning on the bottom of the pan," complained Nell as Aaron returned to the kitchen.

"Turn the heat down, baby," he soothed, "and stir."

"I hope you don't make a practice of storing your furniture polish and oily rags in a drawer. I took the liberty of hanging up the rag in the bathroom." Frieda turned over a piece of silverware beside her plate and screwed up her eyes to make out the inscription. "Where did this come from?"

"That's Nell's," Aaron filled the last of the glasses as Nell brought in a casserole.

"What's that?"

"Mom asked about the silver."

"Oh." Nell placed the bowl on a wooden trivet in the shape of a fish and smiled. "That came to me from my Grandmother Pietering."

Frieda replaced the fork and eyed the table—ivory china, crystal water goblets and matching wine glasses, small bouquet of white and yellow daisies—eyed the covered casserole and oval-shaped bowl of noodles, the cheese asparagus, covered basket of bread, and her own sliced tomatoes. It was a skimpy table, in her estimation.

"Cheers." Aaron lifted his glass of wine.

As they passed around asparagus, bread, and tomatoes, Nell served each of them stroganoff over noodles.

"These tomatoes are great," said Aaron.

"We had so much trouble with cutworms," said Frieda, "I didn't think we were going to harvest *any* tomatoes this year. But Dad poured the Malathion to 'em."

Aaron and Nell frowned across the table at one another.

"What do you call this we're eating?" asked Ernest.

"Beef stroganoff," answered Nell.

"You remember what that is, Ernest. Prell served it when we were at her house for Thanksgiving and you didn't like it."

"Want some more bread, Dad?" offered Aaron.

"Don't mind if I do," muttered the old man sourly before rifling through the basket of garlic bread. "You folks have any plain bread?"

As Nell disappeared into the kitchen, Frieda asked in a
low voice, "Do you have some peanut butter? There's not a
thing on this table that Dad will eat. Except tomatoes."

"Sure," Aaron stood up.

"Smooth, dear," Frieda added before he was out of the
room. "Dad doesn't like the crunchy."

"Guess who we ran into today at the shopping mall?"
Frieda chirped as soon as Aaron returned with a jar of Jiffy
smooth peanut butter. "Your ex-wife." Not batting an
eyelid as Nell crimsoned, she continued. "That girl looked
so pretty. Just like she used to look. And she asked about
you."

Frieda smiled sympathetically at her son. "Don't you
look at me like that," she chuckled. "Isn't it Monument
Bank her father's president of?"

Aaron nodded his head.

"Well, Dad saw on the business page of the newspaper
that Monument Bank had taken over another bank."

There was no reaction from either Nell or Aaron. Ernest
was spreading peanut butter over a slice of white bread.

"I wonder how much money that man's worth?" Frieda
continued. "I can't imagine. Course I'm sure everything
he makes goes in taxes. Deedee's an only child, isn't she?"

Again Aaron nodded sulkily. How much more was he
obliged, by bonds of kinship and hospitality, to put up
with?

"That means all that money will go to her one day, then.
See, Ernest, that's what I told you."

Ernest looked up and showed his teeth.

"We were trying to figure that out. I was sure she was an
only child." Frieda ran her eyes over the room in mute
indictment of Aaron's ineptness in allowing such a gold
mine to slip through his fingers.

"Of course, eventually I suppose it'll end up in little Kim's
hands. If Deedee doesn't marry someone else in the
meantime and have other kids."

"How's the weather been?" burst out Aaron.

"Oh, hot." Her son and Deedee, Frieda was convinced, would someday get back together. Carefully sliding the gravy off gummy noodles underneath, Frieda put a bit of stroganoff on the tip of her fork and popped it into her mouth.

"How often do you get to see little Kim?" she inquired.

"Does anyone need more wine?" Aaron held up the bottle. "They were having a special on this at the liquor store. What do you think of it?"

"Delicious," muttered Nell, whose upper lip was sweating.

Ernest picked up his wine glass and ran a stubby fingertip around the rim. "You know, I can't tell one wine from another. I suspicion it all comes out of the same vat."

"You realize how important it is, Aaron," Frieda resumed what she had been about to say, "to maintain contact with that little girl."

"Mother, I have plenty of contact with my daughter."

"I just want to be sure you realize how important it is that she doesn't forget who you are."

"Mom, for Chrisake, I'm taking care of that!"

"Don't swear at your mother, son," Ernest cocked an eyebrow.

"Well, what do you want? We're taking good care to see that Kim is treated right. I'm not going to lose contact with her."

For a few moments there were no other sounds besides the scraping of forks across plates and the chomping of Ernest on his ice. "Not to change the subject," he rattled the remaining cubes in his glass, "but your mother got a piece of good news yesterday."

On his guard, Aaron replied, "Oh?"

"Tell them about it, doll," urged Ernest.

Frieda laid down her fork and preened like a mongoose. "Well," she began, "you know how the estate business has been dragging on . . ."

"After my grandfather died," Aaron explained to Nell, "he left some property to be divided between my mother and her sisters." Frieda was irked at the interruption. "There have been some sizeable offers, and all of my aunts but Patsy have wanted to sell now for some time."

"Her son Billy Beau is a lawyer and he's handling the estate," Frieda clarified the point. For the first time she looked Nell in the face. "We decided if it could all be handled within the family, that would be best." Unexpectedly, Frieda wrinkled her nostrils and sneezed violently across the table. "My Lordy, what made me do that?" She blew her nose into her napkin.

"So what's happened?" prodded Aaron.

"Oh! Well . . . where was I?"

"The estate's been dragging on."

"Oh, yes. You know how the estate business has been dragging on forever. Mr. Ritter, who owns a lot of property in Curtain, offered us sixty-five thousand for the property, and there are some speculators that want to start up a new addition out there, and they offered us sixty-seven thousand. Why, you know Daddy didn't give but ninety-five hundred dollars for the whole five acres, including the buildings, when he bought it, but there you are.

"Well, Prell's been chomping at the bit to sell the property, sell the property, so she can send her Jacqueline to France for the summer. I think she's crazy. And poor Norma Lou's practically destitute, not a towel to her name without a hole in it. But Patsy wouldn't sell. Daddy left express directions in his will that all four of us had to agree before anything could be done."

"Is there anyone in the house now?" Aaron pictured clearly in his mind the white farmhouse with dormer windows nestling underneath elm and pecan trees.

"Oh, Prell rented it to a family of hippies," answered Frieda irritably. "She insisted. Said we might as well be getting rent off the place. The man — if you can call him that — wears his hair in a ponytail!"

"So what's happened with the estate?" asked Aaron.

"Well, as I said, all of us but Patsy have wanted to sell the place and divide the money. In fact, that's why we drove down here to Dallas today, to pick out my new carpet at Rug World." Frieda's face beamed with pleasure.

"What?" Aaron tried to supply what was missing from his mother's account. "Did you sell the property?"

"My Lord, no!" exclaimed Frieda. "Patsy and Cody bought us out."

"They did?" Aaron was astonished that the four sisters would decide on a split course. "How did that come about?"

"You know Patsy just wouldn't hear of selling the place. Said she couldn't bear to think of it. Then when those speculators made us an offer of sixty-seven thousand—that's thirteen thousand, four hundred dollars an acre, not counting the house—she said she'd think about it. That's what there's been such a stew about for the past seventeen months. Prell wanting her money and Norma Lou on the verge of starvation. And Patsy and Cody just sitting on the matter. I can't deny I've harbored some hateful thoughts toward my own sister. Could not for the life of me figure out what she and that Baptist husband of hers were trying to accomplish."

"So they bought you out?"

"Yes! Prell called me day before yesterday fit to be tied. Said Patsy had driven over in that little red sports car they drive around and told her that they would meet the best offer we'd had and top it by five hundred dollars, minus her twenty-five percent."

"Why would they do that?"

"Don't ask me. Prell said they were both sober as judges. You know Patsy always has been flighty. The first thing you learn with Patsy is not to ask why she does what she does." Frieda had to laugh. She took a drink of ice water before continuing. "So Prell calls me up and says what do I want to do, and I say, well whatever is best for you and Norma Lou is just fine with us. Ernest and me, we don't require a dime from anyone, and I wasn't about to start grabbing after the inheritance at this point.

"So she calls Norma Lou up and that's fine with her, sell the place, and then Prell calls me back again and before she said another word she told me she was going to deduct the cost of her telephone calls from the estate.

" 'Prell, honey,' I told her sweet as pie, 'I do not desire a penny that is rightfully yours. Why don't you just keep a ledger of every phone call you make in this business and we'll deduct it from the estate.' "Frieda rolled her eyes up. "So then she said that it was okay with Norma Lou, and if Ernest and I still agreed, she guessed we could sell our interest in the property to Patsy and Cody."

"Hmmm," Aaron still wondered what Patsy and Cody had up their sleeves. "Have you signed any papers?"

"Sure did. Billy Beau had everything drawn up and brought it around in person for each of us to sign."

"Did you sell the mineral rights?" Aaron arched an eyebrow.

Frieda stopped to think. "Did we do that, Ernest?"

"Oh, I think we did. That's customary."

"I doubt they'll strike gold in that old slough," Frieda laughed. "With my share of the inheritance," she boasted, "the first thing I'm going to do is have my entire house recarpeted. We found a pretty harvest gold shag that regularly retails for thirty-five dollars a yard on sale for twenty-seven fifty. Installed."

"What's going to happen to the house?" asked Aaron later as they were taking their coffee cups with them into the living room.

"That old place?" scoffed Frieda. "I'd hate to live out there and tromp up and down those stairs. Mama always wanted to sell the place before she died and move into an apartment with new appliances, but Daddy wouldn't budge."

"Well, I'd hate to see it destroyed," Aaron sat down on the divan and put his arm around Nell.

"What Ernest and I figure is that they'll keep it as a place to visit on weekends. Cody's been doing pretty well, and they want a summer house."

"In that case," remarked Aaron thoughtfully, "the rest of us could drive up when we wanted."

"After the trash that's in there now," said Frieda in a pungent voice, "I'd want the place fumigated before I set foot in it."

# 24

Nell stayed behind to wash her hair. It was silly, she thought, to take a seven-year-old to the highest-priced restaurant in town.

"Wouldn't you like a Big Mac?" she asked Kim. "Or you could make your own sandwich at the Sandwich Factory."

"You know very well, Nellie," which is what Kim called Nell, "that Daddy said we can go any place I choose, and I choose The Mark." Tossing back her head, the little girl peered down her nose at her father's friend.

The concourse was cool and green after the glare of the parking lot. Like sleek fish in an aquarium, patrons glided from one expensive shop to another, their tans accentuated by simple white or pastel frocks. The din of cascading water in the great sunburst fountain underlay the clicking of high heels on an oak parquet floor.

Kim looked very grown-up in a yellow polo shirt and kelly-green wrap skirt. Dishevelled blond locks bounced about her head as she walked. From the mezzanine drifted down sounds of a cocktail pianist.

"Mommy's brought me here before." Kim surveyed the ground floor as they ascended the escalator.

"Oh?"

"She says it's the *only* place in town that serves a civilized luncheon."

Ferocious mannequins glared at them from shop windows as they approached a cluster of chrome and glass tables set out on the walkway amidst greenery. Expensively dressed women and a few gray-haired men in dark business suits sat chatting over cocktails, crepes, salads.

"What would you like, sweetheart?" The menus were oversized and hand inscribed.

Kim knit her brows. Soft light from the skylight complimented her porcelain complexion, her fine cheekbones. Aaron felt a great surge of love for his daughter.

"When we were here last time," she began deliberately, "I had a chocolate crêpe à la Russe, but I didn't like it."

Kim had taken French since first grade. Each month Aaron wrote out a check to the costly private school.

"But I thought you loved chocolate."

"This was very *bitter* chocolate. It's called 'semi-sweet.' I think that's very curious. It should be called 'bitter.' "

A swarthy, black-moustachioed waiter appeared with a pad. "I'd like crêpes aux Pêches, please, and spring salad without any dressing. And a glass of Perrier," Kim closed her menu and smiled across the table at her father.

"I'll have the same, except for Roquefort dressing on the salad, and a glass of white wine," said Aaron. He was proud and appalled at his daughter's precociousness. With cool gray eyes and yellow hair, spare yet squarish frame, Kim clearly was her mother's daughter. Only in the color of her eyes and in the slender shape of her fingers, perhaps also in the way she cocked her head to one side whenever she was thinking, did Aaron discern any of himself.

For hours at a time, she would study Nell's fashion magazines. The sketch pad she carried back and forth under her arm from her mother's house to his apartment was filled with costumes of her own design. Aaron recognized himself in that creativity. In his adolescence he had covered sheet after sheet of Big Chief tablet paper with floor plans of houses and buildings.

His ex-wife was a connoisseur, a spectator. Never had he seen her produce even so much as a pencil sketch. By inclination and training, she consumed. The choicest morsel, the very heart she consumed and left the rest for someone else to finish. Had she married a much wealthier man, she might have shaped herself into a notable patron of the arts.

Like her mother, Kim displayed a remarkable sense of discrimination. At seven she could suggest an appropriate wine for Coquilles Saint-Jacques or filet mignon. She could match fabrics with seasons. Nestling in the lacquered, oriental jewelry box on her vanity table were tiny pearl earrings, as well as ruby, sapphire, and diamond studs, and delicate, hammered-gold loops. She knew when and how to wear each to advantage. Kim was acquainted by name with the headwaiter of one of the most exclusive restaurants in New York. (Giorgio, normally the maître d'hôtel at The Mark, was on vacation, she had informed Aaron as they walked along the mezzanine. She didn't know the new man.)

Aaron found himself awed by this worldliness, and a little intimidated by it. It was abundantly clear that she was becoming a creature of her mother's world. She had patronized Frieda and Ernest the last time he had taken her to Grandma's, and with cousins Tamra, Buddy, and Randall, she assumed a bored, imperious mien.

What would there be in the way of family memories for Kim? Mondays through Fridays with her mother — the days, themselves, spent in school or with a sitter. Weekends with her father and Nell. She had never known family gatherings of the sort he and his brothers, as boys, had looked forward to so keenly.

No, those were a thing of the past. The grandparents were dead now or stuck away like out-of-season clothes in nursing homes. Only nostalgia, a love of talking about the old days, remained to their less prolific sons and daughters who believed in Planned Parenthood. For their grandchildren, Aaron and Rick's generation, there was little incentive to gather. Gasoline cost too much and they were too busy making ends meet. The wives were all working — when they had remained married. These were hard times for families.

With enormous fondness, Aaron remembered his grandparents' house, at the end of a straight gravel road in a hollow of elm and pecan trees. The white farmhouse had been built on a foundation of red sandstone; a porch nestled like a pocket in one corner along the front. In the summer, purple clematis meandered up the posts, and the porch swing would sway by itself when the wind was out of the south. Dormer windows jutted from the sloping roof across the front, and a red-brick chimney bisected the ridge row.

Behind the dining room at the back of the house was a greenhouse where Grandpa Hale raised orchids and started his tomatoes and cucumbers from seed during the last months of winter. On the other side of the greenhouse, in acid soil along the back wall, grew three hydrangea bushes, one each of blue, pink, and purple.

Grandma Hale would open the door, a white apron pinned to her bodice and a dot of flour on the tip of her nose. "Come in this house," she would cry. "Come in this house. I've been looking for you since eight o'clock. Gunter," she would halloo up the narrow staircase, "the kids are here. Come on."

"I'll be down in a minute."

Fretting in the doorway, Grandma would mutter something in German. "Come on," she would call out again before waddling on bandy legs into the living room and lighting in her sewing rocker.

"It's gonna be a scorcher today," Turner, Frieda's first husband, would moan as Grandma took a handkerchief from her apron band and mopped her upper lip and forehead.

"Is it cool enough in here?" she would ask.

Frieda would assure her it was and give Turner a look. "Did you put that salad in the icebox, Mama?" she would ask. "It's got mayonnaise."

Then Grandpa Hale would clomp down the stairs in khaki pants and shirt and Wellington boots brushed to a sheen. After greetings all around, he and Turner would disappear to smoke cigarettes on the front porch, while Aaron and Rick swung on the tree swing.

Soon the white, four-door Buick belonging to Prell and Hershell Simpson would turn down the dusty road. Frieda could be counted on to arrive early. Prell, on the other hand, was punctual, "neither early nor late" her watchword. Out of the back seat would squeeze Monte, fattish and red-haired in long pants, ironed shirt, and shoes that he never removed from his oversized feet. Wrinkling his nose, he at first pretended to ignore Aaron and Rick, swinging and climbing in the tree. By the time Grandpa Hale had kissed Prell and shaken Hershell by the hand and Grandma had burst onto the front porch, wiping her hands on her apron, Monte would acknowledge his cousins' presence and all three would disappear into the woods.

Mid-morning, while the boys were climbing trees, Norma Lou and Dub Hurry would blow in from Crumb, Dub looking tired with a bowed back and cavities under his cheekbones, Norma Lou beaming with silent pride at the back seat full of vegetable casseroles, a baked ham, her famous butterscotch pie, and a three-gallon freezer of homemade peach ice cream.

By twelve-thirty, Grandpa Hale and his three sons-in-law would be sitting on the front porch with their feet up on the posts, checking their watches and bemoaning the prices of new cars under Harry Truman. ("You all know what 'LSMFT' stands for, don'tcha?" Turner would ask and spit over the side of the porch into the four o'clocks. " 'Lord save me from Truman.' " With a sly grin he'd scratch his balding head while Grandpa Hale shook with repressed laughter, Dub Hurry gave out with a horse laugh and then fell into a coughing fit, and Hershell Simpson, an NCO in the air force, tittered uncomfortably and wondered if he was being disloyal.)

The aromas of baking bread and fried chicken and pot roast wafted out the windows; the three little boys stayed close around the house.

By twelve forty-five Grandma would ask in a worried voice if Grandpa thought they should call Patsy and Cody.

"You know them. They're always late," Hershell would whine from the steps. Grandpa would shake his head, no, and Grandma would go back inside, wondering how to keep the roast hot without burning it.

At one-fifteen Patsy and Cody Fowler's blue Mercury would truckle down the gravel lane. It would ease to a stop in a cloud of red dust, and out would step Patsy with a jello salad. Period. Billie Beau would dart underneath her arm toward his cousins. Cody would unwind himself from behind the steering wheel, arch his back, and exclaim that the damn traffic was terrible.

Down the steps now would pour Grandma Hale, followed by Frieda, Prell, and Norma Lou in a vee like a flight of ducks. She would kiss Patsy's round, painted cheek and go on about the delicious jello salad before reaching up to hug Cody, whose arms gleamed an unhealthy white underneath a mat of curly black hair.

"We better eat," Prell would announce in a rancorous voice, "before it's ruined."

After the thirteen of them had washed their hands and found places to sit around the great table—the four little boys together at one end within easy reach of the fried chicken—grace would be delivered by Cody Fowler, a Southern Baptist, who gave an extemporaneous effusion of thanks for their many blessings, a knack not shared by any of the rest of the family, all less demonstrative Presbyterians who were content with a simple, "God is great, God is good, and we thank Him for our food."

Around the table then went the relish tray: bread and butter pickles and cucumber pickles, deviled eggs, sliced cucumbers and tomatoes.

In the opposite direction ("Which way are we going?"
exclaimed Patsy, laughing easily with the assurance of one
who knew that whatever she said would be doted on) went
the platter of pan-fried chicken, Norma Lou's baked ham,
and grilled pork spareribs ("Who barbecued spareribs?"
asked Prell, gaping at the ceiling. "Hope I don't make
myself sick."). From midway down the long table, Frieda
would ask for plates to be passed to her so she could serve
the pot roast.

In the meantime, the salads—Patsy's jello salad, three-
bean salad, which the boys would dare one another to try,
green salad with tomatoes and onion, spinach salad topped
with slices of boiled egg, and coleslaw—and the vegetables
circulated in either direction. There would be baked
summer squash, pickled okra, corn on the cob, and green
beans from Grandma Hale's garden; one dish of sweet
potatoes with apples, and another of sweet potatoes with
marshmallows on top, macaroni and cheese with mushrooms, a dish of mashed potatoes that kept having to be
refilled ("Sit down and eat, Mama!" the girls fussed as
Grandma Hale disappeared into the kitchen. "She hasn't
eaten a bite yet!"), as well as hot German potato salad,
Harvard beets, marinated carrots, a brown earthenware
bowl of cut-up frankfurters and baked beans dark with
molasses, and a pitcher of brown giblet gravy.

Grandma Hale would return with the bowl of mashed
potatoes in one hand, and in the other, a covered basket of
hot, crescent dinner rolls that disappeared before the basket was set down.

As they ate, five along either side of the table, Grandpa at
the head, and Aaron and Billy Beau sharing the piano
bench at the other end, they laughed and visited, the four
daughters recalling the time when Prell wrote a theme for
Frieda, whom Mrs. Prancethroat had said didn't have the
imagination of a cat, but Frieda didn't bother to recopy it,
just signed her name to the theme and turned it in. Did
they remember how mad Mrs. Prancethroat had been

when she called Mama on the telephone and told her Frieda had cheated on a theme? Mama was so embarrassed.

And the time Norma Lou, who was always so sweet butter wouldn't melt in her mouth, drove nails in Mr. Hauptmann's new tires, a complete set of Firestones? How when Mama asked her why she did it, her chin began to tremble and she said because Frieda and Prell told her to. And how mad Mama was, and when Daddy came home, he never said a word. Just went over to Mr. Hauptmann's and wrote him out a check for a new set of tires. That was the fall when Norma Lou got dust pneumonia and they didn't have any money, and that winter the girls didn't get new shoes. Instead, they stuck cardboard in their old ones where the soles had worn through, and that's what they wore that winter.

After all of them had finished and were leaning back in their chairs groaning, Grandma Hale would get up and her daughters would follow, saying, "Now keep your forks."

Then while the men smoked and the boys slapped at invisible flies on each other's noses, the women chattered as they cleared the serving dishes from the table. In the meantime, coffee brewed and cups and dessert plates were brought out.

Then prune cake, and banana cake with brown sugar marshmallow icing, cheesecake with a saucer on the side of strawberry topping, Grandma Hale's Swedish tea ring, deep-dish peach cobbler, pecan pie, lemon meringue pie, Norma Lou's butterscotch pie, and home-made peach ice cream. There was not so much talking now. Sated from eating, savoring these sweets, these last bites of good food, each person relaxed in blissful fullness.

"Well, there goes my diet," Frieda would lament, and her sisters would commiserate. Their husbands would push back their chairs and loosen their belts and Dub Hurry would ask for a toothpick.

Then, while the men smoked more cigarettes and snoozed in the south breeze on the front porch, and the women washed and dried the dishes, cackling at dirty jokes and recalling childhood escapades, the four boys would troop off to the woods behind the house.

In the lead marched Rick, a full head taller than any of the others, sturdily built and with curly black hair, carrying a stick. Trotting a half pace behind him, Billie Beau Fowler would be spouting orders in an imperious voice and pushing up his horn-rimmed glasses. Aaron and Monte Simpson lagged behind, Monte snorting through clogged nostrils and perspiring through his dress shirt as he clump-clumped through the high grass on feet like shoe boxes.

As they reached the line of shadows cast by the outreaching pecan and oak and elm trees, the boys felt revived. Down a cattle path they trotted toward the stream, not seeing the brambles and vines and blue and yellow wildflowers that flourished wherever shafts of sunlight angled down through the branches.

A low burble of water, like the sound of pigeons. Pulling off hot shoes — even Monte shyly revealing enormous, soft-skinned white feet — they crossed the stream gingerly on mossy stones.

Billie Beau cawed like a crow. Rick scampered off into the bushes after a cottontail rabbit.

"Shoulda brought my BB gun," said Monte.

"You don't have a BB gun," scoffed Billie Beau.

"Do so. My dad bought me a Red Rider for my birthday."

Fidgity with jealousy, Billy Beau boasted, "Well, big deal, I got an Indian bow and arrow. The arrows have turkey feathers on the end."

Wiggling his hips, Monte sneered, "Big deal."

"Let's play cowboys and Indians," said Aaron. "Billy Beau and me'll be Indians, and you and Rick be cowboys."

The two braves disappeared into the forest on the dark side of the river. "I'll be Cochise, you be Geronimo," decreed Billy Beau.

"I'm always Geronimo. I want to be Cochise today."

"Oh, all right," Billy Beau was being generous. "Let's look for arrowheads."

The boys picked their way carefully through brambles, over rotting logs.

"Look out, there's a snake!" screamed Aaron. As if on a spring, Billy Beau hopped into the air.

"Where?"

"There! He crawled under that log."

Their eyes wide, the boys crept around to opposite ends of the thick rotting limb. At an eye signal, they tossed it aside. Underneath they found a green-and-white striped garter snake, coiling on itself. Quick as a tomcat, Billy Beau fell upon it with cupped hands.

"Got him!" he proudly shouted and held aloft the slender, swirling reptile.

"Ugh. Let me see." Aaron stroked his index finger along the snake's spine. He did not ask to hold it.

Billy was grasping the snake just below its head and gazing into its eyes. "If you look in a snake's eyes, it'll hypnotize you."

"That's just cobras in India," said Aaron.

"No, it's not. I read it in a book."

"Well, the book's wrong. It's just cobras in India. There was an article about that in the *Weekly Reader.*"

Carefully slipping the snake into the front pocket of his jeans, Billy Beau changed the subject. "C'mon. We gotta attack the fort."

The two boys picked their way back through the brush, their eyes peeled for snakes, until they heard once again the purlings of the stream.

"There they are," whispered Aaron, peeking around the hoary trunk of a pecan tree. Their plan was to wait until the fort was finished, then attack across the stream.

As they stood next to one another behind the tree, Billy Beau drew the garter snake from his pocket when Aaron's head was turned and held it right beside his cousin's ear.

"Hey," he whispered. Aaron turned to discover the snake's darting tongue not an inch from his nose.

Barely managing not to scream, Aaron clutched both hands around Billy Beau's throat. The snake owner shook with stifled delight and replaced the snake in his pocket.

When Rick and Monte were sitting watch inside their fort, the two Indians burst from behind the pecan tree with a flurry of frightful screeches and rushed into the stream.

"Bam! Bam!" went the soldiers' rifles. The attackers gained the near bank and, dropping to their stomachs, began crawling toward the fort.

Monte aimed a stick over the walls. "Bam! I got you, Billy Beau!"

"You can't see me 'cause it's night."

"Yes, I can. You're dead."

Billy Beau and Aaron leaped over the wall of brush to engage in hand-to-hand combat. While Aaron and Rick wrestled on the ground, the Indian pulled a tomahawk from his belt and, before his foe could reach his rifle, split his skull.

"Woo woo woo woo," Cochise patted his mouth in a victory whoop while his brother expired in a drawn-out fit of agony.

Together now, both Indians subdued the other sweating, red-faced cowboy, who cautioned them to take it easy because of his new glasses.

"Tie him up," ordered Billy Beau. Aaron began pulling at a hairy green vine that was dangling from an oak tree. "We'll burn him at the stake."

"Help me," cried Monte to Rick.

"I'm dead."

"Where's the rope?" demanded Billy Beau. Aaron finished ripping down the lanky vine. With a pout on his face, Monte allowed himself to be strung to a knobby scrub oak near the fort. Apprehensively he watched the two Indians wind the mean-looking vine around his stout mid-section and arms. Then whooping and hollering, they did

their war dance. Motioning for the other two to gather
behind him, Billy Beau declared in a solemn voice that the
prisoner had been condemned to be burned at the stake.
Monte grinned sappily.

"First, though," declared Billy Beau with an awful gleam
in his eyes as he slid his hand into his pocket, fumbled a
moment, then drew out the wriggling snake, "you have to
be bitten to death by this water mocassin."

Brandishing the snake before Monte's eyes that were big
as nickels, Billy Beau let out a bloody scream. With one
hand he pulled toward him the neck of the captive's shirt,
and with the other he dropped the squirming snake inside.

"EE! EE! EEEE!" Monte squealed. Wriggling like an
alligator, thrashing his slippery girth about with prodigious
force, he burst the vine and tore open the front of his shirt.
Buttons popped in every direction. The striped snake
dropped to the ground and slithered off into the under-
brush.

His cousins were howling with laughter, screaming and
guffawing as they rolled about and beat their fists upon the
ground.

"I hope you're having a good time." Monte was red in the
face and the skin on his arms and torso displayed the
effects of rope burn.

"You shoulda *seen* yourself," chortled Aaron, wriggling
his hands over his head in imitation of his cousin's fright
and setting off fresh gales of hysterical laughter.

Picking up his torn shirt out of the dirt and using it to
polish his glasses, Monte was close to tears. He placed his
glasses on his nose, slipped on his shirt, and went over
beside the stream where he had abandoned his shoes and
began to lace them on.

Ever the peacemaker, Rick led the other two over to their
sulking cousin and patted him on the back. "It was just a
joke, Monte," he said with derision in his eyes. "Okay?"

As he continued putting on his shoes, the offended
Monte said nothing.

"Okay?" Rick held out a hand.

"Okay," muttered Monte. Ignoring Rick's hand, he hoisted himself to his feet. "But you guys better never do anything like that again or I'm gonna tell."

\* \* \* \*

The four little boys slipped into the room and sat down together on the floor in the corner.

Memories, memories . . .

"That's too high for me. That's too high," complained Prell. "Get one of those pieces I can sing."

After flipping through the pages of the music book, Patsy placed her hands on the keyboard of the upright piano and began to play.

Oh, you beautiful doll,
You great big beautiful doll . . .

Prell and Norma Lou sang first and second sopranos, Frieda alto, Cody Fowler in his fine bass voice.

Oh oh oh oh
Oh, you beautiful doll.

"Do you know Bob went to college on a musical scholarship?" asked Grandma Hale from where she sat in her rocker embroidering a pillowcase with forget-me-nots.

"Who's Bob?" asked Frieda.

"Bob Bernard, the Bernards' son who lived across the street from the greenhouse."

"What instrument?"

"Tuba. He loves classical music."

Carry me back to old Virginia

> That's where the cotton and
> the corn and 'taters grow . . .

"Well, get some of those pieces I know," shouted
Prell through a gale of laughter.

" 'How Great Thou Art,' " said Frieda.

"Wish I could see the words," Prell poked her sharp nose
closer to the sheet music, then took a step back.

"Do you know the words to that?" asked Frieda.

"Pretty good," answered Prell as Patsy began the chorus.

"Start at the front," directed Prell, as Patsy stopped and
started again with the introduction.

"Tell me when you're ready."

> Oh Lord my God,
> When I in awesome wonder
> Consider all the work Thy hands have
>     wrought.
> I see the hills
> I hear the rolling thunder . . .

Grandma Hale had put down her
handwork and was singing along with those around the
piano. Grandpa and Dub Hurry hummed along with their
mouths closed. Turner was fast asleep on the front porch.

> Then sing my soul
> My Savior God to Thee,
> How great Thou art . . .

they sang, grandly slowing down the tempo,

> How GREAT THOU ART.

"You know 'Doggie in the Window'?" asked Prell.

"Hunh unh," Patsy began the rippling arpeggios of
"Indian Love Call."

"All those pieces you got to warble on," protested Prell. "I can't even warble."

"Go ahead and play it," said Frieda, while Norma Lou closed her mouth.

Again waterfall arpeggios. Then Prell's shrill,

Ooo-ooo-oooh!

As Frieda cackled with laughter and Norma Lou tittered behind her hand, Prell ordered Patsy to proceed directly to the chorus, if she insisted on playing the damn thing.

When I'm calling you-oo oo
oo - oo - oo - oo-!
Will you answer too-oo
oo - oo - oo - oo-?

In the corner, Aaron and Rick were snickering at Monte's pantomime. Closing his eyes, Grandpa rested his head against the back of his chair and Patsy began playing in an overripe, hammy manner.

. . . will come true,
You'll belong to me,
I'll belong to you!

"I wish you'd play right," remonstrated Prell good naturedly now, with a chuckle.

"That's your opinion," retorted Patsy.

"I wish you'd play right, something that sounds good."

Impishly, Patsy swung into a recital version of "Malaguena," then after a few bars, switched to "Bumble Boogie."

"Oh, play 'Sentimental Journey,' " exhorted Frieda. "You've got it in that book. Back at the beginning. 'Sentimental Journey.' "

Patsy now was rolling off "Nola" and twisting her head around to catch her mother's eye.

"Hey, get 'Sentimental Journey,' " insisted Frieda again as Patsy continued playing "Nola."

"Play it." Prell had added her voice to Frieda's.

"Now play it *right*, because that's pretty," Frieda said.

With a bouquet of arpeggios covering the entire length of the keyboard, Patsy set her mouth and began the introduction to "Sentimental Journey."

"Tell me when you're ready," said Prell.

> Gonna take a sentimental journey . . .

"Please play it right! Start over again and play it right, just once!"

Again, Patsy began the introduction, this time at twice the appropriate speed.

"Sing," said Patsy, pausing for her sisters to come in.

"No, not when you're acting like that. Play it right," sulked Frieda.

"I am playing right."

"No, you're not. Now play it right. Please."

"Please play it right," Prell backed up Frieda's request.

At a snail's pace, as if for a funeral, Patsy began the introduction again and turned to grin at her mother.

"Please play it right, Patsy. Just that one piece. I . . ." Frieda broke off in exasperation as her sister gazed up over her shoulder and crossed her eyes.

"Will you please play it right? I don't see why you . . ."

"Please play that right, will you please," cried Prell a last time as their baby sister, having had her fun, squared her shoulders and began the introduction once more.

"You ready now?" Prell asked Cody, who had left the room during "Indian Love Call."

> Gonna take a sentimental journey,
> Gonna set my heart at ease . . .

"Okay, since when do you sing bass?" said Cody to Frieda with a horselaugh.

"Let's do some hymns," suggested Norma Lou out of nowhere.

"Let's go, Goober Sisters," quipped Billy Beau from the corner.

" 'When the Roll Is Called Up Yonder,' " suggested Frieda. "C'mon you boys, you sing, too."

> When the roll is called up yonder
> I'll be there . . .

"That's enough of *that* one!" wisecracked Cody after three verses. "We need another congregation."

"Do you know 'Some Day the Silver Cord Will Break'?" asked Patsy, flipping through the hymnal.

"Well, I don't believe we can sing that," said Cody.

" 'Rock of Ages,' "offered Frieda, following with her eyes the pages flipping past Patsy's fingers.

" 'Rock of Ages,' do that," affirmed Prell.

"All right, let's go," answered Patsy.

"Hit a D," requested Prell.

" 'Rock of ages,' " they began soberly, " 'cleft for me . . .' "

"Hit a D," repeated Prell.

"I like that," said Norma Lou after they had finished the song.

"Find something else you know in that hymnal," directed Frieda. " 'Faith of Our Fathers,' do you have that one in there?"

"Do 'Break Thou the Bread of Life,' " proposed Prell instead.

"Don't have that," replied Patsy, without checking.

"Well, 'Wonderful Words of Life.' Is that in there?"

"Umm, no."

" 'Break Thou the Bread of Life,' " Prell insisted.

" 'I've a Story to Tell to the Nation,' " suggested Norma Lou.

"What would it be under?" asked Patsy.

" 'Sweet Bye and Bye,' " spoke up Cody, instead, to everyone's approval.

Infected by the lively rhythms of the gospel tune, everyone in the room joined in on the chorus.

> In the sweet bye and bye
> We shall meet on that beautiful shore.

"Can you play 'Silent Night' right quick?" asked Frieda.

"We all know that," chimed in Prell.

"Oh, hey, do you have 'Softly and Tenderly'?" suggested Cody again.

"Yeah, that's in here," replied Patsy, ignoring her sisters. "What is it under, 'S'?"

"Yeah, 119," answered Frieda, who had spotted the song earlier.

" 'S' for sick," giggled Billy Beau to his cousins.

> Softly and tenderly, Jesus is calling
> Calling for you and for me . . .

"You really sing that alto," Cody told Frieda.

# 25

When Kim and her father returned to the apartment after their lunch, Nell was vacuuming the carpet. A blue bath towel was wound in a turban around her head. She turned off the sweeper and told Aaron that his mother wanted him to call.

"Well, they've done it!" Frieda screamed through the receiver.

"Who's done what?"

"Patsy and Cody. I guess I should have expected it." Her voice was barely under control.

"What did they do?"

"What she's done ever since she was born. That girl has always been selfish. First comes me, then comes me again, and if there's anything left I might let you get some of it."

"Mom, I don't know what you're talking about."

"Patsy Hale, that's what I'm talking about. She hasn't changed one iota. I remember when she would use all the ice cubes up and never refill the tray. She would drink the last of the ice water and never refill the jug. When I was living at home during the war and she was my size, she would sneak into my closet when I was away doing defense work and take my favorite blouses and skirts and wear them. Then whenever I tried to find them, do you know where they'd be? Dirty, on the floor of Patsy's closet.

"Of course, she was always Mama's favorite, and she knew it. Whenever it was Patsy's turn to do the dishes, her *eczema* would be flared up and she couldn't get her hands in water.

"And how did she repay Mama? I'll tell you how. Right

211

after Mama died, her sapphire engagement ring she had always promised to me, well Patsy hot-footed it in there before Mama was cold and pulled the ring off her finger and took the sapphire out of the setting and had it made up into a starburst cluster for herself.

"Aaron, are you still there?"

"Yes, Mom."

"Well, say something."

Aaron had no idea where Frieda's tirade was leading. "You still haven't told me what Patsy's done."

"The same as she's always done. She's never done anything in her life but take. Take. Take. Take. That's Patsy.

"She would steal my hose out of my drawer and get snags in them. But do you think she ever offered to replace a single pair? Hmph. It was Patsy who just had to have a dog, and then she never cleaned up the yard. Plus I had to keep my Bootsie outside, and she got to keep hers in the house. It was Patsy who got to take piano lessons because she was the baby and by that time Mama and Daddy had a little money. I would have given my eye teeth to take piano lessons. I had the talent. But that was during the Depression and they couldn't afford to buy a pound of butter without charging it."

Frieda broke off to blow her nose. Aaron wondered what Patsy could possibly have done.

"Selfish. That's all she ever was," Frieda continued. "She would use the last sheet on the roll of toilet paper and never put on a new roll. She'd use up all the hot water. And in the mornings, when everyone was waiting around on one foot to get into the bathroom, there she'd be for hours, behind a locked door, primping in front of the mirror. Then when she'd leave there would be her long red hairs in the sink.

"I'm not surprised at a thing she does, but I never thought she'd stoop this low, her and that snake Cody and that shyster lawyer son of hers." Frieda's voice quaked with indignation.

"Mom," cried Aaron, "what did they do?"

"They're putting an oil well on Mama and Daddy's place!"

# Part
# Four

# 26

Bugg, TX

July 5

Dear Patsy,

I don't know where to begin. It breaks my heart, Patsy, that you would do this to your own sisters. What's gotten into you?

In the interest of keeping peace, I've never criticized my brothers-in-law, but is this Cody's doing? Everything that man has ever touched has turned to money. I know that. And I know that business is business. But this!

Patsy, I am just glad Mama's not here to witness this mess. I remember her in the front porch swing saying, "You girls let the men fight until they're blue in the face, but don't you ever let anything come between you."

It's not just the money, although poor Norma Lou couldn't lay out a set of sheets without holes in them if her life depended on it. The fact is, Patsy, our family is coming apart. The very house where our heights when we were growing up are inscribed on the doorframe in the kitchen could be destroyed. Daddy would never allow that doorframe to be painted over.

I never thought I would have to write a letter like this to one of my own sisters. It has given me a migraine.

With love but deeply hurt,

Frieda

Fort Worth, TX
July 11

Dear Frieda,

Come off it!

Frankly, my dear sister, I can't see how you or any of the
rest of them have room to bark. Every damn one of you
were ready enough to sell your interest in the property
when we waved that check underneath your nose.

We did not know that there was oil under the land when
we bought it. Cody and I thought you were all damn fools
for being so hot to trot about selling the property that you
were willing to take whatever old man Ritter was willing to
give you for it. Property's going *up* girl! We tried to tell you
that. But no, you wanted your damn money—now! And if
I'd had to hear once more about poor Norma Lou's holey
tea towels I think I would have just thrown up.

Cody suggested (and in the future, Frieda Teague, I'll
thank you to keep your damn mouth shut about my husband) that we match Ritter's offer and top it if you three
were so all-fired eager to sell off the estate. Just because
you're damn fools doesn't mean we have to be.

It wasn't until after we had signed the papers that oil
people got in contact with us about drilling for oil. You can
believe that or not, but it's the truth, so help me.

Don't think you can pull that line on me about our
heights being marked on the doorframe. Frieda, you know
as well as I do that you didn't set foot on the place after
Mama and Daddy died. The damn house could have been
toted away by fire ants for all you know. Don't forget, you
were willing to let hippies live there as long as you got your
almighty rent check every month.

Your letter made me pretty damn mad, if you want to
know the truth, Frieda Teague. After I read it I tore it up

in pieces and flushed it down the toilet. You had no right to upset me like that. If anybody needs to apologize, it's you.

Insulted,

Patsy


Bugg, TX
July 13

Dearest Patsy,

I just cannot believe the hot weather we've been having. My garden has turned up its toes. All we got out of it were a few early beans and some potatoes. The tomatoes have withered on the vine. They say there's not been heat like this since the thirties. I remember the summer when you were still in diapers and a black old bull snake crawled into the washhouse to stay cool on the concrete floor. I remember Mama screaming bloody murder and Prell and I and Norma Lou ran in and there you were sitting not six inches from the nasty thing, just singing away at the top of your voice. Then when Mama killed it with the hoe, you started to cry.

Patsy, I am truly sorry if I jumped to conclusions. But how do you suppose it would look if your sister bought you out for a few dollars, then turned around and stuck an oil well on the place?

If you say you did not know there was oil there before you bought us out, I believe you. Mama always said we should behave like sisters, which means trusting one another. Let me just say one thing, Patsy, and I want you to think about it and not get your back up. Mama and Daddy left that place and everything on it to be divided equally between we four girls. If there really is oil on the property, don't you think Mama and Daddy would want us to all have an equal share in it? I haven't talked to Prell or Norma Lou, but I know Ernest and I would be willing to tear up the check you wrote us and pretend that transaction never took place. And I imagine the other two would agree to the same. If not, that would be their tough luck.

Dearest Patsy, I do apologize for hurting your feelings. I was so upset and confused I did not know what I was saying. My migraines are so bad at times I can't see straight. And please, will you forget what I said about Cody, who you know I have always thought of and loved as a brother.

Love,

Frieda

P.S. Sorry about the handwriting. I am laying down resting so I can drive to Curtain this afternoon to decorate Mama and Daddy's graves.

P.P.S. I really was very ill when I wrote the first letter and am very weak now but OK, if I don't get tense and upset (my M.D.).

Fort Worth, TX
July 22

Dear Frieda,

My, my, aren't we pitiful!

Yes, dear, you were plenty confused when you wrote that first letter, and yes, I accept your apology. Which doesn't give you permission to horn in on our oil well.

We bought and paid for that property in cash. Fair and square, lock stock and barrel. It's ours. So you may as well go pee against the wind as to think you're going to get a piece of that action.

This won't be like the time I set up a lemonade stand beside the highway and made the lemonade myself and carried out the glasses and the pitcher and a chair to sit on, and then you talked me into letting you help me sell for half the profits.

For your information, dearest, on August 15th, they're going to tear down the house. They say there is oil in the slough where the house stands. The company offered to drill around it, but I told them to go ahead and tear down the old thing if it's in the way. That's for you, Frieda.

Love,

Patsy

Bugg, TX
July 25

Mr. Leonard Shiver, President
Iceburg Oil, Inc.
Headquarters Building
Houston, TX

Dear Mr. Shiver:

I am writing to inform you of a swindle you are taking part in. On August 15th I understand that you are scheduled to tear down a home and drill an oil well where it stood on a piece of land five and a half miles north of Curtain, TX.

That property, Mr. Shiver, is the ancestral home of my three sisters and I, and rightfully any profits made off it should be split four ways. That was the wish of my father, who is currently deceased.

My sister and her husband, Patsy and Cody Fowler, swindled the other three of we girls out of our portion of the inheritance, and now they are planning to hog all the profits.

I am prepared to hire the services of a lawyer to recover everything, which is rightfully ours. However, this would not be necessary if your company would cancel its dealings with the two above-mentioned swindlers.

I look forward to hearing of your decision in the case.

Sincerely,

Frieda Marie Hale Teague

P.S. For many years my husband and I have used an
Iceburg charge card (number 203-4442-1774) and we have
always been very satisfied with your gas.

> Iceburg Oil, Inc.
> Headquarters Bldg.
> Houston, TX
> August 9

Frieda Marie Hale Teague
Bugg, TX

Dear Ms. Hale Teague:

In response to your letter of 25 July: Iceburg Oil has
made inquiry into the ownership of the property to which
you refer. Records indicate that ownership of the land,
including all mineral rights thereto, belongs to Patsy E. and
Darrel C. Fowler. We find no outstanding liens or mort-
gages against the property, nor do we find evidence of any
legal irregularities in its acquisition. We appreciate your
inquiry and trust we shall remain in your service.

> Most Cordially,
>
> Bryan Geoffrey
> Ass't. Director for Public
> Relations

> Bugg, TX
> August 11

Dear Prell, Norma Lou, Rick and Sherri, and Aaron,

I'm xeroxing copies of this letter to send to all of you
because we're short of time.

On August 15th, four days from today, Iceburg Oil will
tear down Mama and Daddy's house. Then they'll begin
drilling for oil in the hole where the house stood.

It's hard for me to put into words what is in my heart at this moment. I am so hurt and insulted and outraged that Patsy is doing this. I suppose this behavior is to be expected from someone who used to cut her toenails and leave the trimmings scattered around the floor.

In a few words, we're getting the shaft (pardon my French). Patsy wrote me this long and tearful letter in which she claims that they didn't have the faintest notion that there was oil under that land. However, the very next day after she sent that lawyer son of hers around to get us to sign the papers, out of the blue, some oil man in a pinstripe suit just happened to knock on their front door and asked them if they owned Mama and Daddy's property, because they wanted to drill an oil well on it.

I'll believe that story when I see snow in July!

The fact is, Patsy and that crooked husband of hers knew from the very first what was underneath that house. Why else would they have been as eager as a bridegroom on his wedding night to buy the rest of us out?

Patsy was so cruel as to flaunt it in my face that she especially *requested* that they tear down the house. She was tired of looking at the old thing, she said. The oil people told her they would just as soon drill around it, and in fact it would have made a lovely office or recreation hall for the men working out there. But Patsy insisted that they tear it down.

Frankly, I am at my wits' end. I have written to the oil company and run into a stone wall. I've been in touch with a lawyer here in Bugg, and he says that, legally, we don't have a leg to stand on. (I don't understand how a swindle like that can stand within the law. It just goes to show once again how all lawyers are crooks.)

I've got another plan. Will you all meet me at Mama and Daddy's place at seven o'clock in the morning on August 15th? As I mentioned above, that's when the work is scheduled to begin. I'm going to contact the newspapers and explain my case and tell them there's going to be a sit-in on the front porch. I'll wager they send reporters out to cover the story. Nothing else has worked. Maybe those Fowlers can be embarrassed into sharing with we three girls what is rightfully ours.

I hope none of you thinks I have flipped my wig. I'll see you the 15th. Don't forget to bring a thermos of ice water.

Love,

Frieda

## 27

Before his divorce, wanting his four-year-old daughter to
remember something of her great-grandfather, Aaron had
taken Kim with him to visit the Clear Lake Nursing Home.

It smelled like wet diapers, disinfectant, and institutional
cooking. Like driftwood in the sun, three old women lay in
wheelchairs on the front porch. With a baby's mindless
expression, one of them picked at motes in the sunlight.
Another worked her toothless jaws and looked straight
ahead out of milky eyes. A third old woman was sleeping
with head awry.

Grasping his daughter's hand, Aaron told a bored-look-
ing receptionist that he wished to see Gunter Hale. Pointing him into a large, linoleum-floored common room, she
picked up a telephone. A squinting old man wearing
slipper-socks, a bathrobe, and a bright orange baseball cap
on his head stopped in mid-shuffle to stare at the vigorous,
dark-haired man and the little blond-haired girl.

Someone with a taste for brilliance had painted the walls
of the room turquoise. An obese woman in a plaid
bathrobe gazed out a window, while in a chair against the
wall another old lady with blue hair in finger waves sat
reading a magazine. As soon as Aaron and Kim sat down
on a brown divan, the woman put down her magazine and
got up with a popping of bones. "Whom have you come to
see?" she asked as she approached them.

"We're here to visit my grandfather, Gunter Hale."

The old woman thought a moment. Then she smiled.
"You must be either Aaron or Richard."

"Why, that's right." Aaron grinned. "How did you know that?"

"Mr. Hale has told me all about his grandchildren. You both have young daughters." The woman patted her waves and looked warmly at Kim.

"That's very perceptive. And who are you?"

"Mrs. Annabelle Mason. I taught history at Curtain High School for forty-four years."

Aaron looked up to see a sturdy black attendant leading his grandfather into the room. "You'll be shocked when you see him," Frieda had warned. She was right. This was an old, old man moving with doddering steps on an aluminum walker. Aaron was appalled. Only a year ago his grandfather had still lived alone in his own house, walked by himself without a cane, driven a car. And Aaron was pierced by a galling sense of guilt. Why for God's sake had he not come out to see his grandfather before now? The old man raised his head and looked Aaron in the face. There was no recognition in his eyes.

"How are you doing, Grandpa?"

Still no glimmer.

"I'm Aaron, Grandpa. Don't you know me?"

Then something happened in the old man's brain. "Aaron . . ." He reached out a frail hand and grabbed an arm. His skin was puffy and dark, like onion skin. Something he tried to articulate came out garbled.

Aaron helped the attendant place the old man in a straight-backed chair with arms. "How are you doing, Grandpa?" He hated inanity. He could think of nothing else to say.

"Fine. Fine." The old man spoke carefully and slowly; his tongue had been thickened by a series of strokes.

Aaron studied his face. The virile, black moustache was now nearly white. His jaws, once muscular, now wore a few days' growth of white beard. The skin hung in festoons. Only the eyes suggested the same man. Rheumy and draped in folds of bloodshot flesh, they seemed to be trying to convey something: isn't this a hell of a state for a man to find himself in!

Aaron presented his daughter. The old man reached out shaky hands to pat her wild, yellow hair. In spite of bloated fingers like fat sausages, it was the light, dandling movement Aaron remembered his grandfather using when touching a flower.

"You don't remember me, do you?" he slurred the words.

Kim looked wide-eyed at the old clown.

"How long was that, Aaron, you brought her to the house?"

"Just after her first birthday." Again a horrible flash of guilt.

The old man blinked away film. For a long time he gazed at the child. "Such a pretty thing," he mumbled.

Aaron glanced at the history teacher, who sat outside their circle. The old man was ignoring her. Then as Mrs. Mason and Aaron began to chat, he turned to her and barked, "Get out of here!"

Giving no sign of offense, the blue-haired lady stood up and, as Aaron rose apologetically as well, told him that he must come again.

"Old bitch," muttered Grandpa Hale as she walked away.

What was there to say? Aaron racked his brains for topics of conversation. Each the old man dismissed with a monosyllable. He would not be patronized. It was not until Aaron asked the old greenhouse man what to do for roses afflicted by powdery mildew that he evoked a response. For several minutes his grandfather worked very hard to talk. The effort seemed to exhaust him. He explained something of the subtleties of growing roses. What to plant next to them as natural insecticide. How to fertilize and prune them. What chemicals to spray to control mildew and black spot.

Aaron recalled how, on hot summer evenings, his grandfather would spray dust off the front porch before watering the fitzers and arborvitae, the lilacs, hydrangeas, verbenas.

How he would pivot unexpectedly and squirt Aaron and Rick with the hose. As they would scream with delight and scamper out of range, their grandfather would chuckle and puff on his pipe. Then how proud he was of the boys after they returned from the war. Both of them had heard retold time after time their grandfather's stories of Picardy and Rheims during the First World War. And about two of their great-grandfathers who had served with the Confederate Army in the War Between the States.

They talked about Aaron's mother and his aunts. The old man's jaws tightened underneath their wattles when he recounted being placed in the home.

That had been as agonizing a decision as Frieda and her sisters had ever had to make. Aaron had followed the increasingly depressing situation through his mother's stories. How from week to week, after Grandma's death, the old man had gone from bad to worse. In spite of pleas from every one of his daughters that he sell the place and move in with one of them, old Hale had stubbornly held on by himself in his own house.

"Why, there's not a one of we girls," Frieda was fond of saying during this period, "who wouldn't be tickled to death to have Daddy come and live with us. Every one of us has the room. And if he doesn't want to stay permanently with one of us, he can rotate when he wants to."

Instead, Gunter Hale had taught himself to cook. After a lifetime of being waited on, he learned to fry link sausages and potatoes, to scramble eggs. He bought beer to drink and cookies to satisfy his sweet tooth.

When they would drive up on weekends, the sisters would cluck their tongues at his dirty habits. He never emptied an ashtray, preferring instead to dump the ashes and butts on the floor. And the bathroom! They would roll their eyes up to the ceiling. He had gotten too lazy even to raise the lid. They could manage though. Each of them agreed to drive up one weekend a month and clean the house and cook and freeze some things for the following week's meals. Things would work out.

Meanwhile his reflexes worsened. Aaron remembered when his grandfather had been able to pluck a fly out of the air. Now his daughters began to worry about his driving the old Ford around town. The fenders became puckered with dents, and the tires were bruised from bouncing off curbs. What would happen, they worried, when — not if, but when — he had a serious accident? What if he should strike a child? Why, he could be sued for every penny.

Call the police station, Prell said, and have them take away his license. Which they did, only to be informed that there was, legally, nothing that could be done. The police were not empowered to lift a person's license because he had gotten old.

One Saturday afternoon, Prell had simply slipped the car keys into her purse. When the old man wanted to go out for a drive and complained he could not find the keys, she told him they were lost. She would take him out for a drive. She would buy groceries for the week ahead. She would be only too happy to do that. The peace of mind she would gain from knowing her father was not rolling about the streets like a bowling ball would be worth the extra trouble.

He had only called a locksmith after she left and ordered a new set of keys cast. At a cost of thirty-seven dollars and fifty cents.

They began to notice a shuffle in his walk and a slur in his speech. He is having strokes, they said to one another. For the first time, the possibility arose of putting their father away in a rest home. They dismissed it. He needed care. That much was clear. But he remained adamantly opposed to leaving his own home to move in with one of his daughters. They would hire someone, some decent Christian woman, to come in once a day to clean the house and cook and make sure their father was clean. It was not something they liked to admit, but he smelled bad. He would wear the same shirt, the same pants for days on end. He must be made to change everything, from the skin out, every day. A trained person could manage that.

They found someone. A middle-aged widow with a black moustache whose parents had come from Italy. She was strong and kind. For six weeks, the girls felt as though a burden had been lifted from them. Not that she cleaned house like their mother, or one of themselves, would do it. But she was honest. And every time any of them came to the house, there was nourishing food in the refrigerator and the house was, if not exactly clean, at least decent.

Gunter ran her off. As he came to realize the loss of his faculties and coordination, he became verbally abusive. This did not bother the Italian woman. But when he raised his steel-tipped cane at her one afternoon while she was vacuuming around the television and he wanted to watch the baseball game, she warned him that she would not take physical abuse. Then two days later he took a swing at her with a claw hammer. She dropped the mop where she stood, dropped it with a clatter to the floor, took down her purse from on top the china cabinet, and drove away.

"We'll have to put him in a rest home now," Patsy began. Prell was noncommittal. But Norma Lou and Frieda insisted no, they couldn't do that to their father. He would have to leave the land and move in with one of them.

"Which of us is equipped to handle him at this point?" Patsy said. "He's losing control of his bladder. What if he falls and breaks his hip? Which one of us is physically able to take care of him?"

Gunter refused to budge. They could beg until hell froze over; they could do any damn thing they wanted. He would stay put. Where he was. He would take care of himself.

Then one hot afternoon in midsummer, he shouted over the phone to Frieda, "The air conditioner's on fire! What'll I do?"

Rattled, she yelled back, "Why, pull out the plug!"

When he did not return to the phone, Frieda jumped in
the car and sped the forty-five miles to the old house. She
found Gunter rocking on the front porch and chuckling
over the incident. She deduced that the air conditioner
had overheated and caught fire. Utterly nonmechanical,
her father had panicked.

So now they began to worry that he would burn himself
and the house down.

Soon afterwards, he fell ill with a kidney infection and
had to spend ten days in the hospital. The girls argued it
out. He could not live by himself any longer. That they
agreed on. Still, he would not hear of selling his place to
move in with one of them. And even if he did, none of
them was equipped, they agreed, to look after his physical
needs.

The time had come to commit him to a rest home.
Against his will. They cried about it. But all four of them
agreed it was the only answer. Their parents' savings,
augmented by Medicare, would pay the bills. There would
be the property to manage and divide among themselves
after the old man died. For although they could take him
from his land, they could not bring themselves to sell it
from under him while he lived.

When Gunter was released from the hospital that hot
September morning, all four of his daughters were there to
drive him to Clear Lake. Still drowsy from medication, he
mumbled that they were heading the wrong direction.

When an attendant in a white uniform met them at the
car, Gunter turned purple. His neck cords thickened to
ropes. Frieda was afraid he would have a heart attack and
die on the spot.

Up the short sidewalk to the front door of the home he
shuffled on the arm of the attendant. Whether from the
shock of his uprooting, or from his illness, perhaps from
his perception of his daughters' perfidy, he suddenly
looked ten years older.

He had come home to stay.

## 28

For twenty-seven straight days, the thermometer had sur-
passed the hundred-degree mark. For six weeks there had
been no rain. After Aaron turned onto the dirt road
leading to his grandparents' house, he could see nothing in
the rearview mirror but dust. Red dust. A quarter mile to
the east of the house, in what once had been pasture, were
situated rusty pipes in long orderly rows like licorice, two
huge pieces of heavy machinery painted gold, a red tin
building, and a canvas-covered pile the size of a small
delivery van. Nobody was around.

As on the occasion of visiting his grandfather in the rest
home, Aaron had been prepared by Frieda to expect a
major change. But he was not prepared for anything of
this caliber. An American flag attached to the corner post
of the front porch hung down listlessly. The glass was out
of one of the dormer windows. Paint peeled from the
clapboards. Shrubs that once had been meticulously
shaped now rambled and reached. Like cornerposts, the
gawky fitzers at the corners of the house clambered taller
than the cornice. Weeds filled the flowerbeds, and sandburs grew underneath the elm and pecan trees, where once
had stretched a green, shaven lawn. On the porch beside
the open front door, covered in a filthy flowered fabric,
sprawled a dilapidated hide-a-bed whose springs stuck
squalidly into the air.

Depressed, Aaron parked beside his parents' Buick.
Except for the ticking of hot metal, everything was quiet.
Red dust hung in the air. As he was wiping dirt from his
forehead, Frieda opened the screen door. As if for a burial,

she was draped in a navy-blue silk suit with matching high heels and bag. A prim, saucer-shaped straw hat balanced atop her head and she was wearing clip-on earrings. Two steps behind her lagged Ernest in a long-sleeve white dress shirt, bus driver's blue tie, and checked double-knit slacks.

"Hi," she warbled to Aaron, who was sweating in a pair of golfing shorts and tee shirt. "I was in hopes you might dress up, son." Perspiration beaded her temples.

"Why?" He was stung, if not surprised, by his mother's obliviousness to the old home's derelict appearance.

"For the cameras. The TV people will be here anytime." Frieda squinted at the diamond wristwatch she wore for special occasions. "I wish the oil people would get a move on. I told the people at the newspapers, and the television stations, and the radio, that we're beginning this thing early."

"You're not serious." Aaron cringed at the notion of their family feud on the six o'clock news.

"Of course I'm serious." Frieda stirred through her purse and drew out a slender, clear plastic bag. "Do you think I should wear my gloves?"

Ernest dropped onto the flowered divan and groaned, "My God, this ain't no style show."

"You hush your mouth." Frieda was exhilarated, as if giving a party. "If I'm going to be on the television, I want to look my best. Be sure you brush off the back of your pants when you stand up, Ernest. That old divan's filthy!"

Aaron was leaning against the corner post and peering thoughtfully down the road. "Are you sure anything is going to happen?"

"According to Patsy, the company starts work today. They're going to demolish this house." His mother gazed about with impetuous fondness. "Our home."

"Have you confirmed that with anyone else?" Aaron asked, wondering whether demolition might not in fact be preferable to existence in this present, forlorn state.

"You can't get anything out of those companies. But it's Patsy's property." Frieda sniffed and fanned herself with the plastic envelope. "Legally. She ought to know when they're going to tear down the house she was raised in."

Frieda checked her wristwatch again. "Six fifty-five. I told the news people seven. Oh, I wish everyone would get here."

"I just can't get over," Aaron remarked softly, "how much this place has changed."

"Isn't it horrible?" Frieda stepped to the end of the porch and craned her neck up the road. "The inside's worse. That bunch of hippies destroyed the inside. They knocked holes in the walls. The bannister's torn off. Every post snapped off at the base. The sink in the bathroom is literally torn off the wall. It just makes me sick."

Aaron shook his head as a green Dodge turned down the dirt road.

"Here comes Prell," Frieda looked at her watch. "It will be seven on the dot when she steps out of the car. You just watch. Neither early nor late."

A blur of green in a red fog, the Dodge pulled to a stop. In a chino skirt, sleeveless blouse, and canvas shoes, Prell stepped out fanning herself with both hands. "Gawd, it's hot!" With geisha steps, she minced big-footed through the dust to the porch. "My Lordy, are we going to church?"

"Now don't you get started, Prell Simpson. I thought since we're going to be on the television, we ought to look halfway decent. Obviously, no one agrees with me."

"Well, my stars! You can look nice without being dressed to the teeth. In this heat, girl, you look ridiculous."

Frieda glared at her sister. "Where's Hershell?" she pouted. "And Norma Lou?"

"Oh, I couldn't pry Hershell away from the air conditioner. And Norma Lou," Prell perched on the arm of the divan, crossed her knees, and bobbed a white canvas shoe, "didn't feel well. You know Norma Lou. Bless her heart, every time anything has ever happened that wasn't all cupcakes, that girl has rolled over on her back and played dead."

"Well, I am disappointed." Frieda's hair hung down in limp tendrils beneath her blue hat. "This was to be a family affair. Look what happens."

"What time does this show get on the road?" Prell was disregarding her sister's griping.

"Well, I assume oil companies get started early. I thought we all needed to be here before anything happened. Surely they'll get here soon."

Aaron snorted, narrowed his eyes to slits, and stared down the road.

"As soon as they get here," Frieda introduced her plan, "we'll all line up here beside the flag. That's important for the cameras. They won't be able to demolish the house with us in the way. Then when they try to get us off the porch, I'll explain how we have been cheated out of our inheritance and that we won't leave until our sister agrees to split the profits from the oil well four ways. Of course," Frieda knit her brows, "since Norma Lou can't be bothered to be here. . . ."

"Now, it will be divided even steven," said Prell.

"What if we're charged with trespassing?" asked Aaron, beginning to find amusement in his mother's zany plan.

"That's where the media comes in," said Frieda craftily. "If we explain how we have been cheated out of what is rightfully ours, then public opinion will force the oil company to do what we want. That's the way the media works. I saw a show on television about it."

"Well," Prell sounded full of doubts. "I just hope Sheriff Rickell doesn't throw us all in jail for trespassing." She snickered. "You'd look pretty silly, Frieda Teague, sitting in the women's jail cell in that hat."

At seven-twenty, Rick, Sherri, and the three children drove in from Jessup. Wary of Prell's smirk, Frieda made no comment on their attire.

Rick sat down beside his brother on the steps, his expression reflecting Aaron's own dismay at the neglected condition of the place. In the past year and a half he had slimmed down, and in spite of his six-days-a-week indoor job at the newspaper, he sported a suntan. As they visited, Ernest snored on the divan, ignored by the three women who were chatting with their backs to him. Reminding both brothers of themselves as boys, the children climbed the pecan tree where the swing used to hang. Even in this hottest of summers, the trees around the house stood stalwart and green. "Have the kids ever been down to the stream?" Aaron asked.

"Hell, *I* haven't been down there in years."

Assuring Frieda that they would be gone for only a few minutes, the two men gathered the children and, treading on shadows that spilt before them on the parched earth, set out for the woods. "We had lots of good times here," Rick recalled. Aaron nodded and bent to pick up a stick. His emotions were muddled: pleasure at retreading this path with his brother and his children and pleasure at passing along to them some inkling of what Aaron and their father had used to regard—more than any other place—as their home; grief at the desolate spectacle it now provided; an indefinable feeling—awe, perhaps—at witnessing these tangible effects of time. Ahead of them, Tamra stepped warily among sandburs and tall weeds in the powdery red dirt, while Buddy and Randall capered and turned cartwheels.

The trees they found shrouded, many of them, in great webs. Gone was the verdant undergrowth of more temperate summers. Little besides thorn bushes and stickers had survived. Even in the absence of moisture, mosquitoes abounded in the shade of the webby trees. After some hesitation, Rick and Aaron decided to continue with the children to the creek. They could not come this far and miss seeing it. As they rambled down the path, Rick confided that life had been treating them well. He had received two raises—substantial, both of them—within the last twelve months. He was taking six hours of night classes at the college and, at that rate and going in the summer, he would earn his bachelor's degree in two years.

There was a lift in his voice, a sense of confidence and serenity, that Aaron had not perceived for years. Happily, he asked how Sherri was liking Jessup.

"She loves it. You know, she's working at the college. She loves her job. We have a little garden in the back yard that she waters every morning."

"Is she taking courses?"

"No, she's decided to hold off until after I finish." Rick paused to shout to the children that the stream lay just over the knoll ahead. "She wants to work on a degree then. In the meantime, she says that one college student in the family is enough."

The stream bed was dry, nothing but a gully with a cracked mud and pebble floor. The brothers' faces registered their shared disappointment: the stream had always been their magical place. Apologizing to the children, Rick promised to return another time, after it had rained, while Aaron assured them that there would be a stream again. Sweating and slapping mosquitoes, they turned back toward the house.

When they reached the porch, Ernest was still asleep and the women were sitting on a plaid blanket that Sherri had brought out from the trunk of their car and spread on the steps.

"Still no show?" Rick wiped the back of his neck.

"They're later than I imagined," Frieda admitted.

Sherri caught Rick's eye. "How was the stream?"

"There wasn't any," said Randall.

"It's dry," Rick affirmed.

"Why, I've never known that to happen," Prell shook her head in amazement.

After a drink of lemonade from the thermos Frieda had brought along, the children ran back out to the trees, while the adults sat on the porch. At a quarter to nine, a pick-up truck turned down the road toward the house, raising a rooster tail of dust. In a few moments it was followed by two more trucks, painted slate blue. On the doors was inscribed the green-and-white logo of Iceburg Oil. Instead of proceeding to the house, the trucks turned east toward the small stockpile of equipment.

"Where are those damn reporters?" Frieda paced back and forth across the concrete porch in her blue heels.

"Why don't you face it, hon?" said Prell. "If you told them to be here at seven and they still haven't showed, they're not coming."

Frieda set her mouth and wiped her temples with a handkerchief. "They'll come," she craned her neck around the post to try and spy what was going on at the supply yard. "When did the Five-Alive News ever pass up a good story? They sounded so interested on the phone."

Aaron caught his brother's eye and shook his head. He saw now that their task would be to shelter his mother from too much disappointment, too much humiliation on account of the incident.

"It's that damn oil company. That's what it is. They've scared the media into not covering the story." Frieda shook her finger. There was a run in one of her hose, and rivulets of red mud trickled down her face. "This is a plot!"

"Calm down, sister," soothed Prell. "Criminy! You'll die of heat prostration."

"I can't help it," fumed Frieda. "Those reporters were supposed to be here. Don't you see? Publicity was to be our ace in the hole."

"Well, they didn't come. There!" Prell had gotten up and was towering over her sister. "The question is, what do we do now?"

"Oh . . . spit!" Frieda stamped her foot.

Attracted by the commotion, the children had run over to the porch. "I want some more lemonade," begged

Randall as Sherri shushed him and opened up the thermos.

"Well, I still say, they will tear this house down over my dead body." Frieda was granite.

"That may be," said Prell in a casual voice, "but what are we going to do?"

Frieda thought a moment. "We'll go ahead as planned. When they come over, we'll be lined up here beside the flag. We won't budge."

"Well, now," Prell said as if getting more than she had bargained for, "I told Hershell I'd be back by five. At the latest. He gets awful testy if his dinner is not on the table at six o'clock."

"You listen to me, Prell Simpson!" Frieda screamed, her crimson face glistening with sweat. "I've put up with about all I can stand. You said you'd do your part. If you rat out on me now I'll. . . ."

For the first time since collapsing on the dusty divan, Ernest opened an eye and sat up straight. "Stop that squalling!" he ordered. He pulled out a red bandanna and blew his nose with a toot. "Now, I don't want to hear another word." Settling back into his former position, he closed his eyes.

"In any case," said Rick as Frieda squatted on the blanket, "they won't tear down the house while we're standing here."

"So?" sneered Prell. "What are we going to do then? Move in?"

"We'll think of something," said Rick. "One thing at a time."

By noon it was obvious that the men who had driven up in pick-ups were not simply ignoring the party on the porch; they were unaware of it. Under a blaring blue sky, four roustabouts hoisted long pipes around, while others alternately revved up and killed the engines of the lumbering, golden machines. A pair of men in dress shirts bent their heads together over fold-out blueprints. One of the drivers began grading a plat.

"What do you make of it?" Prell muttered to Frieda as they sat fanning themselves on the steps.

"They've got something up their sleeve. You can bet on it."

"Well, I don't think they're going to mess with this house." Once again scoffing had crept into Prell's voice. "Looks to me like the well's going in over there."

Frieda angled her palm across her brow. "Maybe," she said after awhile.

By twelve-thirty, they were eating sandwiches and drinking iced tea on the porch. A slight breeze distributed red powder stirred up by the bulldozer.

"Well, I don't know about you folks," announced Prell peremptorily, "but I've got other rats to kill. It's obvious to me those men are not going to bother this house."

"Aunt Prell's right, Mom," Aaron said, looking for a crack in her iron resolve. "They're busy over there." Soon it would be time for Ernest to take his mother home. But she was not ready just yet to give up.

"Who will go with me to see about it?" It was a last-ditch effort by Frieda to press the issue.

"Oh, I'll go with you," said Aaron, while the others indicated assent, as well.

"Come on, then." Frieda was off the steps and tugging at her slip before the others were on their feet. Across a stubble pasture, they made their way toward the two men in dress shirts, who were drinking from Coke cans in the shade of their truck.

"May I help you?" inquired one of the men in a cultivated voice.

"I want to speak to whoever's in charge," demanded Frieda.

The men glanced at one another.

"I guess that's me." Short-haired and deeply sunburned, he spoke with a Deep South accent.

"I am Frieda Teague, and these are members of my family." Frieda gave a half turn to present the others. "This is our family land you're drilling on."

"Hmmm. Well, it's nice to meet you." The oil men exchanged perplexed looks.

"I have it on very good report that you all are going to destroy the house over there." Frieda pointed back to the peeling structure among the trees. "And we just want to let you know that we will not allow that to be done."

"Are you telling us that you own this land?"

"Um. Not legally. It was stolen from us."

The Southerner cocked an eyebrow. "I think you're mistaken in any case, Ma'am. I don't have any instructions to touch the house. As you can see, we're drilling here." He pointed to where the bulldozer was raising dust.

"Are you sure there are no plans to tear down the house? None at all?"

"Here are my instructions, Ma'am." The man pulled out from behind the seat a looseleaf binder and opened it to the first page. "These coordinates indicate the location of the well—where that earth-mover is working. This is the only spot I know anything about drilling."

Prell shrugged her shoulders. "Come on, honey. Thank the man and let's go."

Aaron put an arm around his mother's shoulders. Sweating freely, Frieda nodded to the oil man and started with her son back across the pasture. She was crestfallen. "Let's get out of this heat before one of us dies of sunstroke," she said bitterly.

As they were putting belongings back into their cars, Prell grumbled, "I'll bet Patsy Fowler is laughing her head off right now."

"Oh, it's one of her little jokes, all right," agreed Frieda. "Her name's written all over it."

## 29

"Maybe Aunt Patsy will restore the house," suggested Aaron optimistically.

"Mnff. Patsy doesn't like that old place a bit better than I do," said Frieda. "Nobody in their right mind would tromp up and down those steep stairs or work in that hotbox of a kitchen: no dishwasher, no disposal, no nothing. Just that little dab of cabinet space and a sink. Period. To think that Mama had to live in that gruesome place all her days. I still see her in that hot kitchen in the summertime, her face red as a beet." From the fortress of her womanhood, Frieda shook her head at the pure damned foolishness of men. "Daddy wouldn't hear of moving. I really think he *liked* it out there in that slough."

Aaron had gotten his parents to stop with him at the Red Rooster Cafe in downtown Curtain before continuing home. He was worried about his mother's ability to withstand the heat, which had steadily intensified. She was not an outdoor person, especially in the summertime, when she preferred to stay within range of an air conditioner.

Aaron ordered the special of the day — Patty Melt. Two dollars and a quarter. When he asked the waitress, a brassy-banged two-hundred pounder in a tank top reading "I'm a Pepper," what a Patty Melt was, she licked her pink lips, picked in her ear, and groped for a way to describe it. "Well, it's got a hamburger patty, like you make a hamburger out of, and there's this melted cheese," she drawled the word, "and mushroom soup they pour over it and serve it with a slice of dill pickle." She shifted her weight to the other hip and grinned with her teeth. "It's real good."

"We just want iced tea," Frieda said. Watching the waitress waddle back toward the kitchen on rubber flip-flops, she clicked open her navy handbag. "That reminds me, I must look a fright." She pulled out a rectangular mirror and peered critically into it. "God in heaven, is that me?" She grimaced and inspected her gums.

Ernest sat with a sour look on his face. "Does that sign apply to us?" He pointed to a hand-lettered notice behind the counter:

COFFEE DRINKERS
sit at counter
during "Lunch"

"Ignore it, it's nearly one-thirty. Besides, we're drinking tea." Frieda wiped her face with a paper napkin. She had left her straw hat in the car. Otherwise she was dressed as she had been that morning.

"Why is it there's always a Saltine in the sugar shaker?" Aaron asked gamely. He was ennervated from the heat, and he was very hungry. He had started the day in a rush with a single slice of toast and had not thought to pack sandwiches for lunch. He had been grateful as a hound dog puppy for the half a peanut butter sandwich Randall had dropped off the porch.

Frieda gave him a sharp look. "You always did ask the strangest questions." She began applying fresh lipstick. "What I'm wondering about," she contorted her lips, "is what's the matter with our car?"

Ernest leered. "I told you, I'll take the car to the shop when we get back to Bugg. It's nothing serious or it would show on the oil gauge."

"You and your silly damn gauges." Frieda smacked her lips, looked again into the mirror, and recovered the lipstick with its tin cover. "What about the time we drove to New Orleans to see Tommy? 'Don't worry,' you kept telling me. 'If it's anything serious it'll show up on the oil gauge.'"

She leaned across the table. "Next thing we knew the rods shot up through the floorboard."

"Now, I don't want to hear that story again. I told you, I'm taking care of the car. Let's talk about something else."

Frieda pulled out a coarse-bristled hair brush and attacked her hair.

Aaron wondered at the resilience of their marriage, in spite of the bickering that sometimes seemed to be the only communication between them. Apparently they were as happy as either of them could be. A good part of it was that they were never apart. They didn't have separate careers. They never took separate vacations. They never slept apart. Did they really have it better, living like Siamese twins, not knowing what it was like to be alone?

Honey, their waitress—she had pinned to her bosom a laminated tag bearing her name underneath a printed-HI, I'M YOUR WAITRESS—was bringing a plate of food and an iced tea.

"Where's ours?" demanded Frieda crossly after Honey had served Aaron.

"Well, excuse me!" she squeegee'd back to the kitchen on her flip-flops.

"Don't wait on us," Frieda said. Then she added cagily, "Son, mentioning Tommy just now made me remember . . . "

Aaron sawed his Patty Melt with the side of his fork.

"You know I've never really understood what you said about Tommy . . . near the end before he . . ."

"Mom, there's nothing to understand," Aaron interrupted, then softened his tone. "You heard everything I know. I hadn't seen Tommy for several days. He had been doing better. He wasn't drinking, so far as I know, and he'd kept his job for several months and saved some money. He called me one afternoon at the office. I was very busy with some blueprints that were overdue and couldn't talk. That night was when it happened." Aaron broke off and stuck a bite of meat in his mouth.

"You never said anything before about a phone call."

"Oh . . . I didn't think it was important."

"Well, what did you talk about?"

"We didn't. I was tied up and told him to drop by the apartment that night."

"You never said anything about that before." Frieda was astonished. Ernest also was listening carefully.

Sheepishly, Aaron laid down his fork. "I know," he mumbled as the waitress brought out Frieda's and Ernest's iced tea. "I've thought about it, though. I've asked myself a thousand times, if I hadn't been too busy to talk to Tommy that afternoon, would things have worked out differently?"

Ernest poured a stream of sugar into his tea. "Well," Frieda said, "don't blame yourself, son. If something was to be, then you couldn't have prevented it."

Aaron felt awkward and guilty talking about it. And he remembered more than he was telling.

* * * *

It had been one of those awful days: he'd had a major run-in with a client in the morning, then missed a luncheon meeting of the architects' association because of a dead battery. He was under heavy pressure to supply a set of overdue blueprints by five o'clock.

At four-fifteen his secretary informed him that his brother Tommy was on the phone.

"Tell him I'm tied up now," replied Aaron without looking up.

A few moments later, his secretary interrupted again. It was urgent, Tommy said.

Swearing under his breath, Aaron picked up the phone. Without preamble, Tommy began blurting out some story about a phone call he'd just made to New Orleans. He'd been feeling real down, and that guy China—Aaron remembered, he'd met him at Ruby Red's—had hung up on him. Tommy wouldn't take that. If anybody would hang up on anybody, it would be Tommy, not that middle-aged faggot.

The kid was drunk. As for the tale, Aaron didn't care to be drawn into it right then. With as much patience as he could muster, he told Tommy to cool down. He, Aaron, was absolutely snowed under with work and couldn't talk. He would be free that evening, and Tommy should drop by the apartment after eight.

"Christ, man," Tommy's words remained sharp in Aaron's memory, "you go on back to your work. That's fine. That's just fucking A-OK." Dramatically, his brother had paused before adding, "Just don't expect me to be around when you get finished."

"Come off it," Aaron grumbled. The whining bravado in his brother's voice was repugnant.

"You're the one who's always trying to get me to open up," Tommy was ranting. "Open up! Aw . . . Christ, forget it."

Wanting only to be finished with the tedious matter, Aaron repeated what he had said about being busy and about being available that evening. Then once more before hanging up the phone, he admonished Tommy to pull himself together.

When Aaron arrived at the apartment shortly before seven that evening, he learned from the old lady in the next apartment that Tommy had already stopped by. It had been a strange visit. Freshly shaven, Tommy had knotted a blue silk bandanna around his neck. He handed over to her a cassette tape of Lou Reed's Greatest Hits. He said it was his favorite tape; he wanted Aaron to have it. Then Tommy had ducked his head and slouched down the balcony stairway.

At eleven-twenty that night, according to the account of a witness at the Wander Inn, Tommy had placed his hand on the leg of the man drinking beside him at the bar. The man had responded by sliding a six-inch shiv between Tommy's ribs. A limping, red-faced detective had given Aaron the

meager, explicit details as they rode the elevator down to
the morgue in the basement of the police station the night
of the murder. The assailant had disappeared out the
front door. The newspapers would no doubt ignore the
matter: another tavern knifing. Small beer.

Driving home from the morgue before dawn, Aaron
monitored his feelings. It was like watching someone else's
movements through a one-way window. That other person
was staring out vacuously through the windshield into the
darkness. That other person was feeling—nothing; he had
absolutely no reaction to what he had just learned. It was a
familiar syndrome, honed to perfection by the war: numb-
ing the emotions against overpowering facts. Like a
delayed-action bomb, the experience would no doubt detonate inside his head—but later, when there would be time
to appreciate every irony.

It was not yet five-thirty when he got back to his apartment. Blueprints were spread out on the table. He might
as well get an early start. But he didn't want to do that just
now. Yesterday afternoon he had talked on the phone with
Tommy. Informed Tommy that he was too busy to talk.
Then his brother had driven to a bar and gotten himself
killed. What would happen to the killer? Aaron hoped the
bastard fried. Tommy had just begun to get himself
together; he had been going to make it. Aaron had been
genuinely hopeful. Goddamn, it was crazy.

Who was going to inform his parents? The question
carried the impact of a surprise punch from his blind side.
Aaron should have asked if the police did that. In any case,
it was his place to make contact. He wondered if Frieda
and Ernest still woke up at quarter to six.

Aaron would not go to work today. He did not really
know why. Surely it was owed him, a day off. He wasn't
"grieving," but he did not want to go to the office and carry
on as though nothing had happened. No one at the office
knew Tommy anyway. On the other hand, he didn't want to
have to tell them what had happened and go through all

the goddamn details and have them tell him how sorry they were. He just did not want the hassle now.

How was he going to break the news to his parents? It wouldn't be right to do it over the phone. He would call and tell them he was driving up and that Ernest needed to stay home from work. Would his stepfather be able to take the day off? It would be very important to avoid alarming them over the phone. Although how, for Chrisake, could he insist that Ernest stay home from work until Aaron got there without alarming them?

On the third ring, Frieda answered the phone. Instantly, from her monotone "hello," Aaron knew that she already had heard.

"Mom, this is Aaron."

A pause, then, "You've heard about Tommy?" Her voice sounded dead.

"Yes. I didn't think you'd know yet."

"The police called us."

"Is Ernest staying home?" It was a dumb question.

"Yes, he told his supervisor what happened. He's got the rest of the week off."

"Are you doing okay?" Aaron longed to say something that would comfort his mother. And half-consciously he longed, as well, to be comforted by her.

"Ernest will make the funeral arrangements. We'll let you know."

"Okay." After a long pause, Aaron repeated, "Mom, are you okay? I mean is everything all right?"

"Yes, son. Don't worry."

Aaron swallowed hard. "Well, Mom, I'll let you go. You'll call me as soon as you find out about the funeral?"

"Yes, son. We love you."

After hanging up the phone, Aaron sat for a while, staring at the wall. Then he shuffled to his room and climbed into bed without undressing. For a strange moment, he had a sense that Tommy had stayed out over-night and would be back later that day.

He was hungry. English muffins would taste good. English muffins and tea. But he didn't want to walk to the kitchen to make them. That would be a hassle. He would stay in bed.

All morning, Aaron lay gazing out the window at the milky sky and feeling vaguely that he should get up and do this or that, but desisting. In the afternoon, he dozed off and on until he was waked by the phone about four. It was Frieda; the funeral was scheduled for Thursday at eleven.

Shortly after six o'clock, Rick telephoned. Aaron told him the story of how Tommy had been knifed in a bar, making no mention of his brother's provocation of the attack. Aaron had never acknowledged Tommy's homosexuality to Rick or anyone else. It was the sort of very private matter Aaron instinctively shied away from discussing. If Tommy wanted his sexual preference disclosed, he would have to be the one to do so. In New Orleans, for some unknown reason, Tommy had chosen to share that knowledge with Aaron. As far as Aaron knew, Tommy had thus confided in no other member of the family. Because Aaron believed unquestioningly in his brother's right to privacy, he had never considered violating that confidence.

After agreeing to meet Rick and his family on Thursday morning in Denton, then continue in caravan to Bugg for the funeral, Aaron hung up the phone. He thought of calling Nell, who was visiting her ailing father in Normal. She would probably be expecting a call from him tonight. In a way he was glad she was out of town; none of this was her affair. It was a family matter. Besides he did not want to rehash the details. He was too tired. He would call her tomorrow.

Thursday morning, an hour behind schedule, Aaron headed north out of Dallas on I-35. Under a gauze sky, everything along the road seemed shrouded in dust. The morning had already begun to heat up when he reconnoitered with Rick at Wyatt's Cafeteria in Denton. They were talkative, even witty, the six of them. Rick spilt his coffee and made a production of wiping up the mess; Buddy swallowed a dime, then puked it up. They left the haze behind when they cut east off the interstate.

The previous morning Aaron had gotten up feeling self-indulgent and silly for goldbricking around the apartment on Tuesday. Once again his old self, he had showered and shaved, then driven to work down Preston Road and had a reasonably productive morning. No one had inquired of his whereabouts the day before, and he had not brought up the matter. Tommy was dead. He would not be coming back.

By the time Bugg's water tower came into sight across the rolling north Texas landscape, there was no time to spare. They were late. Straight up the dusty main street they drove to Reiger's Funeral Home. Except for a small sign in Gothic script over double leaded-glass doors, it resembled its shabby, turn-of-the-century neighbors, all of them dug stubbornly into the plain brown Texas soil. Cars and pickups lined both sides of the wide street. Two couples, the men in front wearing cowboy hats, the women behind in pants suits and with scarves tied around their heads, ambled up the brick sidewalk to the mortuary.

The brothers were met at the door by their own reflections in lustrous blue glass. Mr. Reiger, an old tissue-skinned man in navy blue who looked precisely as Aaron remembered him twenty years ago, stood inside the door and mournfully handed them bulletins before they passed into a long, carpeted room smelling of candles and fresh flowers. There at the end of the hall, dead center between the two walls, lay a shiny metal casket, topped with an elaborate spray of white roses. From her place in the front pew, Frieda turned and gave them a wan smile. Then after hugging each of them, and while Ernest shook hands and helplessly showed his teeth, she directed each of them where to sit: Aaron beside her—Ernest was on the other side—then Rick, Sherri, and the children. Frieda smelt of perfume and there were dark circles underneath her eyes.

Looking over his shoulder, Aaron saw his great-aunt Minna, an old bent woman of ninety who was eyeing the casket with a hard disdainful glare. Beside her sat Uncle Hermann and Aunt Agnes, both of them big-shouldered. A burly gentleman unknown to Aaron and wearing a full, wiry beard was striding to the front.

"Who's that?" Aaron whispered to his mother.

"Reverend Bud Fowler," she hissed under her voice as he took his place behind the pulpit. "He's our new preacher."

Like the usher at the door, the minister wore a dark navy suit, although from the rough, blocky cast of his head and a sense he conveyed of being uncomfortable in the stiff white collar, he seemed very much one of the working people in front of him. Slowly and sonorously he began to speak of the vanity of human endeavor, turning several times during the course of the sermon to the metal coffin to declare, "There is where it leads, your dream of earthly glory and riches," and ending with the injunction to exert your efforts "where they will be everlastingly repaid, to the glory of the Lord." Afterwards a soprano hidden behind a curtain sang "In the Garden." Frieda's audible sobs were echoed from around the room.

Aaron felt acutely uncomfortable and wished the ceremony were over. Tommy would surely have laughed up his sleeve at the maudlin bathos of the whole sorry production.

The white-haired Mr. Reiger crept up the aisle with an assistant and proceeded to open the casket for viewing. After rearranging the spray of white roses and raising the lid, they noiselessly stepped away. Inside, displayed like a ring in a box, lay Tommy. That painted wax dummy with its eyes discreetly closed, that was his brother. Aaron felt as though he had been slammed with a two-by-four in the diaphram.

At the end of the service, after the other mourners had filed out past the body and left behind only the family and attendants, Aaron hung back in the pew with the children while the casket was closed. For the first time since

Tommy's death, he was working to subdue his emotions. He sensed that the delayed-action bomb that had impacted three days ago with the revelation of Tommy's death was about to detonate. He knew the explosion was inevitable, but he wished it would not occur now, not before the others. Some motive that Aaron did not comprehend, indeed that he regretted, made him ashamed of displaying before the others the grief he was now beginning to feel. He used tricks to hold at bay the imminent breaking down: studying the cast-tinwork on the ceiling, forcing his mind away from the spectacle of his brother's corpse and his tearful family, biting his upper lip.

On the way to the burial, even the children were subdued. Strolling across the hillside cemetery to the small cluster of mourners at graveside, Aaron looked out across the roofs and elm trees and feed mills of the prairie town. This was where Tommy had grown up; now he had returned for good.

As Reverend Fowler intoned, "Ashes to ashes . . ." and sprinkled a handful of dirt over the flower-topped casket, Aaron glanced sideways at his mother. Holding on to Ernest, a handkerchief to her nose, she looked so goddamned forlorn. Something broke in Aaron. He felt so scrry for Frieda and, pretending to scratch his nose, he brushed away a warm tear. He hoped no one had noticed. Then for the first time since he was ten and his father died and for two days Aaron had bawled in a violent and fruitless effort to get rid of the awful hurt, there were more tears and he was furious with himself, but they wouldn't stop and he stood crying without a sound.

* * * *

"Well, we'd better get a move on," Frieda remarked as she plucked a quarter from her handbag and laid it beside Ernest's tea glass, shattering Aaron's reverie. "I want to get home in time to see 'Days of Our Lives.' "

"Hold your horses," replied Ernest. "I'm still working on my tea."

Aaron still wondered how his brother could have done something so goddamn dumb. He couldn't figure it out. The Wander Inn, with its mixed clientele of bikers and refinery workers, was anything but a gay bar. Didn't Tommy know better than to make a pass in such a place? Had he *wanted* to get himself killed? And if that had been the case, then how much guilt was Aaron's for his indifference to Tommy the afternoon before his murder? Like a hanging thread on an otherwise tightly woven piece of fabric, the affair defied assimilation.

Impulsively, as he sat now with his parents in the Red Rooster Cafe finishing his Patty Melt, it was on the tip of Aaron's tongue to confide the rest of the story to his parents. As if by sharing the story, he could somehow dissipate its burdensome effect on himself. For surely his parents had a right to know the truth about how Tommy had died. Yet he knew what his parents' reaction would be to that disclosure: they would be hurt even worse than they already had been hurt. And the fact remained that Tommy had not intended for them to know.

Wiping his mouth with his napkin, Aaron studied the long fluorescent light bulbs on the ceiling, then looked at Honey, their waitress, leaning against the milk machine and picking her teeth. He read the collection of bumper stickers pasted on the wall behind the cash register, peered at the walleyed cashier with red corkscrew curls and swoop-framed glasses. The old woman grew uncomfortable under his scrutiny and blinked her popeyes once at him before turning away. Aaron regarded this countrified and reassuring place for a long time before choosing finally to say nothing more on the matter.

No doubt he should have insisted on playing more of an active role in his younger brother's life. No doubt he should have projected himself more vigorously as an advisor. He and Tommy, after all, had been brothers.

As were Aaron and Rick, who liked one another, natu-
rally, but who also had plenty in common: had gone
through school together, a string of new schools in which
the handsomer, more outgoing older brother had repeat-
edly smoothed the way for the shyer, awkwarder Aaron.
And there had been the war. More than Aaron preferred
to admit, his own character, his sense of identity, his
values—like Rick's—had resulted from the experience of
Vietnam and from the shitty reception they, as vets, had
received after Vietnam. Those experiences ensured a kind
of sympathy between them. Tommy was of a later generation. Under very different conditions than those Aaron
and Rick had known, he had still been in the process of
finding out who he was.

Why should the simple fact of having had the same
mother produce in Aaron this nagging sense of responsibility for his younger brother's welfare? Hadn't he given
Tommy all he asked for—a place to stay when he had
needed it? Hadn't he sought his brother's confidence, his
friendship—in spite of never having really understood
Tommy? Aaron had gone the distance, he tried to reassure
himself. It hadn't worked out. As with Deedee, he had
failed. Wasn't that the inescapable conclusion?

It had been understood between the two brothers that
Aaron would keep his peace. He had done so. Had
watched as Tommy tried to make his own way. Had
watched him fall. Aaron had kept his peace. Beyond the
fact of blood—the mere, the all-important, fact of blood—
that peace had constituted one of the few pacts, one of the
few real understandings between Aaron and his wild hare
of a brother. Now it was all that remained. A tacit under-
standing. One to which the living brother would remain
faithful.

# 30

It was flatland now, wheat land, not rolling countryside as around Bugg, with silos pitched across the prairie and farm machinery in the dusty back lots of farmhouses. Here and there tough old juniper trees clustered together, if they hadn't been rooted out for farmland. If they had been rooted out, there was nothing at all to keep the eye from scanning the horizon. The afternoon smelled of dusty grass and heat, and the meadowlark's cry spilled through the air. Stalks of wheat the color of stubble jutted stubbornly out of hard-packed earth.

From the compartment in the dashboard Frieda took out a tube of sweet-smelling hand lotion and squeezed a dab into the palm of one hand. "What a pass this family's come to," she sighed and rubbed her hands together, one over the other. "Who would have guessed ten years ago that today we'd have one son in the grave and another living in sin?"

"That's not for us to judge," cautioned Ernest. "That girl Aaron's living with seems to be a nice girl."

"Foot. She's nothing but a whore." Frieda wound her hands around one another like fate. "Mama and Daddy in the grave. Three of we girls not speaking to the fourth one. What a pass we've come to."

As she was replacing the tube of hand lotion in the glove compartment, the motor coughed twice and died.

"Oh, my Lord! The car's stopped."

Ernest turned off the air conditioner and coasted the Buick onto the highway's gravel shoulder.

"What are we going to do? We'll suffocate in this heat."

"Roll the window down." Ernest set the gearshift lever in park and turned the ignition key to the right.

The motor growled but did not fire. A red lamp shone on the oil pressure gauge.

"I told you, we should have had someone look at the car before we left Curtain."

Ernest pumped the footfeed three times, then turned the key. "Damn!" he swore and tried it again. "You get behind the wheel," he told Frieda, "and be ready to turn the key when I give you the signal."

Ernest popped the hood release, stepped out of the car, and propped open the hood. "Damn," he muttered as he surveyed the car's bellyful of piping steel pans and rubber hoses. Continuing to swear, he stomped around the car, opened the trunk, and found a drop cloth.

In a suck of steam an eighteen-wheeler roared past.

"You'll get your water cut off if you're not careful," Frieda clicked her diamond on the steering wheel.

Red in the face, Ernest spread the cloth neatly over the right fender and ducked underneath the hood. "Now," he shouted after what seemed to Frieda, as she sat fanning herself, an interminable span.

She turned over the key. Nothing.

"Well?" she shouted back as another truck swooshed past. "Well? . . . Did you hear me?"

Still there was no response. Lightly Frieda rapped the horn. Twice. As if alerting the driver ahead of her at a stoplight that the light had changed.

There was a thump. The hood shivered. Rubbing his crown, Ernest stood up, enormous, beside the car and glared at his wife through the windshield's sheen. "If you ever do that again," he said in measured tones, "I'll kill you."

For a moment Frieda was speechless. Then, her dander up, she snarled back, "Don't you talk to me like that, Ernest Teague. You've got no call to talk to me like that."

Back under the hood he lowered his head. For nearly fifteen minutes he tested hoses, nuts, and levers.

With a whomp he let the hood fall. "Move over," he opened the driver's door.

"What's wrong with it?"

"If I knew what was wrong," he muttered as if around a mouthful of ball bearings, "do you think we'd be sitting here?"

"You always tell me you know everything," Frieda taunted. "Hmph. You and that silly damn oil gauge. Didn't it tell you anything?"

Ernest ignored the jibe.

"I told you we needed to see what was wrong when it started missing this morning. But no, you wouldn't listen. You never listen. So here we sit. Stuck on the side of the road forty miles from home. In the heat. What are we going to do, Ernest?" Frieda blinked her eyes. "What are we going to do?"

"First thing we're gonna do," Ernest replied, "is calm down. This screaming and crying isn't getting us no place."

Through her nostrils Frieda gathered, then expelled, a lungful of air. She unfastened two buttons of the jacket to her navy silk suit.

"Is there any lemonade left in the thermos?" asked Ernest.

"No, we drank it all for lunch. There was a little bit left but I dumped it out. I was afraid it might sour before we got home."

From down the ruler-straight highway they watched a glinting bead turn into a shiny blue Chrysler. As Frieda patted a hairdo already stiff with red dirt and sweat, Ernest crawled out of the car, grinned a toothy grin, and stuck out his thumb.

WHOOOOOM.

"They never even slowed down," he slumped back behind the wheel.

"Did you see the tag?" observed Frieda in a knowing voice. "New York."

"Damn Easterners."

Then down the sizzling strip of concrete rolled a diesel truck. Again Ernest stuck out his thumb and was bypassed in a wash of foul-smelling exhaust.

"They used to say truck drivers were the most polite drivers on the road," said Frieda as Ernest slid back onto the bench seat.

"Damn truck drivers."

When they did not see another vehicle for eight minutes, Ernest grumbled, "Where is the damn highway patrol when you need it?"

"I don't know," Frieda was fanning herself with both hands. "But I'm about to have a heat stroke."

"Take off those silly hose."

"Oh . . ."

"All right, then, sweat." Ernest shook his head. Carefully, he began folding up his pant legs until they were above his knees, which Frieda liked to say reminded her of cauliflowers. Then after sliding off his black wingtips and rolling down his nylon socks below his ankles, he unbuttoned his shirt and took it off.

"Ernest Teague, you are not going to be seen in public wearing that godawful old strap undershirt."

"I might." Ernest scowled. "A body could have a heat stroke. That's a fact. One thing we can do to prevent that is to keep ourselves cool as we can. If you had the sense of a squirrel, you would strip off those silly panty hose and unbutton your blouse. You can button it up again when someone stops." Pessimistically, Ernest peered into the rearview mirror. "*If* they stop."

Wretchedly, Frieda leaned back into the seat, raised her hips, and began rolling down the stockings. "I just hope I don't see anybody I know," she said.

For another half hour they waited in the oven of a car while an occasional automobile or tanker truck whipped by.

"You didn't notice how far back the last farmhouse was?" Ernest asked. He sat with his black nylon booties propped up on the dashboard.

"I didn't see."

"I was thinking about heading off on foot in search of a farmhouse."

"I don't think you should do that," said Frieda after a while. "It might be miles. And then they might not be at home."

Ernest didn't say anything.

"How far did you say we were out of Peach?" asked Frieda.

"About five miles, if I recollect right."

"Hmmm." Frieda rubbed the half-moons under her eyes. "Surely someone will stop soon."

"If we don't get picked up by six o'clock, I'm gonna hike into Peach."

"Oh, don't be ridiculous. That's five miles. You'd have a heart attack." Seeing her husband bristle, Frieda added, "In this heat, I mean. Without water you'd collapse. Besides what would happen to me? You're not about to leave me unprotected along this highway." Frieda ruffled her shoulders. "At night, yet."

"Well, we got to do something."

"We'll just wait." Frieda felt superior in her woman's patience. "Someone will stop."

Before long, as if to bear out her prediction, an ungainly, slow-moving object appeared on the horizon. White, appallingly white on its great hump, a Moby Dick of the highway, it seemed at first to be a moving van, then a Wonderbread truck, transporting fresh bread to the towns of the prairie. Then, as it emerged out of the waves of heat dancing up from the pavement, they saw what it was.

"I am not riding in a garbage truck," Frieda declared as the clanking vehicle began to grind down gears.

"Would you rather stay here and sweat?" he spat back. "Button your blouse."

Onto the shoulder behind the Buick eased the huge ark. The motor idling, a yellow-haired boy with red cheeks and a wide grin poked his head out the driver's window. "Y'all need a lift?" he spoke in a high voice and snapped a wad of pink chewing gum.

"Sure do," said Ernest. "You got room for me and my wife?" The cab of the truck held two other persons, besides the driver.

"Oh, we can put two on the back," the yellow-haired boy called back. "Ain't but a hop to town."

Ernest had rolled down his trouser legs and put his feet back into his shoes. Now slipping his arms into his white shirt, he hurried along Frieda, who was fastening the last covered button on her silk jacket. Before stepping out, she squeezed her panty hose into a moist ball and stuck it into her purse, along with her comb and handkerchief, and slipped her bare feet into the navy-blue pumps.

Ernest left the hood open and a white handkerchief tied to the aerial. "We'll have it towed in," he explained as his wife walked around the car. "And don't complain."

As they approached the reeking truck, Frieda elongated her nostrils and breathed through her mouth.

The door of the elevated cab swung open and down stepped a frizzy-haired, chunky young woman smoking a cigarette through an ebony holder. She wore skintight Levis and a tank top. After winking at Ernest, she swaggered towards the rear of the truck.

"C'mon ma'am," the driver smiled at Frieda. "You can sit up here with Jim and me." Gratefully she appraised the empty space that was hers on the tattered bench seat beside an old, white-whiskered black man. Placing one foot on the running board, she was about to hoist herself up, when she heard the girl drawl to Ernest, "Come on back here, I'll show ya where to hold on."

Only for an instant did Frieda vacillate. In the shade of the truck underneath the Peach Sanitation Department lettering, the young female worker vibrated in time to the rackety old truck.

"You show me where to stand," Frieda peered testily at the girl. "I hate to take your seat."

With Frieda and Ernest riding shotgun, the white garbage truck started with a lurch. Her shoes in her purse, Frieda stood on the balls of her feet with both arms looped tightly through the grab bar, her hair flapping about her face like a flag, her nose out into the fresh air. One knee jauntily cocked out at an angle, Ernest was hanging on by one arm.

Soon they were passing JoJo's Salvage Yard along the west side of the highway. On the east was Our Place, closed tight as a bunker against the sun. Then Glenda's Glamourette, and a rambling brick ranch house with a basketball-sized blue glass ball in a bird bath on the front lawn and a flock of pink plaster flamingoes posed around it.

Frieda ducked her head down to where her fingers gripped the grab bar and tried to do something with her hair.

The truck slowed down as it neared the two blocks of business district. Two boys were peddling along on bicycles behind the truck and holding their noses and laughing.

At a four-way stop, a new Oldsmobile pulled up behind. Through a tinted windshield a blue-haired woman pointed at the pair clinging to the rear end of the truck. After making a left turn from the stop sign, the truck bumped another block and stopped in front of a red tin building. Across the front hung a wooden sign with peeling letters that spelled out "Peach Wrecking Service."

Down from his perch hopped Ernest, then helped down his wife, who complained of the gravel's sharpness on her bare feet.

"Sure thank you folks," he walked around to the driver's side and popped a salute to the yellow-haired driver.

"Glad to be of help." Like a flatulent hippopotamus, the truck backfired.

Frieda jumped.

"Well," Ernest faced the tin building, "let's see what Peach Wrecking Service can do for us."

Inside, everything was wonderfully cool and dim. A thin, middle-aged man with a deeply lined face was sprawled asleep in his chair behind a desk littered with papers, manuals, directories. In one window purred an air conditioner.

Frieda rolled up her eyes as the cool air hit her. She collapsed onto a low-slung, oily couch.

"How do," Ernest knocked on the desk top. With a forefinger the sleeper pried open one baggy eyelid. He frowned.

"Our car needs a tow-in. Broke down about five miles outside town."

The man lifted his boots off the desk and rummaged through papers.

"Name?" he droned after uncovering a pad.

"Ernest Teague."

"Address?"

"204 Locust."

Suspiciously the man looked across the desk. "That in Peach?"

"No. Bugg."

The man scribbled on the pad then looked up again. "Where's the car?"

"Like I said, it's on the highway about five miles south."

"How much you gonna pay?"

"How much it be?"

"Tow-in five miles, no extras, run you forty dollars. Extras run more."

"I can write a check."

"What's your bank?"

"First National of Bugg."

Wearily, the man exhaled then reached into a desk drawer and pulled out a billed cap inscribed "Eat my dust" in Gothic lettering across the front.

"Where you want it brung?" he limped around the desk to the door.

"Is there a place here that works on Buicks?"

"Yep. Darrell's Garage. It's the only place that works on any cars."

"Might as well tow it there."

"Course it won't do you no good today." There was a hint of a smirk on the man's lips.

"Why not?"

"Darrell's out a town till tomorrow. His son Junior's over there. I wouldn't let him work on my grandson's tricycle."

Stumped, Ernest turned to Frieda. "Is there a motel?"

"Yep. The Palm Beach. Other side a Peach."

Frieda straightened up on the couch. Crossly, she said, "I'm not staying in some town while someone tries to fix that car. I want to go home."

"Well, how do you propose to get us there?"

"You got us in this fix, Ernest Teague. You figure it out." She blew a lock of hair out of her eyes.

"What kind of place is this Palm Beach?" Ernest asked the man.

"Oh. Yer typical tourist court. Don't expect no air conditioning."

"No air conditioning?"

"Naw. Folks kept turning them air conditioners up on high and running up the electric bill. Trixie, she ripped 'em out this spring. Said she warn't gonna be paying them high electric bills another summer."

At a loss, Ernest plunged his hands in his pockets and stared out the window.

"You folks say yer from Bugg?"

"That's right."

"Well, fer a little extra, I could tow you there in my truck."

Frieda's eyes sparkled. "Let's do that, honey. I want to get home."

"How much 'extra' you charge?" asked Ernest.

"Oh . . . lemme see." The man returned to his desk, opened the drawer, and found a pocket calculator. Raising his eyebrows, he punched on the keyboard, wrote down figures, punched some more. "I'd do it fer two hundred dollars."

"My God!" yelped Ernest.

"It's thirty-eight miles from my driveway to Bugg city limits. At five dollars a mile, which is giving you folks something right there, you take the five miles from where yer car sits to here, and the thirty-eight miles from here to Bugg, not counting wherever it is you want it brung, and you got yerself a bargain."

While Frieda shook her head hopefully, Ernest paced back and forth twice in front of the desk, then told the man, okay.

"Before you go," said Frieda, "is there someplace around here I could find something to drink?"

The man grinned. "Lone Star Tavern's a block east on Main Street."

"I beg your pardon!" Frieda was offended. "I mean a Coke. Or a glass of ice water."

"No. There ain't none of them. The Blue Bird Grill over on Main is closed while the owner's in the hospital with a stone."

*     *     *     *

All the way to Bugg, Frieda sat in the middle, her knees discreetly spread to catch the air blowing in through the vent. Hot air was better than no air. Neither she nor Ernest had had a drop to drink since the iced teas four and a half hours earlier in Curtain.

For the first time since before the car had broken down, her thoughts turned to her sisters. Patsy she felt bitter toward. And yet . . . that was Patsy. Always thinking of herself, grabbing the biggest piece of cake. If she had acted any different, it would not have been Patsy.

After it all blew over, she knew deep in the layers of her consciousness, they would patch it up, the four girls. Right now, if Patsy was there beside her on the seat, Frieda would turn and scratch her sister's eyes out. Spoiled brat. But it would be there between them to come back to — the bond they shared as sisters.

If only Patsy hadn't cut so deep this time. She had sliced through right to the quick. Frieda didn't know if she would ever get over the resentment, the hatred she felt right now.

She really was afraid she was going to pass out. Never in her life had she felt so hot, so thirsty, so exhausted, so filthy.

The first thing Frieda would do when she got home — oh, how glad she was that they had decided not to stay over at that pokey motel in Peach — would be to take a long, cooling shower. She would turn the hot water on only slightly, so it wouldn't be actually cold, but cool, like rain.

Later, she would rub moisturizer into her skin. Would it ever recover from the mistreatment she had subjected it to this day? And dust on her Chanel powder and put on a pretty negligee. She would have turned down the central air to sixty-five. She would fix a pitcher of lemonade and she and Ernest could loll in front of the television all evening and drink lemonade with a little rum mixed in it.

"Left at this next corner," Ernest pointed to the stoplight at Eighth and Pine. "There it is."

The tow truck turned into the parking space of Ollie's Garage and stopped.

All three of them got out of the cab. Ernest pulled out his billfold and began writing a check as the man from Peach cranked their Buick to the ground and disconnected the chain that bound it to the truck.

Frieda wandered inside the garage. Several times she had picked up a car for Ernest after it had been worked on, but she did not personally know any of the people who worked there. She was feeling light-headed. Surely there would be a drinking fountain or a Coke machine.

It being near six o'clock, the garage was quiet except for the echoing of her footsteps across the oily floor. She opened a plywood door with "Office" painted across it. Inside there were two men in grease-monkey suits and a woman about her own age.

"Hello," Frieda smiled.

"Are you here to pick up a car?" asked the other woman. All three of them looked curiously at Frieda's disheveled appearance, her flushed face.

"No, we're bringing in one. Our car broke down on the highway outside of Peach. We had to be towed in."

The woman clucked in sympathy as the two mechanics returned to their conversation.

"Is there somewhere I can get a drink?" Frieda ran her tongue over dry lips.

"Sure, hon. Will ice water do?" The woman pointed to a serving cart in the corner with a large, green plastic pitcher on top. Condensation beaded the sides of the pitcher. A stack of cone-shaped paper cups rested beside it.

With a groan, Frieda thanked the woman and snatched one of the cups. Pouring it full with ice water—yes, it was: ice water—she grabbed it to her mouth and, in one gulp, downed the cupful. Then a second cup, and her right temple ached from the cold. A third cup she poured down as the others in the office gaped.

"That woman was thirsty!" murmured one of the men.

She poured out a fourth cup of water and swashed it down.

It was not enough. Frieda was still hot and the water was excruciatingly delicious. More water. She must have more water.

Greedily, she worked the plastic lid out of the pitcher. Then she grasped the container with both hands, lifted it squarely over her head, and turned it upside down. As the onlookers dropped their jaws, ice cubes and water splashed and clattered down over Frieda's crown and the sides of her head and her bare throat, and flowed down inside the top of her sweat-soaked suit.

Never in her life had anything felt so good. She knew she looked like an utter fool. She didn't care. It had been a long and hot, hard day. And she wasn't home yet.

Frieda closed her eyes and shrugged her shoulders to allow the ice cubes to shush down between her breasts. She would hold this moment of pure refreshment, she would savor it, make it stretch.

"What in God's name are you doing?"

Frieda opened her eyes. Ernest stood staring at her. He looked at the other woman and the grease monkeys confounded by the crazy woman who had drenched herself in the middle of their waxed linoleum floor. He looked at the ceiling, then back at Frieda. For a long time they stared at one another, his red lids trembling in irritation and bewilderment, she on the verge of hilarity.

"What in God's name are you doing?"

Frieda tittered. "You must think I'm an idiot." Thoroughly revived now and coltish, she replaced the pitcher on the cart and grinned at her husband before stepping down out of her soggy shoes. "Come on now, don't look like that. I'll fix you a nice pitcher of lemonade when we get home." With that, Frieda Teague bent over, picked up her shoes, and walked out barefoot.

# 31

Aaron sat in his rocking chair by the sliding glass doors overlooking the apartment clubhouse, a row of thirsty sycamore trees, and a deserted swimming pool. He was glad to be back from Curtain. The FM station was playing Vivaldi—ceremonious, mournful, preening music. The reading lamp with a stained-glass shade at his elbow defined a soft circle of light in the darkening room. Aaron sipped from a glass of Scotch, then opened Nell's letter.

Normal, IL
August 13

Dear Aaron,

Am sorry for not writing sooner. Things have been just so hectic. Dad's operation went smoothly. He was in the operating room nearly four hours. Mom has been a total wreck. I'm so glad I took off work again. I'll never forget walking in and seeing Dad lying there in bed that way. He looked so old. With his hair messed up and his face all white and hooked up to that machine—I wanted to yell at him, Dad get up out of that bed and be yourself again!

Aaron, I've decided to stay over a few more days. Mom and Dad really seem to be appreciating my visit. Plus I ran into an old friend who's given me a good lead on a job with a television station in Chicago. It would only be writing copy and learning how to do things for now, but it would be an opening. I don't feel that I can turn it down, if it's offered. I've always wanted to work in television. Am going up on the train next Monday for the interview.

Think about me on Monday, dear, won't you, and wish me luck. I miss you.

For a while Aaron sat stunned. The music on the radio had become strident. He walked over to switch it off, then took his seat again in the rocker and reread the letter.

From the first, he had known that they would not stay together permanently, Nell and himself. Sooner or later one or the other of them would become involved with someone else. That a job would lead to the break, a goddamn job — that was the surprise.

He was jumping to conclusions. A lot of people who interview for jobs never get them. The way Nell was ready to jump at an offer, though, was handwriting on the wall. If not this job, then another. If she was looking for something else, she would find it. Nell was too sharp, too smart, he admitted with pride and chagrin, not to get what she wanted. And she missed Chicago, he knew that.

She would go to live in the city and wear tailored gray flannel suits and meet some well-groomed man nearer her own age with a flat, midwestern accent. And they would raise a houseful of blockheaded. . . . No, he wouldn't become bitter. He couldn't blame her. In fact, wryly, as if she were his daughter, he wished her the best. Never had either of them presumed a permanent arrangement. Accepting that notion intellectually now, with diverging paths just ahead, was a hell of a lot easier than accepting it emotionally.

With an effort Aaron turned his mind elsewhere. He thought of his daughter and of Tommy — how Tommy used to slink through the apartment chuckling in that curious sucking manner. And for some reason he remembered the night he had spent in the apartment of Henry

Lazarus and his wife, whom Aaron had not yet met, shortly after receiving his discharge papers from the Army.

It was a round-cheeked woman with startling, brick-colored hair who hurriedly pulled him into the apartment, then dashed back into the kitchen, yelling over her shoulder that the pasta was boiling over. Immediately a tow-headed child in diapers and a crocheted sweater poked his head up under Aaron's arm and showed him a toothless grin.

"Hey, you old whore!" Henry burst into the room holding out both arms and pounded Aaron on the back. He had put on some weight and his curly black hair was longer than it had been. Scooping up the toddler, Henry pointed to the newcomer and said, "David, this is Aaron," then explained to Aaron that the boy was the son of his wife, Elizabeth, from a former marriage. Aaron smiled and waved. Sideways from the corner of his eye, David regarded the stranger, then clung to Henry's neck.

Aaron smiled again and looked away. After a year in the Mekong Delta, it felt awfully good to be back in Washington again with his friend. Elizabeth brought each of them a glass of red wine, wiped her forehead with the back of a flour-covered hand, and announced that dinner would be ready in twenty minutes. On her way back to the kitchen, she asked Henry if he would make a fire.

Handing the child to Aaron before he had time to object, Henry set about piling logs in the tiny fireplace. When all seemed ready, he struck a match and turned on the gas. As a line of blue flames flowered along the gas jet, a gust of heat blared into the room.

"What the . . . ?" Henry scowled, as heat continued to radiate forth in a sheet.

"Did you open the flue?"

"Oh, Christ!" muttered Henry, grabbing ahold of the flue handle with his hand and just as suddenly yanking it back with a yowl of pain.

David burst into tears. Aaron yelled, "Pull on it with the thing," pointing to the cast-iron poker hanging beside the hearth. As Elizabeth ran into the living room, Henry was tugging open the flue with the fireplace tool.

"My God, what's going on?"

Aaron broke into laughter as David wailed on his lap and Henry shook his glowing right palm.

"Henry, haven't you learned yet to open the damper before you light a fire?" she scolded. Taking the baby from Aaron and patting him over her shoulder with one hand, Elizabeth examined Henry's burn with the other hand and decided that it needed a coating of butter.

Dinner was a wonderful lettuce salad tossed in a sweet exotic dressing, spaghetti, garlic bread sprinkled with parmesan cheese, a fruity chianti wine, and peach cobbler a la mode and thick espresso coffee for dessert. Henry remarked to Aaron that it was exceptional for a child of David's age to eat from the table as he was doing, while his mother beamed.

After dinner Henry grabbed a stack of plates and told David that Uncle Aaron would read him his story tonight.

"C'mon kid," Aaron droned, shaking a fist in the air at his friend. "Let's see what you got to read."

With a tiny hand, the youngster led Aaron into the nursery. There was a white-enamelled crib on one wall and a matching chest on another, a rocking chair with a pillow done in needlepoint of a bouquet of yellow roses in the corner, and blocks, stuffed animals, and plastic cars and trucks scattered around the floor. Underneath the double windows extended a bookshelf filled with puzzles and gadgets and lined across the top with books. The room smelt of powder.

Pointing at the row of books, David looked Aaron squarely in the eye and grunted.

"So that's where they are?" Aaron slid out a large picture book of trains and flashed its bright cover in David's face. "You like trains?"

Responding with a vigorous, negative head shake, the child pointed once again at the books.

"Don't like trains, eh? Well, what else do we have here?" Pulling out a boring-looking *What Do We Do On a Rainy Day?*, he showed it to the kid. No go. A third book, about Old MacDonald's farm, received his approval, and they returned to the living room couch in front of what had become a cozy fire.

Dropping down onto the thick cushions, Aaron realized how worn out he was after traveling all day and gorging the way he had done at dinner. Up onto the couch David scrambled and snuggled in beside him. Aaron put his arm around the soft, squirmy creature, patted him, and proceeded to name over the marvelous animals that inhabited MacDonald's farm.

As he was finishing the last ee-yi, ee-yi, oh!, Elizabeth and Henry walked in with arms about each other's waists.

"Come on, buddy, let's hit the hay!" called Henry to David. "Give Uncle Aaron a hug."

Aaron leaned over as David gave him a wet smack on the cheek, then watched as the child slid down off the couch and toddled into his room ahead of his parents.

After a while, Henry returned wearing a sheepish grin, followed by Elizabeth, glowing and contented. She nestled down on the couch beside her husband.

How natural they seemed together. And how lovely their life together. This icon of family life represented everything Aaron wanted for himself—hopefully with Deedee as his wife. His stomach rolled with anxiety and pleasurable anticipation as he recalled his primary reason for traveling to Washington: to see Deedee again for the first time in over two years. Over the telephone before leaving Bugg, he had arranged to meet her for lunch at the Shoreham. All his hopes were riding on the chance of reestablishing a relationship with that elusive and beautiful woman.

Leave it to Henry to find the women. And this time, he had outdone himself. Aaron took off his boots, toasted his

feet beside the fire, and began to talk about the war—
something he had avoided doing with anyone until now.
After a while Elizabeth fell asleep against her husband's
shoulder, and the two friends swapped tales until daybreak.

Sitting in his rocking chair now amidst the shambles of
his personal life in Dallas, Aaron switched off the stained-
glass reading lamp. In darkness modified only by courtyard
gas lamps shining through the sliding glass doors, he dwelt
again, this time enviously, on the happiness he had witnessed that night at Henry and Elizabeth's. Why in Christ's
name, after two tries, had he been unable to achieve something like it? Why had it proven to be so complicated, so
chimerical a goal?

Things had seemed so simple in the war. You killed
Charlie before he killed you. And that wasn't so bad,
because it was enemy you were killing and you were a
soldier. You were following orders; guilt could be assigned
up the chain of command—at least for the present. If
somebody else fucked you over, another GI, you hit him in
the mouth, or you goddamn left him alone. If you wanted
something—anything: dope, sex, stereo equipment—you
paid money for it. Everything was for sale with a clearly
marked price tag. In the war, everything had existed on a
very clear basis. There were none of these unresolvable . . .
problems.

Like Nell. And Frieda with her godawful band of harpy
sisters that he loved with a deep and unsentimental love.
Or Tommy—what had happened that last evening, and
what was his own responsibility in the matter? Aaron did
not understand these things; he continued to be haunted
by them. Only the break with Deedee had been clean. So
clean, he mused ironically, that sometimes he would give
his left nut to see her walk through the door. Things had
become too goddamn complicated.

Or could it be that in the war, as in domestic matters as
they used to be, things had been just as complicated, but in
different ways? Aaron was tired of thinking. It had been a

long day. He would work with the pieces again tomorrow. Now, he needed to make up the bed in his daughter's room. Tomorrow she was coming to stay with him for a week while her mother was in San Francisco on a case. He would unpackage the new yellow sheets he had bought just last week at Nell's suggestion. Then he would leave the window open overnight so the room would be fresh and airy when the little girl knocked on his door in the morning.